Tucker McBride's

Many Lives

Tucker McBride's Many Lives

Doris Gaines Rapp

Daniel's House Publishing

Huntington, Indiana

Copyright 2020 Doris Gaines Rapp
Huntington, Indiana 46750
website: www.dorisgainesrapp.com
contact: dorisgainesrapp@gmail.com

This book is a work of historic/biographic fiction. Some characters and incidents are products of the author's imagination and are used fictitiously. Conversations were created out of the author's imagination. The timeline of the actual events is compressed.

Cover design is stock imagery from @Dreamstime.com and Shutterstock.com. Put in place by @Debi Lindhorst/The Type Galley. Other images are from the internet

Bible Verses - taken from the King James Version (KJV)

Library of Congress Control Number: 2020911684

ISBN-13: 978-0-9988590-6-4 (paperback)
ISBN-13: 978-0-9988590-8-8 (ebook)

Warning
Tucker McBride rarely thinks before he acts. Learn from Tucker. Do not try Tucker's stunts.

Glossary
For an unfamiliar word with an asterisk (*) beside it, go to the back of the book for a definition or picture.

Dedication

This book is dedicated to Albert and Perninnah Kime, my husband, Bill Rapp's, grandparents. They took in Bill, his older sisters Merry and Beverly, and brother, Jack when the children's mother, Helen died at the age of twenty-seven. Bill was only four months old. Grandpa was seventy-six and Grandma was sixty-six when they began rearing their second family. They were both devoted grandparents, parents to their first family, and dedicated workers in the church and community.

Seven-million grandparents are raising their grandchildren to some degree. Two-thirds of families, headed by at least one grandparent, also have one of the child's parents living in the home. Over two-and-a-half million grandparents are raising their grandchildren on their own.

Bill and I had three birth children, Vicki, Donna, and Jim, then adopted a boy, Vonn, when he was nearly ten-years-old. Later, we adopted two of our grandchildren, Katy when she was six weeks old and her little sister, Amanda when she was seven months. Raising them into the wonderful adult women they are was a joy to our hearts.

Love is everywhere. Reach out and claim your share. You will find your life is full of God's blessed love.

Acknowledgements

I am always thankful to my group of writers, Soli deo Gloria (to God be the Glory) for their positive encouragement and the many times they share their faith.

Thank you to Vicki Borgman for the time and effort she put into editing *Tucker McBride's Many Lives*. Since Tucker is really her dad, Bill Rapp, she is as familiar as I with all his antics.

Thanks to all six of our children: Vicki, Donna, Jim, Vonn, Katy, and Mandi, who managed to grow up without repeating the shenanigans they heard in the stories of "the Dunlap Kid," as one of Bill's pastors called him.

Thank you, Debi Lindhorst, of The Type Galley in Warren, Indiana, for being able to conquer the computer when I can't.

A huge thanks and blessings to all my readers and fans of Tucker. Your enthusiasm and joy of reading *Tucker McBride* prompted *Tucker McBride's Many Lives* and may encourage a third book.

Table of Contents

The Lake Shore and Michigan Southern Railway, a part
of the New York Central Railroad. It runs from Chicago,
Illinois to Buffalo, New York, through Elkhart, Dunlap,
and Goshen, Indiana.

Dots left to right: 1 = Chicago, Illinois, 2 = Elkhart, Indiana,
3 = Goshen, Indiana, 4 = Toledo, Ohio, 5 = Buffalo, New York

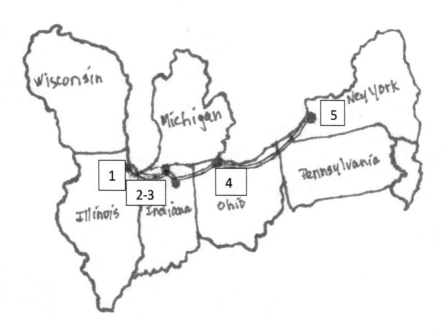

Chapter One
A Clear View

Friday, November 22, 1946

Like a Siamese cat, Tucker McBride seemed to have many lives. He could change the downs to ups in most situations. That day was no different.

Tucker stared out the large classroom window, watching George Sutter and two other friends of his sister, Carolyn, get into a Chevy with Miss Fritz. Carolyn said they were on their way to a speech contest in South Bend. It didn't start for another hour and a half, but they had to get there early enough to register for their events.

Frosty wind leaked around the multi-paned windows allowing the twenty-four-degree temperature outside to cool the room inside. Tucker pulled down the rolled-up long sleeves of his flannel shirt and buttoned the cuffs around his wrists. He wasn't paying attention to his teacher's instruction. His thoughts were outside that November day.

In his head he rambled on and on. *I don't want to stand up in front of people and talk about the news like those in debate class, but it would be great to get out of school early. I can drive already; but I'll take Mr. Gilbert's drivers training class in a few years so I can get out of the building during school hours.*

"Tucker," Mrs. Hunter called out to the last seat in the first row. "Stay with us."

Tucker jumped as the teacher jerked his focus back into the room. His friend, Christy Tree, two rows over, smiled.

Mrs. Hunter turned back to the class. "I know it's Friday, but I have a fun assignment for the weekend." She passed a small stack of papers to the first person in each row. "Please, take one and pass them back."

"There's smeared ink on mine," Freddie Cooper complained as he inspected his purple fingertips. "I can't read part of it."

"Sorry, Freddie. The gelatin in the hectograph pad was over-used." She passed a cleaner assignment paper to him.

Tucker slouched down in his seat grumbling. "Homework, Mrs. Hunter?"

"Alright, Tucker." The teacher lowered her black wire-rimmed glasses and glared at him. "Wait until I tell you about it before you start complaining."

Tucker shook his head in disbelief. "But, Mrs. Hunter, I have plans for the weekend. Tomorrow's my birthday and we have a game in the morning."

"Well, Happy Birthday in advance, Tucker. But I think you'll have no trouble doing this assignment." The tall, lanky teacher watched as Freddie, in the middle of the third row, received his fresh paper. Pointing to the lines on the printed form, she continued. "The image on your paper is called a Family Tree. Since we're talking about Indiana History, I'd like you to fill in the blanks with the names of your family ancestors who first came into the state. If you know the date, tell us that, too."

Josh Merriman gasped. "But my family moved here from Pennsylvania last summer."

"Did they leave the rest of the family in Pennsylvania?" Mrs. Hunter asked.

"Yes and no. Dad's family is there, but Mom's family is here."

Mrs. Hunter smiled. "Moms count too, Josh. Tell us about your mother's family and when they moved into Indiana and why."

"My family came in a long time ago, on the Erie Canal," Tucker blurted out.

Mrs. Hunter frowned. "Well, I don't know about that."

"Well, I do," Tucker interrupted again.

The teacher ignored him and continued. "For many of you, the "why" will be farming."

Tucker rolled a piece of lined paper into a tube. Crouching down with his chin on his desk top, he put the paper to his mouth and mooed into the cylinder, hoping to project the heifer sound to the other side of the room. Tucker imagined himself as the famous ventriloquist, Edgar Bergen, with his dummy, Charlie McCarthy.

Mrs. Hunter sighed heavily. "Okay, Tucker, that's enough."

Tucker grinned sheepishly. "How'd you know it was me?"

"You're taking up our time, Tucker. Please be quiet." She took a deep breath and began again. "Your family may not have come to farm. Just tell us why they came to Indiana."

"Why they came?" Tucker wiggled around a little, repositioning himself until the back of his neck rested on the seat back-rest. "But that will take a long time."

"The class wants to work, Tucker." Mrs. Hunter grabbed Tucker under his arm and eased him out of the chair with a slight pull. "You're excused."

Tucker's eyes bulged. "I can go home?" He couldn't believe what he heard.

"No, young man, I didn't say that." She ushered him toward the door. The often-refinished, old hardwood floor squeaked as they moved toward the classroom door.

"Oh, my, my, my," Anna Fredrick whispered, drawing out each singsongy, mocking word. "Somebody's in trouble."

"It could be you, Anna." Mrs. Hunter turned and frowned. The space between her eyebrows knitted tightly.

Anna studied the wood pattern in her desk top with her finger nail and whispered. "Yes, Ma'am."

Out in the hall, Tucker wondered what his teacher's next move would be. She always seemed fair to him. Now, she puzzled him.

"Tucker, the last time I had you stand in the hall so the class could work, you went down to the auditorium and watched them practice for the Halloween program."

Tucker smiled. "Yes, Ma'am. They were sure good, especially Tubby Alexander. For a baseball player, he can sing good."

"I imagine so. But, that's not why you're in the hall. For a seventh grader, you should know better. This time, you'll have a quiet place to think about proper classroom behavior." She unlocked the janitor's closet with a skeleton key and pointed inside. "Turn that bucket over and have a seat." She reached in and pulled the string attached to the light bulb mounted on the wall. "I'll be back and pick you up when the kids switch classes."

"Okay," Tucker agreed and up-righted his galvanized lounge-chair. In the hall, he heard the key turn in the lock and sat down.

When he heard Mrs. Hunter's brown oxfords click on the tile floor as she walked back to the classroom, Tucker looked around the small space. The janitor left his collection of cleaning rags, mops, and bottles of Windex scattered among the other cleaning supplies. The most interesting part of the closet was the metal ladder attached to the west wall. The pipe-like rungs stood away from the wall just enough so he could get his foot safely on the round steps. He didn't stop and ask himself, "Should I?" Not even once.

There was no hesitancy in his charge up the ladder. Whatever he would find going on outside had to be more interesting than the nothing that was happening where he was. With a bump from his shoulder when he stepped onto the top rung, he lifted the trap door in the ceiling and hoisted himself through the opening.

It was cold on the school roof. The icy air whistled around his neck and blew down his shirt. He tried not to think about the temperature. Over on the Minutemen track, the senior girls' gym class was rounding the second bend. It was too cold to have much of an outdoor class but Tucker thought the girls were probably warming up running at top speed.

"Wow, they're good," he breathed into the visible breath around him. Tucker hunkered down on his haunches with his arms pulled tightly around his body. From there he watched the girls work out in preparation for a cross-country track meet the next day. He convinced himself the bright sunshine would soon warm his bones. Regardless of the chill, he'd rather sit on the roof than on a bucket in the closet.

• • • • •

In the classroom, Mrs. Hunter glanced at the Regulator clock that hung on the wall. Time passed rapidly, as it always did for the teacher. Students saw time passing as inchworms, measuring the clock-face one minute at a time in tiny loops. She nearly spoke aloud. *I'd better check on Tucker.*

Mrs. Hunter stepped out of the classroom into the hall while the students were reading a chapter of Indiana history. Smiling, she unlocked the door and opened the closet. "Tucker..." she stopped short. Her mouth flew open, gasping at the empty storage room. "But ... how?"

Her heart beat wildly as she looked up and down the hallway. "He couldn't have gone anywhere."

"Who, Virginia?" another teacher asked.

"Oh, Randolph," Virginia Hunter blushed, averting her eyes in embarrassment. "We'll talk about it later." She hoped that Tucker would turn up before she had to explain her strange form of discipline.

Mr. Crawford smiled. "Greg is waiting for your class in the music room. That's their next rotation."

"Thanks." She waved weakly as she turned back to her room. "Okay, everybody, Mr. Jordan is waiting for us."

• • • • •

Up on the roof, Tucker thought about the assignment. He loved looking at the old pictures of family he found stored in boxes in the attic. He had to admit, the homework could be fun. He might even take some of the photos to school if Gramma said it was okay. Suddenly, he startled when the gym teacher blew her whistle. The runners were coming in off the track, walking back in the building. Tucker jumped up, lifted the trap door, and slithered down the ladder, two rungs at a time. He had just hit the floor and sat down on the bucket, when he heard the key in the lock.

"He was right h—" Virginia Hunter opened the door. She needed to finally confess to Randolph Crawford how she may have lost one of her students.

"Hi, Mrs. Hunter." Tucker strutted out of the closet with his hands in his pockets, past the two flabbergasted teachers.

Virginia Hunter didn't ask why the cupboard was bare. She just slowly closed the door and relocked the closet.

To Tucker, Mrs. Hunter, his favorite teacher, looked tired. He wondered if she would benefit from a little relaxing time on the roof. But he didn't mention his form of sitting in the upper deck of a stadium. He thought no one knew he'd gone up top anyway. He smiled as he headed to class. "Guess we'll all be glad the weekend is here," he commented as he turned back to Mrs. Hunter. "That homework assignment will be fun. I'll ask Gramma and Grandpop for names and dates as soon as I get home." Tucker loved his family and could listen to his grandfather's stories of their early, pioneer lives as often as Grandpop would share them.

Mrs. Hunter said nothing.

Chapter Two
A Hit and a Miss

Saturday, November 23, 1946

Like that same Siamese cat, Tucker could leap straight up from a standing position right under the basketball hoop. He had the Concord Minutemen Junior High gymnasium crackling with excitement. The aroma of buttered popcorn and caramel apples from the concession stand added the snappiness of autumn and high energy to the room. With only a few minutes left in the pre-season game, people stood more than they sat. Basketball games before Thanksgiving were a time to show-off what the fans could expect. Tucker and his team tended to show-off a lot.

Tucker whirled past his Elkhart friend, Johnny Washington, and couldn't help but smile. Tucker was too friendly not to say, "Hi, Johnny" even if he was on the opposing side. "See ya later," he teased as he dodged around big, sweaty Steven Golickey from Elkhart Central School, leaped straight up off the floor, and sank the basketball through the hoop. "Wahoo!" he shouted out through a toothy grin.

Tucker's heart pounded so hard he could hear the thump, thump in his ears. He couldn't believe it. His basket tied the score with three minutes left on the clock. His team might win their first game of the season, and he just may play the hero. The crowd roared as the stands on the "home" side erupted with cheers from students, parents, and friends. Tucker's multi-directional attention spanned the room. Rev. Dailey and his wife, Janice, were sitting on the front row with the team. Tucker could see her cling to her husband's arm until his plaid cotton shirt nearly pulled from his shoulder.

A tall, gangly Elkhart player threw the ball inbound. Freddie snatched it up, turned, shook off an opposing player and darted around the lanky string bean. Twisting right, then left, he jumped and let the ball fly. The ball rolled around the basket slowly, keeping the excited spectators in suspense, before it bounced off the rim and hit the floor.

The fans' sighs were so heavy it sounding like the whole room sprang a leak. Still, their enthusiastic encouragement spurred the team on.

A hush fell over the room as everyone waited with excited anticipation for the next play. In the heavy silence, Freddie's dad called out, "That's okay, Son."

Ray Owens from Elkhart had the ball and dribbled it down the court. Each bounce echoed in the room, whump, whump, whump. His shoes squeaked and slipped just as he sprang up to try for the point that would win the game. Pain was obvious on Ray's contorted face when his foot met the floor again. He crumpled and landed in a heap on the hardwood.

Tucker's scattered attention snapped to his own new high-top basketball shoes. He beamed with pride. He had saved the money he earned from detasseling corn to buy the special Converse shoes. "Tucker, watch your man," he heard the coach yell from the sideline.

The young Minutemen moved as a team, watching, blocking, scrapping with the man they were guarding. With new energy from a feeling of success and power, Tucker scooped the pebbled-leather ball off the floor and dribbled it toward the key. Back and forth from one side of the court to the other, in and out, he pounded the floor in rhythmic bounces. The clock, high on the wall, ticked loudly.

"Shoot," Betsy yelled from the stands.

Tucker knew he had to maneuver into the best position to make the shot. Maybe his sister could see something he couldn't. Perhaps she saw the second hand on the clock clicking by.

Tucker whirled, turning his back to the Elkhart player who waved his arms wildly in Tucker's face, continued dribbling to a perfect beat, pivoted back to his right, jumped, reached, and watched the ball clear the basket without ever touching the rim. The single, ending blast from the timing gun reverberated off the walls and bounced off the rafters.

The timekeeper recorded the winning basket on the scoreboard as the crowd erupted with shouts and cheers. Mrs. Cooper rushed onto the floor joining Freddie as together they jumped up and down, laughing. Anyone would know she was Freddie's mother. Her red hair matched Freddie's in every way except length.

Freddie's dad leaped down from the stands and pounded Freddie on his back in excitement. "Great win, Son. Great win." Turning to Tucker, Mr. Cooper threw his arm around the boy's shoulder and shook him vigorously. "What a basket, Tucker. Great job!"

"Tucker," Coach Milton grabbed Tucker's shoulder with a firm grip and patted him on his back. "You did it."

"Thanks Coach." Tucker appreciated his coach's support. But, as he looked around, he saw that the other guys had parents in the gym. Moms and dads brought their son, sat on the hard, wooden bleachers all the way through the game, jumped to their feet with each basket, and flew out of the stands when the game was over, win or lose. Tucker had no parent there. Uncle Jacob had to work a half-day that Saturday morning. Thank goodness his uncle would be home by lunch time when the family would celebrate Tucker's thirteenth birthday.

Tucker's bubble began to burst as moms and dads embraced their sons with shouts of praise. Dads, home from the war, were especially excited about cheering on their sons. Tucker knew Johnny Washington's dad, killed near Merkers, Germany when a sniper's bullet took him out, wouldn't be there. Johnny's mother, Goldie, a friend of Gramma's, was shouting and laughing however. She hugged Johnny, then turned and momma-hugged Tucker as well.

Goldie stood back, her eyes beaming. "Your mama would be so proud of you, Tucker."

"Yes, Ma'am. Thanks," Tucker agreed but wondered. His mother died when he was so young, he didn't get to know her. Maybe Mrs. Washington was just being kind.

"Hey, Tucker," Johnny bounced closer. "You did great. But ... wish you hadn't." He playfully shook Tucker by the elbow. "Then we would have won."

"I know," Tucker laughed. "Say, Christy and I are going to Goshen the day before Thanksgiving. Want to come along?"

"What ya going to do?"

"Go to a movie." Tucker shrugged and grinned.

Johnny looked at his mother who nodded. "Sure."

"I'll call you," Tucker added as people patted him on the back. Everyone was there; but Tucker's grandparents couldn't come. They rarely ventured out of their routine: home and garden, family, and church. They expected Tucker to learn to be on his own. But it was obvious other parents saw things differently. Even whinny, uppity Anna Frederick's parents ran onto the floor, yelling, laughing, and congratulating the players. Janitors, pushing everyone off the playing floor with heavy, wide brooms, laughed and joined in the fun.

"Anna's a cheer leader, not a player," Tucker complained to Freddie.

"I heard that." Christy laughed as she jumped playfully on Tucker's back, her blond hair bounced as she landed. "Cheerleading is a sporting skill that has to be practiced just like basketball."

"Yeah, I guess." Tucker didn't really think cheerleaders didn't deserve a hearty cheer. But, looking around at the support of all the parents was just another example of what was missing, or he never had.

"Okay, brother," Betsy darted up behind him and gave him a bear hug. "You did a great job. You even made the winning basket!" She gave him a playful jab in the ribs. "You're a real athlete."

Tucker laughed as he joined in the fun. "You're the athlete, Bets. The Daisies invited you to try out, not me."

"Well, yeah," she laughed with wide eyes. "The Daisies are a professional women's baseball team, Tucker."

"Right," Tucker agreed with a grin.

Christy's jaw dropped. "Snazzy! Betsy, you're going to be a professional baseball player?"

"I might have been," Betsy rolled her eyes, "if Gramma hadn't said no." Betsy said no more.

Tucker knew that Betsy was the best baseball player around. But, when Gramma said no, Gramma didn't change her mind.

Tucker looked around as families began walking their sons toward the boys' locker room. "I'll shower and be ready in a minute."

"We'll be over near the concession stand." Betsy started walking with Christy close behind. "I'm thirsty."

Betsy pulled a Jefferson nickel out of her pocket and handed it to the student in charge of concessions. "A coke please."

"Super," the student swooned. "This is one of the new coins."

Betsy smiled, took the small bottle, and sipped. "I have another nickel with me if you want a coke, too, Christy."

"That's nice. But ... mother says—"

"What? What does your mother say?" Betsy quizzed.

"Never a borrower be." Christy's chin turned up in resolute determination.

"That's fine, Christy. Then, I'm not lending you anything." Betsy handed the counter girl another dime. She gave Christy the coke and shoved a chocolatey, butter brickle smelling bar in her pocket. "The coke's a gift. I just ask a favor in return."

"Okay," Christy drew out slowly.

"Today is Tucker's birthday." Betsy looked up as Tucker came out of the locker. She quickly added, "I'd like you to come to lunch. Oh, and Tim won't be there."

Christy smiled and whispered. "I'm sorry, but I'm glad Tim won't be there. He always calls me by my full name, Christmas Tree, because he knows it makes me mad."

Betsy choked on a large gulp of fizzy Coke. "I'm sorry, too, Christy. You remember Tim has been in North Carolina at boot camp? Christy, boot camp is over now. So, he'll be home later."

Christy rolled her eyes. "I remember when he came back home for a while after he hurt his ankle; and, I remember when he left again."

"Well," Betsy drew out slowly, "he'll come home for a few days before he ships out. Uncle Jacob is supposed to pick him up at the bus terminal in Elkhart this evening."

"This evening? Thanks. I'll stay away. Tim is a tease." Christy watched for Tucker. "About lunch, what will your grandmother say?"

"About what?" Tucker walked up using his blue bandana handkerchief to finish drying his dark, wavy hair.

"I just asked Christy to join us for lunch since it's your birthday." Betsy took Tucker by the elbow and steered him out of the gym into the bright but chilly November morning.

He buttoned up his black and red checked jacket and pulled the earflaps of the matching hat down to cover his wet hair. "I feel like I'm being herded." Tucker laughed and sucked in the sun.

"You are," Christy giggled.

Tucker turned and took each of them by their hand, pulling them along. "Move, girls. Hustle. Cake awaits."

Chapter Three
What a Birthday!

Tucker walked with Betsy and Christy the two blocks back home. The beautiful colors of autumn usually peaked before late November. In 1946, it was no different. Gorgeous purple wisteria and the golden leaves of the tulip poplar had already fallen for Uncle Jacob to rake into piles. The remaining freshness of the evergreen trees sent the fragrance of cedar across the narrow streets of home. There, it mingled with the earthy, smoky wood of Mr. Stuart's pile of burning leaves next door.

Tucker's very detailed imagination took over the moment. In his mind, he was riding his red sorrel horse with its flaxen mane and tail in the high ponderosa pine forest of the southwest. As the mighty steed climbed higher along the woodland path, the crystal blue sky overhead came closer. Rugged songs of cowboys filled his head as he smiled. Tucker drank in the beauty of the late November day as he mentally zoomed back to the present. The three of them cut across the back yard, careful to step around the piles of leaves he helped Grandpop rake onto the strawberry plants to hold in the moisture and insulate the roots.

The trio jumped up the steps and entered the house through the side door off the small porch. Betsy threw her coat over one of the large brass hooks of the corner coat rack as she shouted, "Gramma, can Christy stay for lunch since it's Tucker's birthday?"

The family's very own hero, war-dog, Joe, wound himself around Tucker's leg. "Hi, Boy," Tucker said as he bent down and scratched behind Joe's ears. "Smell that food, boy. Did you beg Gramma for some?"

"Nein*." Gramma smiled and pointed to the door. "Joe was a good boy. Christy, your potbellied pig showed up looking for you. I told Joe to herd her back home, just like the dog did when Tucker was little."

Christy's eyes popped. "Rosie? She was here?"

"For a few minutes. Joe followed her short legs as she waddled away." Gramma winked. "And, ja*, Betsy," Gramma said slowly. "There will be plenty of food today." She walked out to the kitchen and took a pitcher of milk out of the refrigerator.

"Mrs. Moyer," Christy gasped, following her. "You got the new refrigerator. It is beautiful." The new Frigidaire sparkled with a fresh-scrubbed shine.

"Danke schön," Gramma said with a twinkle in her voice. "But, always remember Christy, only the love of Jesus is beautiful. A refrigerator is helpful."

"Yes, Ma'am," Christy agreed. "I can see how helpful it will be. No more ice deliveries."

Tucker lifted the lid of one of the pots on the stove. The smell of browned meat wafted up with the steam.

Tiny, the silky terrier, yapped and fussed as she jumped up, with all four feet leaving the floor at the same time. Obviously needing all eyes to focus on her, she twirled her body a little in all directions.

"Yes, Tiny, I see you." Tucker assured the little dog. Grabbing her on an up-jump, he nuzzled her close and tucked her under his arm. "The noodles you made yesterday, Gamma … we're having them for lunch? I was hoping we would." As usual, Tucker was hungry. New refrigerators could wait.

"Ja, one of your favorites. Roman Swartz dropped off a little roast yesterday in exchange for the use of your granddad's train whistle. We're having beef and noodles with mashed potatoes."

The Moyers watched every penny. Joseph's eighty dollar a month pension from years of working on the railroad, wasn't a lot of money for a family of seven. If their youngest daughter's four children hadn't come to live with them after she died, Rebecca and Joseph Moyer would have spent their later years traveling up and down the South Shore-Southern Michigan rail system on Joseph's railroad pass. Except for their trip to Colorado to visit Gramma's cousin, the governor, traveling was no longer a goal of retirement and hadn't been for over twelve years.

"Christy, you call your mother and ask if it's alright with her for you to stay for lunch." Gramma pointed to the crank telephone* hanging on the wall in the dining room. "You can share in Tucker's birthday dessert."

"Birthday cake … yummy," Christy said with a smack to her lips.

While Christy used the telephone, Tucker helped his grandmother set another place at the table. "Why did Roman Swartz want to borrow the train whistle? He's Amish."

"It was interesting." Gramma took another drinking glass with yellow flowers, and a cream-colored dinner plate with gold scallops, out of the cabinet. Brushing fine hair from her forehead that kept popping out of her rolled up bun, she thought for a moment. "Our Amish friends don't use modern conveniences, cars and such, but their children love trains. So, he borrowed the train whistle for his children's Amish school. The children won't learn about *building* trains. They'll learn how to read the schedules since they do *travel* on trains. The whistle will add a little fun."

Tucker put the wooden whistle Grandpop had whittled out of a piece of the 1933 Christmas tree trunk to his mouth and blew. To Tucker, the sound was both a forlorn call in the blackness of night and an exciting invitation to adventure.

Christy replaced the trumpet-shaped telephone receiver on the side hook. "She said sure, Mrs. Moyer. Thanks for inviting me."

"Good, Christy." Betsy's smile filled her face.

"Sit, sit," Gramma instructed as she took her place at the foot of the table with Grandpop at the head. She nodded … "Joseph."

Grandpop bowed his head and offered a blessing over the food. Before the deep "Amen," he added, "And, thank you Lord for Tucker's good aim." Turning, he chuckled, "Well, Tucker, I hear you already got a birthday present."

"I did?" Tucker dropped his fork on his plate.

"Ja, somebody said you became a basketball star today. That seems like quite a gift." Grandpop rubbed his wrinkled, sandpaper hands together.

"I hadn't thought about that," Tucker nodded with a smile as he spooned some mashed potatoes with hot melted butter onto his plate. Two large scoops of beef and noodles danced across the mound of spuds and a helping of green beans added color to the side. During the war, the government butchered beef cattle for the hungry boys in boot camp, which left little for families on the home front. So, the aroma of shredded beef was like perfume to Tucker. He poised his knife and fork artfully over his filled plate like a band conductor before the downbeat. With a plunge of his fork, he dug in.

"I'd say you're hungry, Tucker." Christy sat back in awe. "Are you going to do all your birthday growing today?"

"My what?"

"Mom said I only grow for a month or so right after each of my birthdays. If she bought clothes as a present a few weeks before I turned a year older, I'd outgrow them the week after we finished off the cake."

"Uh-oh," Gramma gulped.

"Gramma?" Betsy asked.

"Wait." Gramma got up from the table and retrieved a present from the sewing room, a little space off the dining area.

The gift, wrapped in plain white paper, had no bow. But, to Tucker, it was beautiful.

"Go ahead, Tucker," his grandmother coached. "Open it."

When Tucker pulled the string wrapped around the package, a pair of green and white athletic stirrup socks fell out. He picked up the soft fabric and rubbed it on his cheek. "Team colored basketball stirrup socks!"

"Better start wearing them," Gramma cautioned as she sat down, leaning her knuckles on the table for support. "If Christy's mother is right, you might outgrow them before Christmas."

Carolyn watched as Tucker began shoveling in his lunch again. "It looks like you enjoy the noodles." With big-sister-concern, she pointed to his plate of food with her fork. "Better slow down."

Uncle Jacob smiled a quiet smile. "He's been working hard this morning, Carolyn. I suspect a second plate of noodles wouldn't even fill him up."

Tucker glanced at Carolyn with a grin, remembering the Heath bar Betsy pulled from her coat pocket on the way home from the gym. He snatched it from her hand like a hungry dog, nearly inhaling the sweet chocolate covered toffee. Betsy didn't complain about losing baby-sitting money. She laughed, took out a second bar, a Baby Ruth, and divided it with Christy. Everyone knew Tucker could eat a vat of homemade noodles even if he had first wolfed down a whole candy bar.

Tucker polished off the last bite of noodles and sat back. The large serving bowl was still half full of food but he didn't know if Gramma had plans for the leftovers.

"Ja, Tucker," Gramma drew out slowly, "you can have seconds. You too, Christy."

"Thank you." Christy spooned a small helping of fluffy potatoes onto her plate and covered it with the beef, noodles, and savory broth. "Did you get your genealogy homework done, Tucker?"

Tucker ladled and talked at the same time. "Gramma and I went over it when I got home from school yesterday. On her side, my great-great grandpa, Jacob Franks, came to Indiana on the Erie Canal in 1849 from Summit County Ohio. He was a farmer. Gramma's going to sign the paper that says they came on the Erie Canal, since Mrs. Hunter wouldn't believe me."

"Swell," Christy put down her fork. "They came in 1849? Wonder if you'll win a class prize for having the oldest ancestors in Indiana?"

"A prize?" Tucker thought about it. "A large trophy would be nice - one with a farmer behind a plow." He grinned as he dug into his food. "On Grandpop's side of the family," Tucker said as he swallowed, "Great-grandpa Daniel Moyer moved to Indiana from Pennsylvania in 1887. Grandpop told me about the time, when they were living in Pennsylvania, he and his mom and sister waited for dinner for his dad to come home. When he came in, he said he was late because a guy named Booth shot President Abraham Lincoln. Great-grandpa had waited in town for the telegraph announcement telling if the president was alive or not."

"Wow," Christy gasped as she looked at Tucker's grandfather with a fresh respect.

Tucker always liked that story, then realized, "Hey, Great-grandpa farmed, too, so the trophy would work for both sides of the family tree. Grandpop was already twenty-five when they moved to Indiana. Right?"

Tucker's grandfather used his knife to push some noodles onto this fork. "Ja. I was gone all week working on the railroad, so I lived with my parents on weekends before I married."

"My goodness," Christy threw her head back. "You guys have been here a long time. My grandfather moved to Indiana after World War One, not after the Civil War."

"That may be the case with Dad's family, too." Tucker cleaned the last bit of food from his plate. "Gramma knew that

Dad's mother died when he was nine-years-old. A family in Michigan adopted one of his brothers. Dad never saw him again. John and Estella McBride took Dad in. He changed his name from Dawson to McBride."

Uncle Jacob finished his food and sat back with his cup of cream-filled coffee. "Enough ancient history," he interrupted. Removing an envelope from where he had hidden it under his napkin, he handed it to Tucker.

Tucker smiled, peeled back the flap, removed the card, and pulled out a five-dollar bill. Laying it on the table, he smoothed the bill with his fingers.

"With all the overtime I've had, almost like before the end of the war, I couldn't get to Goshen to get you a new shirt from Garland's Department Store. You run over sometime soon and get one. And, Happy Birthday."

"Thanks Uncle Jacob." Tucker had grown to like nice clothes. Maybe not all the time, but he graduated from clodhopper shoes at school to brown oxfords. The metal plates on the soles of the clodhoppers clacked as the boys walked down the hall and made deep scratches on the hardwood floors. The janitor had them banned from the building. On Saturdays, the work boots came out again.

Grandpop dug into his blue work shirt pocket and pulled out his brown, wood trimmed, two-blade pocket knife ... all polished and sharpened. "No wrappings, but I want you to have it for your birthday."

"Grandpop," Tucker gasped. It was his grandfather's favorite pocket knife. Tucker had seen him carry it every day. "Are you sure? You're still using it." Tucker couldn't let himself think of a time when Grandpop would no longer need his knife. He secretly worried about it at night, when darkness had over-taken the day.

"I'll manage." His grandfather reached over and patted Tucker on the shoulder. "I know you like the knife, and it's important to me that you have it."

Tucker sniffed as his eyes filled with water. "Thanks, Grandpop."

"Well, now, ya daresn't get any of those tears on my other present." Gramma went out into the kitchen and came back with a pie. "I have a nice birthday cake to share with everyone; but this sugar cream pie is all yours, Tucker. Happy Birthday."

"And mine," Christy grabbed the pie, pretending to snatch it from in front of him. "Your grandma said I could share in your birthday dessert."

"Birthday cake is dessert, too," Tucker teased.

"Yes, I believe I'll have some cake … right beside my piece of pie." Christy smiled so big the three freckles on her nose danced in place.

Betsy looked up sheepishly. "My piggy bank is empty, Tuck. So, I have a unique present. Uncle Jacob said he'd put up a basketball hoop for us this afternoon. For your birthday, I promise to not make more baskets than you for the next week."

"Oh sure." Tucker snickered. "You? Five-foot-tall-Betsy? That'll be the day." He took his table knife and cut a medium piece of pie, ready to plop it on Betsy's dessert plate. "For your great sacrifice, here's some pie to go with your cake."

"Well, Tucker," Carolyn began, "I don't have to work at the telephone office until after lunch today. I wanted to be here for your birthday. You must remember, Tucker, my paycheck isn't very big and what I can save, goes toward my wedding after I graduate from high school. So," Carolyn, no taller than Gramma, straightened, "for your birthday, I agree to take you into Goshen to see a movie. I'll pay for your admission, and you can invite a few friends. But they'll have to pay for their own movie ticket."

"Gee Carolyn, that's great." Tucker couldn't believe his ears. Carolyn often didn't like the movies he wanted to see.

He wondered if she would decide which movies were on her okay-list. For now, he wouldn't bring that up.

Christy got up from the table, picked up Tucker's empty dinner plate along with her own, and took them out to the kitchen sink.

"You don't have to do that, Christy." Tucker's grandmother hurried over to the sink and pumped some water over the dishes. "You're a guest."

"I enjoy it, Mrs. Moyer." Christy looked back at the table. The family had finished eating and was sharing in the birthday fun. "I have no brothers and sisters. I like all the love and hub bub around here."

Gramma rolled her eyes. "Ja, hub bub." She picked up a two-layer chocolate cake and started back into the dining room. "Christy, please bring the dessert plates I have stacked there on the counter."

"Cake time," Gramma announced. Small candy basketballs Carolyn made from sugar dotted the baked masterpiece. When Gramma began singing *Happy Birthday* the rest of the family joined in, laughing. The cake was so large, careful, equal pieces wouldn't be necessary. She simply slabbed off generous hunks and passed them around the table.

Uncle Jacob tapped his fork on the side of his dessert plate. "That's not all, Tucker." Leaning forward, he added, "I hope it's okay with you."

"What is it?" Tucker creased his brow, puzzled.

Uncle Jacob spoke softly. "Well, it's not really a *what*, it's a *who*."

"A who?"

"You can't outgrow this present," his uncle said with a laugh. "Your dad is coming by soon with Noah Dominick."

"Old Noah?" Tucker's eyes popped. He knew Noah. Tucker had cleaned up his yard and weeded his garden during the summer after Noah tripped and injured his arm. "Will he drive over in his 1925 Maxwell* with the crazy paint job?"

"Not this time." Uncle Jacob paused, and then grinned. "Chicken feathers, that stuck all over it when he re-painted the car, didn't add much, did they?" The entire family erupted in laughter.

Grandpop took over the conversation. "Remember last summer when Noah told you he'd like for you to have his 1931 Model A?"

"Right," Tucker drew out. "Tim said I couldn't have it."

Betsy jumped in. "Tim over-does the big brother thing sometimes."

"And, that was wrong." Gramma agreed. "But it was easier for him to say no all the time to things you wanted, keeping you two younger children under his thumb, than it was to risk not saying anything, and one of you got hurt."

"But it wasn't his decision to make." Grandpop smacked his hand on the table with authority. "Your grandma and I decided the Model A would be a good project for an ingenious boy like you. Your dad will follow Noah and drive him home."

Tucker couldn't say anything. He was afraid the magical words would dissolve. He knew he remembered seeing the old Ford in Noah's faded red barn, tucked away toward the creek. He also knew Noah's crooked little house was just down the road from where his father lived.

Finally, he shook his head in amazement. "So, Dad and Noah Dominick are coming soon … to bring Noah's old Model A Ford … for me?" Tucker's smile worked its way across his face. "Snazzy! What a great thirteenth birthday present!"

Chapter Four
Wheels but No Wherewithal

Tucker transferred his third piece of pie to his other hand as he slipped his arm through his sleeve. He finished putting on the jacket out on the side porch. When the last big gulp of sweet pie filled him up, he looked for a place to flip the remaining bite of thick creaminess. Joe skittered off the porch and pranced in the yard, like a wide receiver ready to catch the quarterback's toss.

Tucker's grandfather opened the door part-way and spoke around the edge. "Ya daresn't throw Joe over the porch railing some pie. Bugs you could draw."

"Okay, Grandpop," Tucker agreed and shoved the last full, sweet chunk in his mouth. Together, he and Christy sat down on the porch steps and waited for the Model A to show up.

Christy smiled and stole a glance behind her to see if Tucker's granddad was still there. "I like the way your grandfather talks."

"It's Pennsylvania Dutch," Tucker looked back and smiled. "He's been in Indiana since he was twenty-five-years-old. He's eighty-nine. Wonder how long it takes to lose an accent?"

The two sat huddled as the wind blew icy cold, like winter had snuck in without warning. Christy folded the full skirt of her shirtdress with the Peter Pan collar her grandmother made from blue oxford cloth, behind her knees and tucked it in beneath the Levi's she wore underneath. The day before had been balmy and dry, but, that Saturday afternoon, dark clouds gathered in the corner of the sky.

The dampness of the afternoon seemed to seep through Tucker's jacket and penetrate to his bones. He could smell the earthiness of the musty dirt Grandpop had tilled in the garden. Regardless of the cold weather, Tucker's excitement over the Model A was amazingly hot and hung in the air like jungle mist, almost blocking out the coldness of the day.

Tucker's head was full of anxious noise. *Hurry up. Where is he? Hurr-y up.* Tucker didn't blather on so anyone else could hear, however. For a compulsive talker, it was amazing that he was too excited to prattle.

Rosie, Christy's pot-bellied pig, waddled around from the backyard and squatted down at Christy's feet. "Does Mom know you walked back over here, Rosie?"

"Rosie can find you anywhere, Christy. Almost like Joe," Tucker said with a smile as the dog sniffed at the short, stout pig. "Right, Joe?" He nuzzled the war hero's ears.

Tiny danced around on her four hairy paws, forcing her little wet nose between Tucker's hand and Joe's ears. "Yes, yes, Tiny. I know you're here." He pulled the small dog onto his lap. Tucker thought she felt like she needed a good brushing where the curly hair on her underbelly matted together with a few damp Autumn leaves.

Christy sat quietly for a moment, patting Rosie's full round side. Tucker could hear Rosie's tummy gurgle from where he sat. Finally, Christy smiled mischievously, slowly shook her head, and whispered, "Tucker Dawson, not McBride? I wouldn't have guessed it."

"Uh-huh." Tucker agreed but didn't take his eyes off the street. He sighed as another feeling of emptiness flowed over him. "Dawson ... more family I don't know."

The humming and chugging of passing cars and the distant ringing of a bicycle bell were the only sounds he heard. A Dodge sedan, the interurban bus, and a new 1946 tan Plymouth went by, but not the old Ford.

Across Moyer Avenue, Rev. Daily walked through the church parking lot from the parsonage. "He has his days mixed up," Tucker pointed as the pastor started up the back steps of the church.

"He's a day early," Christy agreed with a chuckle. She pulled her navy blue, double breasted, peacoat more tightly around her, hugging her body, as she rocked back and forth.

Tucker sat there for a while. He thought about the old car and how Tim muscled in and prevented his great opportunity to get one a few months back. He could have gotten the A last summer before Tim left for the Marines. "Grandpop said Tim had no right to tell Noah I couldn't have the old Model A."

"I know," Christy agreed. She paused, digging the toe of her brown oxford into the little weeds that popped up through the cracks in the sidewalk. "Your grandmother said Tim was just trying to protect you from getting hurt, Tucker." Neither one of them said anything for a minute. "You'll have to admit, you do dangerous things sometimes."

Tucker remained silent and looked out to the road again, hoping Noah would get there so this conversation would stop. Instantly, an exciting distraction popped into his mind, as it often did when he was anxious. The tense anticipation, waiting for the car of his own, melted from his face. "I've got an idea."

"Oh, no," Christy moaned.

He jumped up from the steps, reached around behind the wooden lattice panel that blocked the space under the porch, and pulled out a mason jar he stashed there a few weeks before. The cool area under the porch, with its three and a half foot headroom, was the perfect place for Tucker's private treasure chest. That's where he hid another pint jar, the one from Schmidt's Dairy he'd filled with Indian Head pennies, and an old tin box in which he stored his collection of bottle caps.

"What ya got?" Christy asked as she started following him down the sidewalk and across the side street toward the church. A little parade followed, including Joe-the-protector, Tiny-the-rascal, and Rosie-the-large-ham-on-cloven-trotters.

Tucker laughed as he turned the glass jar around in his hand. "Gramma canned these tomatoes a year ago. When I brought this jar up from the fruit room in the basement, she said the lid had lost its vacuum and the seal popped. She told me to throw it away." He slowed as he neared the brick corner of the church. "I had other plans for it."

"Tucker, no," Christy gasped slowly with a crocked grin. "It only works with over-ripe fresh tomatoes."

"Never you mind." Tucker brushed the thought away with his hand and turned to the animals with a firm command. "Stay." He opened his jacket and jammed the jar inside his red plaid flannel shirt, making sure he tucked the tail tightly into his jeans, and closed his jacket around him. "Hope I don't break anything," Tucker mumbled as he stepped on the protruding water spigot and wrapped his fingers around the nearest down spout. Wondering if he looked like Batman scaling the wall with his bat-cape flowing out behind him, he peeked in a church window. Pastor Dailey had just settled in to work at his desk. Tucker jumped down, waved a "follow me" gesture to Christy, and slipped into the church through the side door with Christy at his heals. Down the hall a few steps, careful not to click on the tiles, the two slipped silently through a narrow door in the hallway and darted up the winding stairs to the belfry.

As Tucker pushed the trap door open at the top of the steps and eased into the tower-like space above, the wind blew even colder from inside the open-air steeple. "You'll wish you had your knit hat on up here," he cautioned Christy as he took her hand and helped hoist her through the opening.

Black tar paper wasn't the only thing that covered the floor of the tower. As he took a few steps, his shoes made ticky-tacky sounds. Looking down, the corners of his mouth drooped into a near-gag. "There's pigeon hooey all over the floor. Your high-top galoshes would have been perfect for this belfry." He tried to ignore the filthy floor, covered with gray and white lumpy stuff, breathed in a gulp of fresh air, and pulled out the jar of spoiled tomatoes from under his clothing.

"Oh, Tucker McBride, you are not...." Christy held her fingers up to her nose as she stared at the jar.

"Sure ... why not?" When he opened the canning jar, a putrid, rancid odor escaped and hung above them like a cloud of acid rain.

"Tucker, no—" Christy grabbed her mouth and gagged.

He reached into the jar, wrapped his fingers around a large sloppy red tomato that squished through his fingers, waited for a passing car, then flung it at the windshield with his best baseball pitch. The lumpy part of the tomato splatted across the surface of the pane, as the stinking juice oozed down the glass.

"Hey!" Tucker heard the driver yell as his front wheels swerved a little into the crunchy gravel of the berm.

Christy had already ducked below the half-wall that surrounded the tower, careful not to get her clothes in the poo on the floor. Tucker only stooped down in a shot, far enough his eyes could still see over the side. He chuckled softly.

"Tucker, get that slop out of here," Christy choked out a muffled plea.

"Still have some." He eased up slowly and looked over the side until he spotted another car. His eyes lit up when a two-door coupe approached. The car looked familiar, but he didn't take the time to figure out who it belonged to. He was having so much fun, caution and common sense seemed to have floated away on the foul stench of tomatoes.

"I'm watching for a small car; the smaller the target, the more points toward my Olympic blue ribbon." His grin nearly burst his face as a smaller car got closer.

Christy shook her head in disbelief. "The first-place winner of the nasty poison throwing event?"

Tucker stood up as the 1940 Studebaker Champion came nearer. "Okay!" His elation bubbled over and must have splashed on his brain. Rather than aiming at the windshield, Tucker thought the open driver's window was a better challenge. With a full thrust of his shoulder, he shot the last two rot-filled tomatoes at the half rolled down window.

To Tucker, the next seconds were a blur. A woman screamed, veered off the highway and into the ditch at the side of the road where she jumped out, staggered back into the street wiping the rotten tomatoes from her face. Half bent over in the middle of the road, the tall woman gagged, threw up on the pavement and her white coat, while other drivers grabbed their steering wheel, skidded to a stop, and honked their horn.

Tucker looked at Christy, grinning. "Wonder who she is."

Christy nearly choked. "Mrs. Hunter, Tucker. It's Mrs. Hunter."

Tucker's face drained of color, while his eyes grew huge and his mouth popped open. "Our teacher? That Mrs. Hunter?" His stomach rolled and pitched like a small boat in a hurricane.

From the side yard below, the sound of Joe's deep throated barking muffled the high pitched yap, yap, yapping of Tiny, and nearly drowned out Rosie's frantic squeals, adding chaos to the racket out front. Tucker peeked over the side; this time as inconspicuous as possible. "It is her!" he gulped in a hoarse whisper.

He nearly dropped the canning jar as he fell to the floor of the belfry like a lead baseball at home plate. "Run...! While she can't see us," he whispered loudly. He searched his pants on both sides of his body for any evidence of squishy tomatoes or bird dropping smears. Then, in a flurry of frantic fuss, the two bounded down the steps, two at a time, paused at the door, slowly eased themselves through the opening into the hall with the appearance of total calm. They strolled the few steps toward the outside door and cautiously pushed it open, as if a Bible Study session just ended. Tucker felt guilty. He finally made himself come to the reality that no Bible was involved in his previous activity. Tiny yipped and jumped, wiggling herself into a ball of fuzz. When Joe fell into step beside him, Tucker remembered: acting more grown up had been a goal of his since last summer.

"Don't look at the highway," Tucker whispered as they started across Moyer Avenue. Swooping Tiny off the ground, he held her in his left arm, while with his right hand, he muzzled her mouth. Granted, the silky had never bit him, but her little teeth felt sharp. "If we don't pay any attention to the hub bub on the road out front, maybe they won't notice us."

"What hub bub?" Christy asked as she watched to make sure Rosie had crossed the street safely.

Together, with their normal pets, on a normal day, they sat down on normal steps as any normal young people would, completely unaware of the strange, not-so-normal happenings on the road out front. Light snow flakes began to fall, hardly big enough to count, but large enough for Tucker to change the subject.

"The first snow of the season," he said with a smile and stuck out his tongue to feel the freshness of the star-shaped icy crystals.

Christy lightly jabbed him on the arm. "Just you wait, Tucker McBride. When there's enough snow to have a snowball fight, consider yourself challenged."

Tucker turned and stared her down. "Bring her on, my friend."

Christy glanced again in their teacher's direction. "Simon Winkler just brought some towels out of his store so Mrs. Hunter could wipe off some of that gunk." Both sat in silence for a few more seconds. "She's still kinda bent over her car," Christy whispered.

"Did she look over this way?" Tucker asked without looking toward the commotion. He could almost feel the slime on his own skin. He compulsively rubbed at his face, like the time Tubby Alexander hit him in the face with a pie at the school carnival, and Tucker couldn't stop wiping off the pumpkin.

Christy smiled a surprised smile. "She didn't look this way even once." As Christy watched, the street began to clear of the little circus and her eyes brightened. "Snazzy. Look Tucker."

Tucker slowly got to his feet as the 1939 Packard he had been watching for pulled off South Main Street and stopped at the sidewalk. Behind his dad's green car, an older model Ford chugga chugged in front of him. Tucker's grin completely covered his face. He summed up his excitement with Christy's favorite word, "Snazzy."

Chapter Five
Trying on an A for Size

Tucker watched as a well-groomed man in worn clothes opened the Packard's door and stepped out. "Happy Birthday, Tucker."

"Thanks, Dad." But Tucker didn't move. Tension between him and his dad had eased in the last few months, but not completely lifted. He just couldn't complete his feeling of "belonging". Too many people were missing, too many he hardly knew. When the Army released Joe, it helped. Since Tucker's valiant dog finally came home, long after the war was over, the German shepherd became the glue that patched together Tucker's idea of family. He reached down and scratched the top of the dog's head between his ears.

"Christy," Tucker's dad greeted, "it's good to see you again. Glad to see you celebrated Tucker's birthday with him." Sean McBride slowly walked half-way up the sidewalk, looking toward the road. "What happened on the highway?" he asked as he squinted his eyes in the direction of the woman still bent over the hood of her car.

Christy conjured up the most innocent face Tucker had ever seen. "Did something happen?" she asked.

"Something did," Sean's voice faded out as they all watched the lady brush her dress frantically.

"Yuck," Mrs. Hunter squealed loud enough Tucker could hear her from the side porch. "Yuck, yuck, yuck," she shuddered, swiping at her dress, and looking around, first at the little grocery, then the church, Moyer's house, and the house on the other side.

Tiny jumped at the noise, anxious; but Joe took a more watchful stance with his ears alert and his gaze fixed on the road. "It's okay, boy," Tucker reassured him. "Wonder what's going on," Tucker shrugged. Although, he could almost feel on his own skin, the gunk Mrs. Hunter experienced. He chose to look past the lady soaked in pukey, rotten tomatoes. Tucker looked up, "Hi Noah!" Tucker smiled as he pointed to the 1931, blue, two-door Ford Model A Noah pulled off the road and parked half on the grass at the side of the house.

Tiny wiggled and jumped, following Joe to the old car now parked beside the house. The two dog-friends sniffed the tires together.

Mussed and tattered, Noah Dominick slowly pulled his bent body from the '31 Ford, an appropriate antique car for an antique old coot. "Well, now, birthday boy, here 'tis."

"Hot dog!" Tucker exhaled every breath in his body. He stood for a moment as his eyes popped. Could he believe the A-Model car was really his? He could feel his heart going giddy-up.

"Get in," Noah insisted. "It's your A-bone*. Key's in the ignition, and the starter is the button above the accelerator."

"A-bone yes, it's a classic with good bones. But I won't customize it." Tucker looked at the car then at his dad. He didn't move but waited for a silent signal.

"Noah, the boy's only thirteen. He doesn't have a driver's license yet."

"A license?" Noah took off his slouchy, brown felt hat and tapped the rim on his lips. "Do ya have to have a license to drive these days?"

"Well …" Sean drew out slowly, "yes. We all need an operator's license, to prove we can drive."

Noah scratched his stubbly beard and checked his pocket watch. "Really? Um … maybe I'd better get one."

"Say, Tucker," Sean continued chattering, "thought you might want to know. My ex-sister-in-law, Polly Rayburn, said your little brother, Bobby, and his mother are visiting in Goshen over the holiday."

Tucker's heart leaped in his throat. *Someone else I hardly know.* But he didn't say it aloud. "I haven't seen Bobby since he was five, before he and his mom moved to California."

Sean smiled wide. "They haven't been back since then, least not that I heard."

"You don't know where your son is or what he's doing?" Tucker's tone was more cheeky than curious. He knew his own life ran parallel to his father's. His dad lived only a few miles away, but their daily lives rarely crossed. Tucker snapped back to reality and stopped.

Noah motioned to Tucker. "Go on, get in. Your dad has to get to work, and he's gonna take me home first."

"Okay," Tucker looked to his dad for a sign of disapproval. Nothing. The car's chrome door handle felt smooth in his hand, not worn, still as spectacular as when it was new. Tucker felt giggly inside but didn't want to show excitement. He wanted to get in with a grown-up air.

Inside the car, it smelled like the chickens that roamed all around Noah's barnyard with their feathers tucked into the A model's seat cushions and floating from the ceiling. Tucker muffled a gut busting laugh when he thought again of the paint job Noah did last summer on his own car, complete with white and brown feathers embedded in the new paint. Tucker rolled down the driver's side window, airing out the fowl aroma. "This feels great." However, Tucker had to admit, if only to himself, the smell inside the car was not as exciting as the fact the car was his. Every odor from the old barn mingled with the chicken perfume: cat droppings, soggy hay, moldy pigeon feathers, and stale old everything, all blended to create an aroma Tucker thought best labeled—Barn Stench*.

Christy eyed the short, square frame of the fun-size car, and couldn't wait. "I'm getting in. I want to see the inside of heaven, too." She ran around, yanked the door open, and popped into the passenger seat. She wiggled and adjusted her coat, seeming to build a permanent nest. Wrinkling her nose, she looked at Tucker and mouthed, "Baking soda bombs."

Tucker snickered and nodded but said nothing about the odor. "I'm going to start it, Christy." Tucker reached for the key, and then stopped. "Are you sure you want to stay in?"

She paused for a minute. "Do you have any idea how to start this thing?"

"Yep, I sure do," he bragged.

"Nein*, Tucker, nein," Grandpop yelled as he darted out of the house, his fist waving in the air. "Ya daresn't move that car, Tucker. Confound it, Sean, what were ya thinkin'?"

Sean threw his hand to his mouth. "Sorry, Joseph, he didn't say he couldn't drive."

"He can drive, he's just not old enough to be on the road," Grandpop bellowed, still agitated. "And, I need to know if the car can be driven first. Jacob can check it out. He just finished eating."

"Right. Sorry again." Sean started to turn to leave, his head down.

"Sean," Joseph called to him after he calmed down. "Thanks for helping Noah bring the car. Tucker will have fun learnin' 'bout it. It's a great present." He added, "Noah, 'tis a wonderful thing, your givin' the boy a car of his own."

"You have quite a young man there, Mr. Moyer," Noah said with his fingers to his cap in a respectful salute. "He has helped me many times and I can't always pay him. He rode by on his bike two weeks ago and saw me struggling with my storm windows. Once he got me down off the ladder, he washed each one of them and put them in for me. I couldn't give him nothin'. This is the least I can do."

"Thanks, Noah," Tucker said with an embarrassed grin. "You don't have to pay me. I'm happy to help you." He stopped and ran his fingers over the dashboard. Regardless of the dirt and dust, Tucker thought it was the most beautiful car he'd ever seen. "Sure am glad you decided to give me the car though. Thanks."

Tucker ran his hands down the matte-black, four-spoke steering wheel and across the horn button in the center. Was it possible? Did he really own his own car? He made pantomime gestures of beeping the horn and laughed.

Grandpop leaned in the open window and patted the boy's shoulder. "Go ahead, Tucker. It's okay."

Christy covered her ears with her hands. Her eyes sparkled with excitement.

Tucker couldn't resist. He pounded the horn with excited glee. *Ahooga. Ahooga.* Tucker smiled; his voice lowered to a reverent pitch. "Nothing sounds as good as an Ahooga horn."

Chapter Six
The Car Ride

Tucker's dad left to take Noah home before going to work at Garland's Department Store in Goshen. It would only be a few hours of Saturday work. Thanksgiving would be Thursday and one of Sean's responsibilities was to decorate the store windows. The display would only be up one week, a transitional window between the warmth of Thanksgiving and the Christmas splash of red and green that would continue in the larger store window to the right.

Tucker touched every dial and gauge, while Christy sat in the car and waited patiently. "Except for some dirt ... and the smell of course ... the inside is pretty much okay," Tucker finally determined after careful inspection. "The mohair* upholstery is pretty good, no tears...still a little soft even."

"Right," Christy agreed reluctantly. "But, the outside—"

Tucker started to laugh, then stopped. "Wait, I don't know what I'm laughing about. I'll be the one to clean off all that stuff."

Christy tried to muffle her own chuckles. "Wonder how many pigeons it takes to get that much poop on a car?"

"Maybe one," Tucker observed as he looked past the steering wheel and out the front window, "if it has good aim. The car's been in the center of the bull's-eye for years. It was sitting in the same spot in the barn and hasn't moved."

"Wonder if the car came into Indiana on the Erie Canal?" Christy mused as she looked around inside the old Ford.

"Hardly," Tucker laughed as he turned. "Grandpop said the last canal boat docked in Huntington County in 1874. That's twenty-five years after Gramma's people came into Indiana, at Canal Lock Four in Roanoke, and almost fifty years before they made this Ford."

Christy paused for a moment. "Wonder what it would be like to ride on a canal boat."

"I remember a book I saw in the school library called *Canal Town*." Tucker closed his eyes and enjoyed the pictures in his mind. He saw himself as the tall lean man on the cover, in a gray felt top hat, with a canal lock and boat behind him. He imagined himself running to the dock, making a flying leap, and jumping on board the long flat boat. Oh, the places he would go, and the people he would talk to. He could almost feel the movement of the water beneath him. Then he realized it was only Joe, who had jumped in the car when Christy got in, moving around at Christy's feet.

Tucker's eyes sparkled as he continued dreaming of possibilities. "Yeah, I thought about riding down the canal and watching as the locks opened and closed. I dreamed of spending a summer working for a lock keeper. Together we'd raise or lower the water so the packet boats* could safely maneuver along the canal route." Silent for a while, he sat there thinking and remembered an old song.

> "Low bridge, everybody down. Low bridge, 'cause we're coming to a town. And, you'll always know your neighbor, you'll always know your pal, if ya ever navigated on the Erie Canal."

He smiled a memory-smile. "The good stuff has already passed, like canal boats, cattle drives, and laying the great railroad tracks."

"Railroad tracks?" Christy's eyes popped.

"Sure. I've looked at Grandpop's pictures of train wrecks and damaged bridges and trestles all my life. Grandpop was the foreman of the bridge building and repair crew." Tucker sat there remembering as snowflakes fluttered through the open window. He wondered what it would have been like to stand on top of a train bridge when the temperature in northern Indiana was 10 below zero. "I always thought that would be fun. I may not be able to have an exotic Erie Canal adventure, but the train? Now, that's something else. A canal boat's construction reminds me of the square, flat boxcars that go by on the rails through Dunlap." Tucker leaned out the window as his uncle came up to the car. "Uncle Jacob?"

"Hop out, Tucker. I'll give the car a once-over."

"Thanks." Tucker and Christy got out and Jacob got in.

"Tucker?" Freddie Cooper asked as he slowed his dad's old-fashioned high-rise bicycle. He slid off the back and parked it near Moyer's gate. "Where'd the classy classic come from?"

Tucker patted the roof of the A and caressed the still shiny metal with his fingertips. "It's mine."

"Yours?" Freddie squealed. "How? When?"

"Hey, is this an interrogation, Freddie Boy? You bet the A is mine." Tucker pointed with his thumb over his shoulder to the back of the car. "Raise the rumble seat*, get in and try it out."

Uncle Jacob got out again and started around the front of the car. "I'll get a few tools from Dad's shed. While I get them, you can take the kids for a ride ... but, just around the block."

"Yeah!" Tucker pumped his fist with enthusiasm and got back in the driver's seat. He was so proud he worried his hat might get too small. Christy took the front right seat and Freddie piled into the rumble seat. Scrunched down, with sky over his head, Freddie rolled himself into a tight ball. It was about 25° F outside. He pulled his orange cap down over his red hair and covered his ears.

Tucker grinned. Freddie looked a little like he was sitting in the trunk with the lid open backwards. Tucker checked out the dashboard, and located all the knobs, switches, and levers. "I watched Tim start his Model A often enough, I got the pattern down to a smooth rhythm." Tucker saw Christy roll her eyes but said nothing. He'd show her.

He turned the fuel shut-off-valve to the "on" position and put the shift stick in neutral. Next, he moved down the spark retard lever on the steering column. On the right side, under the steering wheel, he pulled the accelerator lever down two notches, turned the key in the ignition to "on," pulled out the choke, put his foot on the starter button on the floor, turned the spark advance lever up, and pushed the throttle up slowly. It spluttered, rattled, and shook like a rocker with a tomcat trapped under one rail.

"She sounds a little rumbly but she's running." Tucker was so excited he thumped his hands on the steering wheel in glee.

"She?" Christy slouched down in a pout and folded her arms across her chest. "So…which *she* do you know that is square and rattles when she walks?"

"Well, now …," Tucker began as he pulled in behind the church and drove across the parking lot. "If I think long enough, I'm sure I can come up with several *shes* who rattle."

They both laughed until Christy saw where Tucker had turned. "Where ya goin'? Your Uncle Jacob said you could drive around the block."

"I know," Tucker agreed with a tease, "but, he didn't say which block."

At the highway he turned left and immediately right again onto County Road 13 across from his home, over the railroad tracks, then turned right onto the Old Goshen Road. Driving west for about two miles, they came to the Elkhart County Home.

"There are a hundred and thirteen rooms in that old building. Carolyn calls it Gothic style. Not sure what that means, but it sounds good. People work on the farm and then have a bed to sleep in at night." Tucker shivered as they passed. He wondered, what would have happened to him, Tim, Carolyn, and Betsy if Grandpop and Gramma hadn't taken them in? Would they have ended up living in that big, cold institution?

Christy watched as they passed the old white building. "Mom said there are all kinds of people living there: orphaned, old, poor, and even mentally ill."

"I know," Tucker said softly. "Kinda like our house, without the mental ones of course." He slowed the old Ford as he neared the corner. "I'll turn at the next road past the home, and then double back to the railroad tracks there on County Road 13."

Christy was quiet for a minute, then calculated, "So, for you, the block you're going around is a two-mile square, or eight miles all around ... the ... *block*."

"Sounds right," Tucker agreed as he turned the corner and started down the second two-mile stretch.

"Look," Christy pointed to Frank Moody's house.

Tucker heard the noise before he saw Frank's truck. He could hear the crunch and crackle produced by the red Chevy as the truck rolled back and forth in the driveway. "That's the easiest way to get the green husk off the black walnuts ... run over them."

The gentle snow already covered the taller grass in the fields. Rays from the early afternoon sun made it look like sparkling magic had dusted the ground and bare branches of the overhanging trees.

"Oh, look," Christy pointed to the field off to the left. "The corn maze from October is beginning to look like a huge snow sculpture. I'm surprised it's still standing."

"Want to stop and go through it? No one's around though. We might get lost."

"Tucker, we are already way too far from your house." Christy's voice took a serious tone. "Your uncle said he was coming right back to check out the car."

"I guess you're right," Tucker agreed reluctantly. They made the final turn and headed up the last two-mile leg of the "Tucker-block". As they neared the railroad tracks just down from the house, the car began to sputter.

"Tucker, what's wrong with the A?" Christy sat up straight, straining to see out the front window.

"Don't know yet," he spoke softly and listened to the spitting sound. As they approached the tracks, Tucker began to hold his breath.

"Tucker, why are you holding—?"

The A-Model gave one last exhale and stopped at the peak of the incline, straddling the tracks perfectly, as if Tucker had aimed the car to fizzle-out in a perfect balance on the tracks. He sighed deeply. "We're out of gas."

"Out of gas?" Christy screamed. "Why didn't you stop before you started across the tracks instead of stopping on the top?"

Tucker stuttered as much as the car had, before it hung up on the rails. "I hoped we'd make it."

"Look!" she yelled again as she pointed down the tracks at an approaching huffing and puffing steam engine.

Freddie began banging on the back window with his fists. "Tucker!" His voice sounded panicked. "The train!"

"We ran out of gas." Tucker called back over his shoulder. "I can't get it started again."

Freddie jumped out of the rumble seat and ran around to the driver's window, his coat pulled tightly around him and his teeth chattering. "Unless you want your Model A reduced to a pile of steel, you better think of something." He checked the approaching train again. "I'll push, you steer."

"Hurry!" Christy kept her eyes on the train as it got closer, her hands trembling.

"Christy, you steer and I'll help Freddie push," Tucker commanded. He grabbed her coat sleeve and pulled her toward the steering wheel.

"I can't drive," she choked out, her hands waving in panic.

"You don't have to drive, silly." He yanked her arm again and forced her hand onto the wheel. "It won't run without gas. Just steer."

Tucker jumped out, ran around, and heaved his shoulder into the left side of the back bumper. It started to move but when he saw the tires wedge sideways in the tracks, he had to make a new plan. "Hold the wheel tight!" He shouted to Christy around the side of the car.

"I'll try!" Christy bellowed back. She clutched the wheel between her hands. Through gritted teeth she shouted back, "Okay, try again." Looking down the tracks she squealed out, "And ... hurry!"

The warm ground mixed with the light snow and turned the dirt under Tucker and Freddie's feet into a melted, sloppy, muddy covering. Tucker puffed himself up and began to lean into the fender, pushing and shoving the Model A from behind, with Freddie helping at his side. Slipping and sliding in the slush, the coupe's tires locked and skidded across the tracks. Tucker shot a glance down the rails, vibrating with the weight of the heavy steam engine and cars behind it. The closer the chuff chuffing sounded, the larger the engine seemed to grow. The approaching train's whistle sounded fearful and forlorn as the brakes hissed, screeched, and tried to slow to a stop.

When the Ford finally cleared the tracks, Tucker and Freddie hopped to the other side, turned, and waved at the engineer. The man in the blue striped hat and coveralls waved back, pulled the leaver for more steam, and resumed the speed as the pufferbelly passed.

"Whew," Freddie gasped, doubled over at the waist, and groaned to get his breath.

Tucker laughed, grabbed Freddie by his coat and joggled him with gusto. "Thanks!" He shook his head in disbelief. "We sure came close."

"Tucker!" Christy yelled frantically from the car.

Tucker couldn't believe his eyes. It wasn't over. The A-Model kept silently rolling on, no engine, no power.

"Put the break on," he screamed and started running. With the car still moving, he jumped on the running board, grabbed the passenger side door, jerked it open. and slid through the open door. "There, that's it," he pointed to the foot pedal on the right. "Stomp on that one!"

Christy quickly shifted her foot to the brake pedal as Tucker grabbed the wheel and let the car coast to the side of the road. "Tucker McBride," she got in his face and yelled, "you nearly got us all killed!"

"Sorry." But he didn't spend any time feeling guilty. Getting out of the car just as Freddie recovered enough to join him, he looked back in the car. "Are ya comin'? We're almost home. No lollygagging. I'll bring some gas back."

"No lollygagging?" Christy mouthed back. "Freddie and I aren't the ones who drove eight miles out of the way." She strutted off in the lead. "Well, come on," she ordered.

Tucker and Freddie stomped the mud from their shoes and fell in step behind her. Tucker didn't think he liked being behind. With each step, he remembered. During the years his grandfather worked on the railroad, Grandpop hopped off the train at that very spot and walked the few blocks back to the house. Now on foot, Tucker traced his grandfather's footsteps home … and finally wondered if he'd be in trouble when he got there.

Chapter Seven
Sunday Rest Day

Tucker opened his eyes early on Sunday morning to the wonderful smell of crisp bacon and the familiar melodies Gramma played on the piano. Each Sunday before church, she practiced the music for worship. Tucker awakened a couple of hours before, but he didn't want to get out of bed. The first thought that popped into his mind about 4 AM was Gramma's reaction to his round-the-country-square the previous day.

He remembered as clearly as if Gramma were standing beside his bed. She said, "Sorry you took so long to go around the block, Tucker." Her tone was calm and sweet; but dug into the guilty spot in his head like a woodpecker on a dying tree. "When you didn't come right back, Uncle Jacob went over to his fiancée's house. Jacob and Nona were planning to go to Notre Dame in the afternoon. When they remembered the team was playing at Tulane, in New Orleans, he and Nona decided to go to a movie this afternoon. So, the car's not ready to drive."

"Yes, Ma'am," Tucker remembered saying. But, as he lay there in bed that morning, he thought: *So much for driving any more for a while.*

"Jacob said you need more gas in the Model A," Gramma went on calmly. "You'll need to take some money out of your underwear drawer." Gramma hadn't looked up from Grandpop's sock she had on her darning egg*. She only paused as she pulled the thread through the toe. "Go over to Butch Randolph's station with Jacob's gas can and fill it up.

I notice the price is 21 cents a gallon today."

Tucker stewed about the events on his birthday for the next several hours of the morning. Finally, he sighed deeply, threw back the covers, jumped out of bed, and into his jeans. Down the steps two at a time, over the banister, and a perfect landing on the hardwood floor of the entry hall.

"Tucker," Carolyn gulped, "you're not wearing that to church, are you?"

"No," he sassed. "Is it what I usually wear?"

Carolyn smiled and patted his shoulder as he walked past her. "You don't have much time. Wash up, change, eat some Wheaties, brush your teeth and get out the door in twenty minutes."

But he thought, *I don't need instructions on getting ready for church.* "Uh-huh," he mumbled. One of Gramma's small mixing bowls was just the right size. He pulled one from the cabinet and dumped in almost a fourth of the entire box of Wheaties, then added milk. With the bowl in his left hand and a spoon in the right, he stood at the kitchen window, wolfing down the cereal as fast as he could.

"It's still there, Tucker," Grandpop chuckled as he walked up behind him. Together, they stared at the Model A through the window glass. "Too bad ... ya daresn't drive today. After church, Jacob is going to Nona's for lunch, radio music, and a few games of Scrabble. He'll have to look at the car tomorrow after work."

"And, you can't look over the car yourself, right, Grandpop?" Tucker slurped the last spoonful of cereal, put the bowl in the sink and pumped some water into it from the hand pump.

"You know I can't drive, Tucker. I figured there was no need to learn what's under the hood." He poured a little more coffee into his cup. "Now, hurry along."

• • • • •

The sanctuary was full that morning, just four days before Thanksgiving. Gramma was playing the hymn, *"Now Thank We All Our God"* on the old church pump organ as the service ended. The flowers Bitty Miller made from bright ribbons and fabric, along with leaves she had preserved in the fall, filled the alter with color and beauty.

Tucker and Christy eased past members of the congregation as everyone started filing out of the pews after the service. Gramma pushed the pump organ pedals with all her strength, filling the sanctuary with song. She was so short, she nearly stood as she pumped. She continued playing the thanksgiving song then switched to *"Be Thou My Vision."* Church friends gathered and talked about the week and their current aches and pains.

Aunt Cora and Uncle Jerry hurried out to their adult Sunday school class. Tucker wondered what Aunt Cora would bring for lunch later when they came for their weekly Sunday meal. There was always the dish of scalloped potatoes. However, he thought he might have heard her tell Gramma something about a pineapple upside-down cake.

"Hi, Tucker," a boy maneuvered his way up the aisle as other worshipers tried to ease their path to the back.

"Johnny Washington!" Tucker reached out and shook his friend's shoulder. "I didn't see you."

Johnny smiled and grabbed Tucker's arm. "Mom and I were driving down to Lake Wawasee at Syracuse to meet with some cousins for lunch. We'll gather in the camp hotel. We got to your church late, but Mom wanted to stop in here for part of church. She's going to Sunday school. Are you guys staying?"

"Sure," Tucker took Johnny's arm and pulled him by his shirt in the direction of the Junior High classrooms. "You remember Johnny Washington," Tucker called back to Christy.

Christy hurried to keep up. "I sure do. Your mother directs the choir at the A.M.E. church in Elkhart."

"Right," Tucker agreed. "Their choir came out and joined ours for a concert last summer."

"I remember, Johnny. You were looking at old issues of *The National Geographic Magazine* in Moyer's attic for pictures of Merkers, Germany. A sniper killed your dad, you said. But, the black G.I.s themselves weren't recognized in magazines or on newsreels."

"Wow," Johnny's face glowed in amazement. "You have some memory."

"She sure does," Tucker agreed. "She remembers stuff I'd rather she forgot about."

Up the steps and down the hall, they darted into Birdie Kline's Junior High Sunday school classroom. "Good morning, Mrs. Kline. You remember—?"

"Johnny Washington." Mrs. Kline's smile took over her face. She quickly reached out and gave the boy a hug. "Goldie's son." As short as she was, the boy of thirteen met her eye to eye.

"Yes, Ma'am." Johnny smiled and followed Tucker over to a few empty chairs in the semi-circle on the left side of the room.

Most of the girls had on a variation of the same clothes: a pleated, plaid skirt; a sweater turned backwards and buttoned down the back; and white bobbysocks with saddle shoes or penny loafers. It was like a uniform with a selection of colors.

Christy sat beside Tucker, then Johnny, and Freddie plopped down beside Johnny. Christy shuddered. With them lined up in a row, would they chatter all through class?

Mrs. Kline picked up a large blue platter. "Mrs. Cooper brought in a plate of chocolate chip cookies." She handed the plate to Freddie. "Please pass your mother's cookies to the class. Anna, if you give each one a napkin that would be nice."

Freddie grinned as Anna Frederick came forward. "Thanks, Anna." He blushed as the girl passed him.

Soon, the room was quiet as everyone bit into the chocolate wonders, but, not for long. "Woe is me," Anna moaned. "I got chocolate on my sweater."

"Miss Woe is at it again," Yvonne Sherbet rolled her eyes.

"Anyone as short as you, Yvonne, should complain about getting chocolate on their knee caps." Anna straightened up as tall as she could. "I don't think knees are very pretty, with or without smudges."

"That's why you wear such long skirts, Anna," Tucker snickered. "So your knees don't show."

"No," Freddie burst out, "She wears long skirts because it's the style, and Anna is stylish."

That's it, Tucker thought but didn't say aloud. *I knew Freddie likes her.* He surprised himself with his own grown up behavior, keeping his mouth shut in favor of his friend's feelings.

Darla put her coat back on. "Is Sunday school over, Mrs. Kline?"

"No, Dear. That was just a cookie. You're probably chilly because it's been snowing and your body isn't used to the below freezing temperatures." She got out her felt board and took out a box with various felt-fabric characters. "Our lesson today is about Paul's shipwreck. Acts 27:23-25."

[23] For there stood by me this night the angel of God, whose I am, and whom I serve,

[24] Saying, Fear not, Paul; thou must be brought before Caesar: and, lo, God hath given thee all them that sail with thee.

[25] Wherefore, sirs, be of good cheer: for I believe God, that it shall be even as it was told me.

Gilbert, Raymond, Ralph, and Darla listened intently to the lesson although Darla had put her stocking hat on along with her coat. Tucker wondered if Darla would be able to hear the lesson with the hat down over her ears. Anna fussed with her handkerchief, trying to get the chocolate out of her top, and Yvonne started writing notes on the back of the church bulletin she took from her pocket.

Freddie held his hand to the side of his mouth and whispered to Tucker past Johnny, "How's the car running?"

"Car?" Johnny's voice was merely a strained mumble.

Tucker covered his mouth and slid down in his chair. "Can't drive it, yet."

Christy pretended to cough and covered her mouth with her handkerchief. "His uncle was out and about yesterday and will be gone today. He wants to go over the car first."

Johnny moved to the edge of his seat. "Car? What car?"

"My car!" Tucker blurted out.

"Your car?" Anna barked back "You have a car?"

Tucker jerked around in excitement. "I sure do."

"My, my, my," Mrs. Kline drew out slowly, her small glasses bobbing up and down on her nose. "A car? Well, that's nice Tucker. Paul from the Bible didn't own a car and certainly not a boat. He boarded a ship with another captain. The skipper was sailing in the Mediterranean Sea on the way to Rome. They hit a sandbar and ran aground on the island of Malta." Her face lit up with excitement like she was talking about her best friend. "What would you do, Tucker, if your ship wrecked?"

"Swim, I guess," he thought aloud. "That sure would be an exciting adventure though." He leaned back and folded one foot over the other. "I was just thinking about riding on the Erie Canal. If they ran aground, I don't think you'd even get your feet wet."

"Interesting," Birdie Kline began again as Gilbert jumped in.

"We flipped our speedboat over on the lake last summer."

"Hey, Johnny," Tucker whispered off to the side, "remember, Carolyn is takin' us to a movie in Goshen on Wednesday. No school with Thanksgiving the next day. Can you go with us?"

"I forgot. Going to Goshen sounds like fun. Who's *we*?"

"Christy, Freddie, and I," Tucker whispered. "We'll go early and see if we can find Bobby."

Johnny's mouth curled up into a question mark. "Bobby? Who's Bobby?"

Tucker looked around the room to see who might be listening. Gilbert was still talking about their speed boat accident on the lake. Tucker put his napkin to his mouth as if chasing the last cookie crumb. "Bobby is my half-brother. We had fun before his mom took him to California when he was five-years-old. I wanna see if I can put a piece of my family puzzle in place."

Chapter Eight
Sunday Evening

Aunt Cora and Gramma washed, dried, and put away the Sunday dinner dishes before Cora and her family went home. Uncle Jerry would spend the evening in front of his ham radio set, contacting other ham operator-friends around the country. Tucker often laughed to himself about Jerry's love of all things electronic, since his uncle grew up in an Amish family where they didn't even own a telephone. Uncle Jerry was a brilliant man. Most of the people in the neighborhood didn't understand him, but Jerry belonged. He was family.

Tucker eyed the clock. Jack Benny's radio program would begin in an hour. Tucker always made a big bowl of tapioca pudding and a pan of buttered popcorn on Sunday evenings. He'd have it ready before Don Wilson introduced Jack, Phil Harris, Eddie "Rochester" Anderson, and Benny's wife, Mary Livingston.

Tucker got up from the living room floor where he poured over the Sunday comics. "Gramma, I'm going to make the pudding so it can cool a little. Will you want some?"

Gramma placed the crocheted cross she used as a bookmark in her Bible and gently closed the leather cover. "Ja, Tucker. I'll be ready for some coffee and food when you have the tapioca cooled a little. I like it warm, so I won't have to wait too long. Jacob already got out the violin stand you made for his birthday. He'll get out his violin soon. I'll come out to the kitchen and make the coffee here in a bit."

The red box of tapioca pearls was on the top kitchen cabinet shelf. Tucker pulled it down along with the bottle of vanilla, got out eggs and milk from the refrigerator, then smiled. He liked the sameness of his Sunday evenings. It felt safe and gave him another feeling of home. The side doorbell rang just as Tucker folded in the last of the beaten egg whites and placed the bowl on the dry sink* in the summer-kitchen. It was cool there, a few steps down off the kitchen.

When he raced back up and into the kitchen, he saw Gramma struggling to get up to answer the door. "I'll get it, Gramma," he offered in his usual willingness to help.

"Ja, Tucker. That's gut," she said with a mixed expression of appreciation and pain.

Grandpop's eyes popped opened when all the movement began. He and Gramma followed Tucker to the door. "Well, Rev. Daily, come in."

"Sorry, I came so late in the evening," the pastor apologized. "A few weeks ago, the congregation voted to buy an item for the church and it didn't get here until now."

"I hadn't heard about a purchase." Gramma put her hand on her hip to help her sore back stand straighter.

The pastor smiled. "Well, put your hat and coat on, Rebecca. Let's go over to the church."

"Now?" Gramma gasped, while dutifully taking her coat off the hall tree by the door. "Oh, wait. I'll put on the coffee before we leave." She slipped her arms into her coat and fixed her brown hat to her head with a long hat pin* through her hair. "You coming, Joseph?" She walked out to the kitchen as she buttoned up her coat and pumped water into the coffee pot.

"Ya," Joseph said as he stood and stretched. "When we get back, I'll eat some tapioca and then go to bed. I believe 4 AM will come just as early tomorrow as it did this morning."

"Ja, Joseph. I think you're right." Gramma came back from the kitchen, stepped out the door, and inhaled deeply. "It's crisp and clean out here. Smells gut."

Tucker ran ahead across the street, clutching his coat as he ran. The sun had already gone down. A multitude of stars blinked across the sky. Mesmerized by all the twinkling lights above, Tucker stumbled across the church driveway, staggering right, and left. Inside the church, he stole a guilty glance down the hall and saw the open tower door; but he pretended he didn't notice.

"In here," Pastor Daily announced as he led the way and held the sanctuary door open.

The whole family stopped at the entrance into the large worship room. The place still smelled like the candle wax Penny Cooper used to make the tapers for the altar. Tucker closed his eyes and inhaled the quiet of the room.

"Come on in," the pastor encouraged and walked backward in the direction of the front of the church. "Rebecca, the church has bought something for you to use and the organists who follow you."

"Gramma," Tucker gasped. "That's a new organ."

Gramma's eyes filled with tears as she walked slowly to the new Hammond organ. "Oh my."

Sandra Moyer, Tucker's cousin, sat on the organ bench and smiled as her grandmother walked up. "It's ready for you to try a chorus or two, Grandma."

Gramma slid onto the polished wood of the bench seat, and viewed the keys at a much different angle than from the round adjustable seat that sat at the pump organ. "I really don't need this fancy thing. If the kids have everything they need, shoes and stuff, that's all that's necessary." She gently placed her hands on the keys and stretched to reach the foot pedals. "I wonder if I'll lose the rhythm of the hymns if I'm not pumping while I'm playing the keys. With her hands on the keyboard again, a few bars of *Amazing Grace* filled the room.

Tucker's smile covered his face ... until he saw a familiar figure walk up the center aisle. Tim, not in military fatigues, but in his jeans and blue button-down shirt, walked up the aisle carrying Gramma's very familiar canning jar.

"Tim," Grandpop called out when he saw him. "Welcome home. You look gut."

Gramma came down from the organ loft to greet Tim. "Gut to see you, Tim. Are you hungry? We have some leftovers in the refrigerator."

"Sure, Grandma." His smile faded when he saw Tucker. "I hear you got that Model A from Noah Dominick," he barked.

"Yep," Tucker answered but said very little more.

Tim held the tomato jar out to Tucker. "I found this up on the floor of the bell tower. It looks like Grandma's jar."

Tucker looked at the glass and then at Gramma. What could he say that wouldn't get him in more trouble?

Gramma watched, not taking her eyes off the face of each grandson. "Have I ever stored my canning jars in the belfry of the church?"

Tucker couldn't believe his ears. Had Gramma lied? He thought about what she just said and realized it was a question not a statement. Tim hadn't even asked if the jar was hers and she hadn't said it was or wasn't. She asked a simple question.

Tucker scooted past everyone and darted out of the church. Perhaps Gramma saved the car after all.

$$\bullet \bullet \bullet \bullet \bullet$$

Over at the house, the tapioca was perfect. Like Goldilocks' porridge, not too hot, not too cold. Tucker got out the old popcorn popper with the red wooden handle and crank, the bacon grease Gramma saved from frequent breakfasts, and some butter from the new refrigerator. Within minutes and after three poppers-full, the whole house smelled like salted, buttered popcorn.

He got out a bottle of grapefruit flavored Squirt for himself. Gramma made a fresh pot of coffee.

Tucker carried his small mixing bowl full of tapioca, the Squirt bottle, and the huge helping of popcorn he dumped into Gramma's blue enamel pan into the living room.

Tucker had avoided his brother since they got back to the house. He didn't want to rehearse the canning jar rigmarole again. Still, looking at his own gigantic mountain of corn, he felt guilty. "Tim, the popcorn is ready. There's another Squirt in the refrigerator."

"Any Coke?" Tim looked away from the radio just as Don Wilson began announcing the start of the program.

Tucker smiled when he saw Tim's relaxed expression. Maybe the topic of the fruit jar was off the table. "Uncle Jacob knew you were coming home and brought in some Coke yesterday." Tucker found his empty spot on the floor and settled in.

"Tonight," Don Wilson began at 7 PM, "it's just four days before Thanksgiving. Jack welcomes all those who will join him for turkey and dressing."

"Ah, turkey and dressing," Tim sighed in bliss. "Real food."

Tucker watched his brother unwind like a tight scarf from around his neck. "Glad you're home," he said with a genuine smile.

"Glad to be home, Tuck," Tim said in return as his eyes slowly closed.

With Tim home until after Thanksgiving, life was comfortable, predictable, and safe. Just like every Sunday, Gramma read her Bible after Aunt Cora's family went home while Grandpop sat in his Morris chair and completed the crossword puzzles from the Elkhart Truth Newspaper and the South Bend Tribune. Everything was the same and Tucker was comfortable with that. The one difference was the new organ at the church. Tucker wondered what the change would mean. Maybe, Gramma's legs wouldn't be sore on Sunday afternoons. He worried about her all the time.

Chapter Nine
Who's Dumber than a Dummy?

It was Monday and Tucker had to get to school. He could see no reason for school that day, or the next day either, for that matter. The Thanksgiving break would start on Wednesday but, in his opinion, the students should have the whole week off. Certainly, every teacher in the school would have to know, Tucker wouldn't be able to concentrate on what they were trying to teach so close to vacation days. How was he going to sit still? And, his ability to listen was a whole other issue.

He slipped into the kitchen, got out the big box of Wheaties and filled his bowl. Standing at the window, he saw that snow had stuck to the ground and colored his world white. His thoughts raced back to a winter day when Bobby was still living with their dad. At two and a half years younger than Tucker, that would have made Bobby about five when Tucker was seven or eight.

In Tucker's recollection, it snowed so hard during the night they cancelled school the next day. Bobby's mom, Charlotte, had to work in the morning and Gramma said Bobby could come to Tucker's house and play in the snow. They took shovels from Grandpop's workshop and dug out a snow cave in a five-foot tall drift in the back yard. It was a good day. Tucker wondered if Bobby had seen snow since that time. Snow doesn't fall in the desert of southern California.

That Monday, a day in the winter snow would have been much better than sitting in a classroom, even if the snow only skimmed the surface of the ground. If Bobby was still in

Indiana, Tucker imagined he would enjoy it. Those thoughts made Tucker feel like he was wilting inside. He didn't like the feeling. Tucker would have to do something to make the day interesting.

Gramma patted him on the back. "Tucker, you'll come home for lunch. Be sure to take back to school the box of clothes I'm donating to the Holiday Rummage Sale. You can take it down in Grandpa's wheelbarrow or your old wagon."

"My wagon?" Milk shot out of Tucker's nose as he gasped over the image of him pulling his little red wagon to school.

"Jawohl," she shrugged emphatically. "That should be a problem?"

Tucker heard his grandmother's emphatic, *Ja*, with the addition, meaning *Yes, indeed.* He rarely talked-back to Gramma, but panic took over his senses. "No, Gramma," he protested, but with no enthusiasm. "How's a guy supposed to face his friends while pulling a toy wagon?"

"Your wagon isn't so little, Tucker," Gramma said with a twinkle in her eye and a pat on his shoulder. "I'm sure you can figure out a way to do it. Maybe a basket on your bicycle."

Tucker felt his face drain of color as a vision of himself on his first bicycle, complete with training wheels and wire basket, pedaled before his eyes. "I'll figure it out Gramma." He finished his breakfast, grabbed his coat, and opened the door.

"Tucker," Gramma put her hands on her hips. "Don't forget your books."

"Right, thanks Gramma." His Math and Social Studies books lay exactly where he left them on Friday after school, on the top of the pie safe in the dining room. He dutifully collected his text books and three-ring binder before running out the door and down the steps. Tucker darted through the backyard gate, cut down the alley, and came out across the street from the school.

"Tucker, you're here early." Freddie waved as he ran up the street toward him.

"Good Freddie, I hoped I'd find you."

"How come?" The two hurried into the school and started down the hallway by Mr. Waggoner's classroom door. "What ya got in mind?"

"Don't think I can stand these two days of school. They should have just given us the whole week off." Tucker opened his hall locker, stowed his coat, and exchanged his Math book for his Science text. "I have an idea."

"What?" Christy heard the last of their conversation as she came up behind them. "What idea?"

Freddie rolled his eyes, "Tucker's bored."

"Oh no." Christy stopped and stomped her foot. "What this time?"

Tucker shrugged his shoulders and grinned. "Just a little fun." He stopped before going into Mrs. Hunter's classroom and added, "I'm going to run home for the lunch hour and come back early. Can you two be back in a half hour?"

Christy's eyes narrowed. "Yes ... why?"

"I have a fun project."

Christy sighed deeply, "Again ... why?"

Tucker walked into the classroom and sat down just as the bell rang. *Why?* The question rattled around in his head while Mrs. Hunter said something about two days before Thanksgiving vacation. "Two days of school, that's why," Tucker mumbled.

Mrs. Hunter looked up from her attendance sheet. "What's that, Tucker?"

"Huh?" Tucker looked at her, startled.

The teacher rubbed her chin, apparently trying not to smile. "You said something about two days?"

"Yes, Ma'am." He looked around at all the eyes staring back at him. "How many of you agree with me?" he asked the class. "There's no need for two days of school this week," he said with a large shrug. "No one would be able to pay attention."

"You're probable right, Tucker," Mrs. Hunter slowly moved in Tucker's direction. "That's why we're going to do something different. This morning, we'll have a nice film in place of a text book lesson."

"Great!" Tucker's slump straightened. "What's the name of it?"

"I thought it might be interesting to combine science with daily activities." She got even closer and gently touched Tucker on the shoulder. "It's Science in the Kitchen. We'll learn how to can vegetables and fruit properly. We'll see how to process them so they don't lose their vacuum seal and … the tomatoes spoil."

Tucker swallowed hard. All that he could choke out was, "Should be interesting."

• • • • •

After lunch, Tucker had everything loaded in his old Radio Flyer, wooden cargo wagon. He camouflaged the wagon by wrapping it in Grandpop's extra gunny sacks. Grandpop kept many tan burlap bags in the loft above his workshop. He covered each layer of garden vegetables with the sacks, storing them for the winter in the root cellar, a pit buried in the back yard.

"Gramma, I'm going back to school," Tucker announced as he stepped in the door and grabbed up the peanut butter and jelly sandwich he left on the corner of the table.

"So soon?" Gramma looked up from folding the laundry she, Aunt Cora, and Grandpop had done early in the morning and had dried already. When Grandpop hung the sheets on the lines in the basement near the coal burning furnace, they dried quickly, but lacked the sweet smell of sunshine that clung to the fabric when hung outside.

"Sure, Gramma. Freddie, Christy, and I have a project at school."

"Ja, gut," Gramma said as she tossed the end of a white muslin sheet to Tucker. He put his sandwich down and held the opposite end to make it easier for Gramma to fold.

"Okay, I'm leaving. I have the clothes you want to donate." He added the last part so Gramma wouldn't ask more questions or check out the wagon now rolling incognito. To Tucker, his often-used wagon looked less like a child's toy and more like a low-slung, open-air army transport.

Peanut butter, grape jelly Gramma put-up in September, all on her homemade bread was T-bone steak to Tucker. He savored every bite as he hurried down the alley called Jewel Court and back to school. He polished off the last bite as he looked around for Christy and Freddie near the tall double side door.

"What ya got there?" Christy asked as she shook her head.

Tucker nodded and breezed past her. "Let's hurry. I want to have everything set up before most of them get back from lunch." Tucker took the big box out of the wagon and started to take it inside. "We'll talk about it as we build."

Freddie tagged along behind. "Build? Build what?" He picked up the clothing items Tucker dropped along the way.

"Freddie, hang up your coat in your locker." Tucker opened his own locker and put his coat inside. "Now ... come in here," Tucker said without answering Freddie's question. He led the way into the same janitor's closet he spent some time in the previous Friday and turned on the light.

Christy stopped at the door and wrinkled her nose, "The closet?"

"Sure." Tucker quickly closed the door as soon as Christy's aqua colored, pleated skirt cleared the doorjamb. "I have Gramma's clothes she's donating to the Holiday Rummage Sale." He started pulled them out a piece at a time. "Here's some string and large rubber bands. Good," he said as he came to a white pillowcase. "Gramma said there was a set of pillowcases in here. Carolyn spilled some red fingernail polish all over one of them. She bought Gramma another set." He held it up to the light. "See."

"How did she do that?" Christy looked at the case. "She's always so careful."

Tucker selected several pieces of clothing. "Tiny jumped up on her bed and knocked the bottle over." He held out the pillowcase in one hand and shoved shirts and out-grown pajamas inside. From the bottom of the box, he fished out a large ball of purple knitting yarn Gramma had included in the donation box. She didn't like the color after all. "Okay, Christy, tie it off about halfway down."

She cut off a piece of yarn and tied the stuffed case as instructed. "Dare I ask if your grandmother knows you have her knitting yarn?"

"Well … I'm sure she does. She's the one who put it in the box. And, it finishes everything off. In fact," he looked up at the clock above the door. "Christy…" he picked up the box from the floor, "you take this box back out to the wagon and park the whole thing under the tree in Benton's front yard across the street. They're at work right now. I'll get it out of their way right after school."

Christy picked up the box to leave, and then turned back. "What will you guys be doing?"

"We're going to build a dummy."

"A dummy?" Christy and Freddie sang out in unison.

"A dummy. Now hurry." Tucker began stuffing a T-shirt full of some of Tucker's other outgrown clothes as Christy slowly opened the closet door.

"See you in class," Tucker called after her in a strained whisper. He and Freddie stuffed a shirt and a pair of pants with clothing as fast as they could until they had used all the pieces, except the white lace curtains Gramma had added to the bottom of the pile. Tucker started to put it aside, and then smiled. They gathered the shirt at the wrist and the pants at the ankles with rubber bands. He smiled again as he looked mischievously at the hand-me-down lady. Before Tucker threw the rummage-sale girl over his shoulder, he wrapped the long lace piece around the "head," down the shoulders, and motioned for Freddie. "Come on."

They climbed back up the ladder Tucker had used a few days before. On the roof, the two leaned the dummy against the school's chimney as Tucker cut off a long length of yarn with his pocket knife. Freddie took one end and together they strung up the poor gal as if she were on a hangman's noose in an old western movie. With a shoe on each side of the ladder, they slid down the steps like firemen at the local firehouse. Their task completed, they quickly burst through the closet door.

"I'll run the yarn over to the wagon and you get into class. I'll be back before the bell rings."

"You only have about five minutes," Freddie warned.

"I can do it." Tucker darted out the door taking giant steps down the sidewalk, ran across the street to where Christy had parked the wagon, dropped the yarn in the basket, and hurried back to the school. Hustling into the classroom, he slipped into his chair just as the bell rang.

When Tucker turned to the window, he saw the eighth-grade gym class filing out toward the baseball diamond. They looked like they were cold already with their hands wrapped around their middle as tightly as they could. From his assigned seat in class, he thought he could see their skin turning an interesting shade of icy blue.

Suddenly, he saw Dotty Yoder, running and dancing onto the field. She turned back to face the school building and let out a shriek that could cut a hole in the snow clouds. Her voice still echoed in the air when several other girls looked in the direction she pointed. They too let out gut churning screams.

Tucker's fellow classmates jumped to their feet and hurried to the window. From where they were located inside the building, none of them could see what was so terrifying.

"This is an announcement," the principal came across the loudspeaker. "Remain calm. Our Vice-Principal, Mr. Saltsburg, went outside to see what other students had reacted to." Tucker, Christy, and Freddie looked away from the window. The entire class was still on their feet as the three dummy builders gravitated toward one another, like magnets made of a similar iron.

"Wonder what's going on?" Tucker asked, as innocent as a puppy near a half-chewed shoe.

"I don't know," Freddie joined in the charade.

Christy said nothing but shrugged as she stole a sheepish glance at Mrs. Hunter.

Again, the intercom crackled. "I'll let Mr. Saltsburg tell you what he found."

There was a shuffle of feet picked up by an open microphone and broadcast into the classrooms before the vice-principal spoke. "I investigated the situation that produced the extreme reaction, and we would like your help. We're offering a reward of a free ice cream bar from the bookstore every day for a week. We'll award that treat to anyone who can tell us, who hung the bride on the school's chimney?"

"The bride?" Classmates all chimed together.

Tucker McBride winced.

Chapter Ten
The Ghost of Dummies Past

The end of the school day was stubborn in coming; almost as stubborn as Tucker in his refusal to admit he had anything to do with hanging the dummy on the schoolhouse chimney. Those two-degrees-of-stubborn made the school day creep along for Tucker.

Anna Frederick's mother sent pumpkin cookies to school which Anna passed around after the dummy situation settled down. Everyone in the class got one. That was the problem. One. Tucker could still smell the spicy delights from his desk near the back of the room after the cookie plate passed. His hunger added another layer of angst to his itchy need to get out of school.

Everyone moved to Mr. Alexander's English class next, then finished the rotation down the hall and around a corner. At the end of the school day, Tucker sat in Mr. Crammer's Math class, staring at the clock ... 3:28, 3:29. Each minute seemed like an hour as anxiety leaped in his stomach. Didn't anyone know, Mathematics was the worst possible subject for Tucker to study during the last class-period of the day.

Ringggg – 3:30 had finally arrived.

"One more day to go!" Tucker cheered as he picked up his books and maneuvered his way around other students. He sucked in his belt buckle, until he squeezed out the classroom door. Reaching over Anna's shoulder, he grabbed another cinnamon-smelling cookie and zig zagged on. Up the hall toward the front of the building, he turned left. The school office was in the middle of this space, an area Tucker would have preferred to avoid. Looking neither left nor right, he sashayed past the brightly lit office door with exaggerated steps, thinking he was less conspicuous, but appeared more so. At the next hall-intersection, he continued down the short hall that led to his locker, back to Mrs. Hunter's classroom, and the side entrance.

"Mrs. Hunter," Tucker nodded in her direction but kept his eyes on the row of lockers.

"Tucker," she acknowledged in return.

"Hey, Tucker," Christy hurried over. Her locker was just a few keys down. "What ya doin' after school?"

"Going to look under the hood of the Model A." He paused with his hand on the locker.

"And, after that?" She pushed her books in Tucker's direction and put her coat on while he held the texts. "Thanks," she said as she took them back.

"What'd you have in mind?" Tucker watched Christy for a sign that might tell him what was up. She seemed to be saying something without saying anything.

"Well, I'm not interested in duplicating the Science lesson." Leaning forward she whispered, "I don't want to can a few jars of tomatoes." She looked over at Mrs. Hunter and stifled a laugh.

Tucker rolled his eyes as he reached for his locker door. Pulling it open, he let out a shrill, whistling teakettle-like scream, joined by Christy's high-pitched shriek that could imitate the high register of a lyric soprano. The bridal dummy, with large crazy buttons sewn on for eyes and a grotesque mouth, was sitting in Tucker's locker waiting for her designer. Over his shoulder, he heard the laughing voices of Principal Dillard and Vice-President Saltsburg. Behind them, a few students gathered to see what all the kerfuffle* was about.

Tucker nearly picked himself up off the floor. He slowly turned, "Good one" he congratulated the principal. Calmly, he took the dummy out of the locker and propped her up against the wall. "Will you please ask the janitor to take these clothes to the back of the gym where they're gathering clothes for the Holiday Rummage Sale?"

"Oh, so they belong to you, Tucker?" The principal had a "got-ya" grin on his face.

Tucker shrugged. "I found them in my locker, Sir. Possession is nine-tenths of the law. So, I'd like to donate these misplaced clothes to the sale."

Mr. Saltsburg bumped Dillard in the arm with his elbow. "It's always good to hear when our students have understood and can apply class lessons. Let me see, since the dummy was in your locker, it now belongs to you. You can decide what to do with it."

"Sounds right to me." Tucker put on his coat and took the one text book he needed ... Math.

"Well, then, you have a good evening." Mr. Dillard smiled.

Tucker and Christy hurried out the side door together. The sun dissolved all the snow clouds making the walk over to pick up the wagon and then back to his house feel almost warm.

"You asked what I had in mind. I wondered if we could do our Math together."

"Math? Me?"

"Mr. Crammer has been talking about angles. Thought your grandfather could help us if we need help."

Tucker's mouth popped open. "Grandpop?"

"Sure." Christy looked down the alley towards the Moyer's back yard. "He's always making things out of wood. All those boxes, cabinets and inventions of his include various angles ... how to cut them, and how to put them together." She stopped talking as they neared the house.

"Ya daresn't mess with Tucker's car, Tim." Grandpop's voice sounded firm. "He couldn't get it months ago because you said no. You shouldn't have done that. Now, it's his car."

"Grandpa," Tim raised his voice, "I wasn't going to hurt anything." He looked up at Tucker. "I was going to go over it for you and see if everything was okay."

"Really?" Tucker couldn't believe what Tim said. It was only a few months back he told Noah to sell the car to someone else because Tucker couldn't have it.

"Really, Tuck." Tim confirmed with a smile.

Grandpop looked at Tim with narrow eyes. "No bargaining or manipulation, Tim. He's not going to share the A-Model with you."

"I know, Grandpa." Tim grabbed the nickel-plated handle of the hood on the right side, raised it, and looked under the hood. "It looks to me like Tucker can handle himself better now and acts more grown up. Thought I'd help him while I'm home."

"Thanks, Tim. Grown up? Great." Tucker spoke of his growing maturity aloud. But, inside, Gramma's lace curtain flapping in the cold breeze on top of the school building filled his mind. At that moment, he wished he wasn't pulling a little red wagon behind him.

Chapter Eleven
A Home for Tucker on Paper

"Mr. Moyer," Christy began as she approached the Morris chair, where Grandpop sat with his feet up, "Tucker said you'd be good at this kind of question."

"Oh, he did?" Grandpop said with a smile. "Let's hear it."

She looked at the Math sheet the teacher had passed out. "Mr. Crammer developed this last Math problem to apply some of what we've been learning." She read the problem aloud.

"This is his homework question. *You are going to design a living room or dining room you may like in your home someday. Draw the room 1:12 scale. Draw rectangles, circles and other geometric figures to scale to represent the furniture you would put in the room.*" Christy folded her arms across her chest. "First of all, what does 1:12 mean?"

Tucker stumbled over Joe, veered into a dining room chair, and stuttered, embarrassed that his grandfather wouldn't know seventh-grade Arithmetic. "Christy, Grandpop hasn't taken a Math course in a long, long time."

"Ja, of course, Christy. It means a one inch to the foot scale. Tucker, 1:12 just means every inch equals a foot or 12 inches. You can cut that down so one-half inch equals 6 inches, or in other combinations."

"It would be easier to leave it at 1:12," Tucker said with certainty. "Less math." He sized up the sheet again. "Gramma, where's a ruler?"

"Same place as always, Tucker." Gramma walked in from the kitchen with the potato peeler in her hand. She wore the long sleeved, dark flowered cotton house dress she'd changed into after Grandpop put away the laundry stuff. Reaching in one of the patch pockets of the large bib apron she wore over it, she pulled out a hanky and wiped her fingers. "There's one in a drawer in the middle of the bookcase. There's also a measuring tape in the sewing box. That might work better for the furniture."

"Wait a minute," Tucker stopped and dropped his head on the table with a thud. "The living room is 20 feet long. That would be … at one inch equals a foot, 20 inches. Our notebook paper isn't twenty inches long. How can we draw it to scale?"

"Of course, you can draw it," Gramma said as she walked back into the kitchen and came back with her new electric iron and some grocery sacks.

Tucker perked up as Gramma's positive attitude seemed to sift through the anti-Math-shield he always had up. "What's all that for?"

She spread one of the large tan bags on the table and tore it down the seam, where the glue attached the front of the sack to the back. "Next, sprinkle a little water on a linen tea towel. Then, put the paper on the ironing board and lay the dampened towel over the paper. Quickly press out the wrinkles and folds. Cut off any raggedy edges around the paper."

"Gramma, you're a genius!" Tucker jumped up, darted in past the sink and out into the summer kitchen. He fished out the ironing board, folded and stored between the wall and the dry sink, and carried it into the kitchen. He paused for a minute and inhaled the savory aroma of browning steak bites Gramma was frying, the first step in the surprise supper she had in mind.

"Don't take too long, Tucker." Gramma cautioned as she picked up another potato. "I'm fixing supper in here."

Tucker pumped a little water into Gramma's laundry sprinkler bottle and took it to the dining room where he would be out of the way of the work triangle: sink, refrigerator, and stove. He smiled. "I have one geometric form right anyway."

"I'll separate the four brown bags and you iron." Christy offered.

"Four?" Tucker puzzled.

"Two a piece," Christy worked quickly. "If I mess up on one, I have another one ready, without getting out all the stuff again."

Tim came in through the summer house door and walked through to the dining room. "Well, if it isn't Miss Christmas Tree," he mocked.

"Tim, I have a yard stick in my hand," Christy sassed back. "You sure you want to tangle with me?"

Tim's face lit up. "Listen to you. You're getting strong, Miss Christy."

"Now, get out of my way, Tim. I don't want to hurt you."

Tim laughed. "You do know I just finished Marine boot camp."

She raised the yard stick. "So, you have well-trained boots. Now you need to train your mouth."

"Think I'll get an apple and get out of your way." Tim dropped the teasing, then turned to Tucker and whispered. "She's got gumption."

Christy didn't even look up. With the thick sack-paper all smoothed out and trimmed to shape, Tucker and Christy sat down at the table and began their project.

Gramma pointed to the other room. "Christy, there's a yard stick in the sewing corner. Kinda long for the smaller details but better for sizing the room and marking out the dimensions."

"Yes, Ma'am, thanks." She jumped up, retrieved the stick and together, she and Tucker planned out their work. They shared the longer measure to mark out the boundaries of each of their living rooms. Twenty by fourteen feet, became twenty by fourteen inches on the large grocery sacks.

"Okay," Tucker looked around. "You measure the coffee table and I'll measure the sofa."

Christy asked, "Do we have to put them in the same place as in this room?" She began to find out how many inches long and wide the table in front of the couch was.

"You don't like where the furniture is now?" Grandpop asked with a twinkle in his eye.

"Oh, no," Christy stammered. "That's not ... I didn't mean ..."

"Now, Pa, you're teasing the girl." Gramma picked up the instruction sheet. "It says, 'You are going to design a living room or dining room you may like in your home someday.' So, it is your room, designed the way you would like it to look in your own home."

"Good," Tucker held out the measuring tape in each hand. "Here Joe." He put the dog at one end of the couch with an end of the tape in Joe's mouth. Then, he checked the measurement at the other end where he held it straight. "Six feet, Christy. So, on paper, my sofa would be six inches long."

"Now, measure the depth of the sofa while I see how wide the chair is." She took the yard stick over to Grandpop's recliner and began marking off the width. "Tucker, how many chairs do you want in your home?"

"My home?" Tucker stopped and looked around. "I'll have a home someday? Whoever would have thunk it?"

"I've thought of my home." Christy held the yard stick in her hand and gazed out the window. Her eyes shone like she could see her living room in her mind.

Tucker looked around the room and smiled. "I'd want one just like this."

Chapter Twelve
A Slide or a Slip

After supper that evening, Tucker wondered out onto the front porch. Joe joined him, just inches from his heels. The newsboys and girls had already folded their papers for delivery. Grandpop was balling up the string they left for him to braid into rope.

"How much rope do you have now, Grandpop?" Tucker picked up a few pieces of the string that had landed on the front steps.

"Don't you never mind," Grandpop said as he stopped and watched the cars pass by. "A lot."

"The road is busy tonight," the boy observed, counting the cars at Butch Randolph's Sinclair gas station across the street. "Butch has a real backup of customers. Why is he open so late?"

Grandpop sat down on one of the tulip shaped metal chairs* on the wooden porch and continued to wrap up the string like Gramma's ball of yarn. "A lot of people are going to visit family with a four-day Thanksgiving weekend comin' up."

The front door squeaked when Gramma opened it a little. "Tucker, are you warm enough?"

"I'll be in in a minute," was his simple, never to admit limitations reply. "Grandpop, were there this many cars on the road when you first moved to Dunlap?"

"Tucker, there weren't any cars when I moved to Dunlap, just horses, buggies, and wagons. It all changes.

Someday, there will be stores and businesses all along the street, from Elkhart to Goshen."

"Joseph," Gramma scolded, "don't you fill the boy's head with such nonsense."

"Just read it in the National Geographic Magazine. Farmland will shrink and businesses will take over." Grandpop limped a little as he stood up and moved across the cold porch.

"Hey, Tucker," Freddie called out from the yard. "Dave Mueller and I are going down to the creek. Want to come along?"

"The creek?" Gramma gasped. "You'll catch your death of cold."

"We're not going swimming, Mrs. Moyer." Freddie shivered and zipped up his coat. "We're going to slide on the ice."

"Well, Tucker, I don't know."

"He'll be alright, Ma." Grandpop went into the house and hung his coat on the hall tree in the entry. "Tucker knows when to come in at night. Night just comes a little earlier at this time of year."

Tucker stepped in the house and inhaled deeply. Inside, it still smelled like the browned meat, sweet onions and tempting garlic in the shepherd's pie Gramma made for supper. She never fixed that before, and he wished she'd fix it again. Made with beef, not lamb, Uncle Jacob said it was really cottage pie. When Tucker remembered Freddie was still waiting, he turned and stuck his head back out the door. "Freddie, I'll meet you around by the side door." Tucker hurried through the house, picking up his hat and gloves as he darted through.

"Only an hour," Gramma warned.

"I have my watch, Gramma." The door banged, followed by the added snap of the storm door.

Freddie waited at the side of the house as Tucker came out. "We'll meet Dave over at his house."

Tucker hopped on his bike and hustled to catch up. Two and a half blocks down, Dave waited in his front yard.

"What's that thing with him?"

Freddie blinked and tried to focus. "Don't know." The sun was much lower in the sky and brought a glare to the street south of the house. Freddie squinted in Dave's direction. "He said we'd go sliding on Big Blue."

"Big Blue?" Tucker began to ride no-hands on the ice … until the bike started to slide. He grabbed the handlebars as he felt the tires go in both directions at the same time. "Who is Big Blue?"

"I don't think it's a *who*." Freddie slowed and pulled into the driveway. "I think it's a *what*." The driveway gravel crackled as the boys parked their bikes.

Dave pointed to a spot up by the house. "You guys can leave your bikes up there. It will take all three of us to push Big Blue down to the creek."

"That's Big Blue? It isn't blue at all." Tucker looked at the huge metal basin-shaped tub. "What is it?"

Dave bent down and put both hands to his back. "It's my dad's old cement mixer."

Tucker leaned his bike against the garage. "Looks like no cement mixer I've ever seen."

"It's not the big round one like you're used to," Dave explained with his hands waving about. "A small, flat one like this is for mixing up smaller batches of concrete."

Tucker looked it over from front to back. The trough-like* structure lay flat to the ground. The sides were two 2 by 12 boards, with a heavy gauge galvanized tin bottom. It was eight feet long and three and a half feet wide. The great thing about it, to Tucker's thinking, was how it slanted up in the front like a Christmas sleigh. An over-sized hoe with silver dollar sized holes, that lay at the bottom, was for pulling the concrete from the front to the back, mixing it completely.

Dave explained the process as he bent to push the contraption. "Dad put in the gravel, a few bags of cement, some water, and mixed it with that big hoe-like thing."

Tucker started to help, then stopped. "Does your dad know you're taking Big Blue down to the creek?"

"Well, no." Dave stood up and thought. "He did say I could slide around in it on the ice."

Tucker threw both hands in the air in justified surrender. "Oh, well then, let's go." Tucker added his own push-power and Freddie joined in.

Even though it was huge, the three boys shoved and pulled Big Blue to the end of the street, through the snow-covered grass with ice crystals crackling as they slid along, and down the little hill to the icy creek. They stopped at the stream's edge, now perfectly still and covered in ice, and sized up their fun-potential.

Tucker touched the toe of his shoe to the ice and shook his head. "It doesn't look very thick."

"Maybe not," Dave agreed, "Then, we'll just use it as a boat."

Freddie brightened up. "Let's do it."

They pulled the flat cement mixer turned toboggan, to the top of the incline above the creek. Tucker piled in the front, then Freddie. Dave gave a running shove and jumped in the back as the galvanized sled slid down the hill. Big Blue bumped at the bottom of the approach hill, bounced, and went airborne for about three yards. Then ... plop, it dropped in the middle of Yellow Creek with a thud and a splat. Did it glide gracefully across the ice?

"We're sinking!" Freddie yelled.

Tucker grabbed the sides. "It's too heavy, Davy! I told Gramma I wouldn't be swimming."

"Get out," Dave ordered. But the creek bank was yards back. If the three went over the side, they'd land in the freezing water.

Tucker jumped out of the skiff-like mixer, not knowing if the water would come up to his ankles or over his head. The creek bottom, like the adjacent fields, rolled up and down along the stream, creating deeper pockets in some areas than in others. "Thank goodness it's only about three feet deep here."

The boys shivered almost as soon as they hit the water. Tucker knew they'd have to get out of the creek as soon as possible. Each boy's teeth seemed to chatter in a different pitch and tempo, providing a strange harmony and percussion of sorts. That, however, wasn't what Tucker was worried about. It wasn't safe to stay in the icy water for very long. Tucker had read about hypothermia in one of Uncle Jacob's magazine. If he could get the other two to move fast and get them out of the semi-frozen stream, he saw no need to scare them. "Move, move, move," he yelled as he herded them like cattle out of the water.

They stood on the bank, soaked to their bones, their lips turned purple, and shook until their teeth rattled. No one said anything for a minute.

Dave stood frozen in shock, looking at the spot where his dad's cement mixer sank into the creek. The bow of the so-called boat stuck above the water. "How do we get this out of the creek?"

Tucker grabbed the other two by their coat sleeves and pulled. "We don't get it out now, Davy. Tomorrow, we'll borrow Ben Sherman's horse, Lightning, and hook the mixer-turned-sled up to the saddle horn. Now, we need to go home, take hot showers or bathes, and get on dry, warm clothes."

"I don't know," Dave hesitated and looked back at the creek again. "My dad will kill me."

"Well, good," Tucker insisted. "Then you won't have to die a more horrible death from pneumonia if you don't get warm fast ... right now. Not being able to breath because your lungs are full of gunk will be more gruesome than if your Dad gets after ya." Tucker turned and started running back to Dave's to pick up his bike.

"Wait for me," Freddie called after him.

Tucker didn't even turn around. "You catch up."

"Okay, okay," Dave gave in reluctantly.

Tucker could hear the thump, thump of two sets of soggy boots lumbering from behind. By the time they arrived back at Mueller's house, Tucker rang the doorbell and tackled Dave around the shoulders. When Mrs. Mueller opened the door, Freddie helped Tucker push Dave in. "Here Mrs. Mueller. Davy got wet. Make sure he warms up."

"Wh...?"

Tucker didn't wait. He knew he had to get home as soon as possible when he heard his speech begin to slur. He threw one leg over his bicycle and hoped to make it home.

Before he even got out of the Mueller driveway, he heard the bellow of a water buffalo, or an angry dad. A shrill yell pierced the night sky, "What?" Tucker cringed and wondered what it would be like to have a dad who yelled and imposed consequences.

Tucker called back over his shoulder. "See you tomorrow after school, you guys."

Freddie peeled off from Tucker's path and headed toward his house, while Tucker pedaled on home. He parked his bike in the corner of the side porch and opened the door.

"Oh, my, my, Tucker. What happened?" Gramma jumped up from her sewing chair where she was mending Tucker's jeans while listening to the radio. "You're soaked."

"Yes, Ma'am. Dave said we could use his dad's old shallow cement mixing trough to slide on the ice down at the creek." Tucker explained as he tried to take off his coat while shaking so hard his hands didn't want to work.

"The ice isn't yet thick enough for ice skating, let alone a heavy galvanized tub." Grandpop sat his recliner back up. "Grandma will hang your coat on the back of a chair in front of the oven. I'll go up and get you dry clothes." Neither Gramma nor Grandpop raised their voice even one note.

Gramma got the afghan she had laying on the back of the sofa and went into the kitchen. "It's too late for your grandfather to pump water into the buckets and heat it to fill the wash tub in the summer kitchen, so ... no bath. Go in the bathroom, take off your wet clothes, put on the dry ones except your jeans, and wrap this afghan around you."

Tucker went into the small bathroom under the stairs and began peeling off his wet clothing. There was no tub or shower in the house, but the little bathroom, put in just a few years past, was a blessing. No more walking to the out-house along the backyard path in rain or snow.

"Here Tucker," Grandpop called through the bathroom door.

Gramma announced, "I just filled the kettle for bedtime tea a bit ago." She went to the sink and began using the Myers hand pump to fill the kitchen sink. When it was half-full, she poured the boiling water from the kettle into the sink, refilled the kettle, and put it back on the stove top. "Now get up here on the drain board and put your feet in the water. As your limbs begin to warm up, I'll add hot water again. You must start with slightly warm water, not hot. But, you'll soon warm up."

The porcelain drain board where Gramma turned her freshly washed dishes upside down to drain dry or wait for drying with a tea towel, was an extension of the sink. With one swoop, Tucker grabbed the edged of the drain board and leaped up on top. With the colorful afghan around his shoulders, he swung his feet into place over the sink.

Tucker held his breath as he eased his feet into the warm water. He had run cold water over icy hands in the past, when he'd been out on a winter day, and he knew how painfully hot that felt. What would warm water do?

With his feet in the warm water, the pain slowly subsided. Gramma came back in the kitchen two more times to add more hot water.

"Now, you sit there until the water gets cool." Gramma handed him a dry tea towel. "Then, dry your feet and hop down. I'm going in to listen to Lux Radio Theater." She turned then asked, "What have you learned, Tucker?"

"Not to believe Davy Mueller," he blurted out. But inside he thought, *Families sure are different.*

"Gut. Not believing everything people tell you is gut," Gramma agreed. "Check things out for yourself before you act."

Tucker fussed about the evening. He really didn't want to miss one of his favorite radio programs. It was good, Gramma and Grandpop both had a little trouble hearing. Out in the kitchen, at the volume Gramma set the radio, Tucker could hear the program come on in the living room.

"Lux Radio Theater," the announcer sang out with a deep flourish to his voice and background music. "Tonight, Greer Garson and Walter Pidgeon with reprise their roles in Metro Goldwyn Meyer's 1944 screen play, *Mrs. Parkington.*"

On most Mondays, Tucker would sprawl out on the floor, and wait for the program to begin. This night, he figured he wouldn't miss much since he could hear it in the kitchen. When his feet felt toasty warm, he dried them off, released the drain plug, and hopped down.

A sauce pan from the cupboard, milk from the refrigerator, and the cocoa box from the shelf, soon turned into bone warming hot chocolate. He slipped on the dry jeans Grandpop had fetched and carried the cup of hot chocolate into the living room turned-radio-theater.

"Did ya warm up, Tucker?" Grandpop asked.

"Yep," he said. But he thought: *In more ways than one. Wednesday will be better. It can't be worse.*

Chapter Thirteen
The Horse and the Cement Mixer

After school on Tuesday, the doors burst open with a herd of stampeding holiday-anticipating students behind the push. Tucker hurried along the school sidewalk without running. He didn't want to spoil the fact he reached his goal of not getting into trouble during the whole day.

"Tucker," Christy called after him. "What's your hurry?"

Tucker turned and slowly walked backward. "Remember what I said at lunch. I have to see if we can borrow Lightning here in a few minutes."

"I'll help," she offered as she pulled her red plaid scarf more tightly around her neck.

Tucker shuddered as he remembered yesterday's adventure. "Gramma would be very unhappy if she found out you fell in the creek."

She caught up fast. "Hey, I wouldn't want to get wet either. But I'd like to watch …."

Once on the street, Tucker stuck out his thumb hoping to hitch a ride to the Sherman farm. It wasn't far out of town, but the few miles would take more time than Tucker wanted to invest in the mixer project. After all, it wasn't his fault Mr. Mueller's cement mixer was now at the bottom of the creek.

"Mom doesn't want me to hitch hike," Christy backed off slowly.

Tucker stepped further into the street when he saw Tubby Alexander's car pull out of the parking lot south of the school and turn north. He was a friend of Betsy's and had picked up Tucker before. "That's smooth, Christy. I'll let you know how it goes."

Tubby spoke through his window. "Where ya goin'?"

Tucker leaned on Tubby's door frame. "Out to Sherman's to borrow their horse."

"Hop in. I'll take you out." He looked back at Christy. "Are you coming, too?"

Christy took a step toward the old Dodge sedan. "I'm not supposed to hitch hike."

Tubby looked in the rearview mirror. "You're not hitching. I know Tucker. He needs a ride and I'm giving him one. If you're with Tucker, you can ride, too."

"Oh, that sounds good." She folded the full circle, light weight wool skirt around her so she wouldn't sit on the cold back seat with nothing but her slip for padding, and slid in. Tucker got in the front. "A friend just picked us up," she repeated to herself." Then she asked, "What's your name?"

"They call me Tubby, Tubby Alexander," he said as he put the car in first gear and headed out across the highway.

"Tubby?" Christy asked with raised eyebrows. "You're as skinny as a fence post."

Tubby chuckled. "You noticed that, too? It beats me where the name came from. Mom said I was a chubby baby. Who knew the name would stick forever?" He shrugged and went on. "What ya need a horse for?"

"We had a small problem sliding on the ice down at the creek last night."

"Right," Tubby said with a laugh. "There was no ice."

"Exactly," Christy agreed.

They rode north across the tracks and out into the country. At the Sherman farm, Tubby turned down the lane, maneuvered into the barnyard, and pulled the car around to face it back out again. "I'll wait three minutes. If no one's here, I'll run you back home."

Tucker opened the door to get out and Christy followed. "Thanks," he told Tubby.

A heavy odor the large pigsty gave off, wafted through the afternoon air. To Tucker, the stench from the pigpen seemed multiplied by the number of hogs in the puddle. "Pee-yew," he nearly gaged.

"That's gold you smell." Tubby laughed, put the car in gear and settled in for a short wait. "My grandfather says that's what pure gold smells like." He hung his arm out the car window. "Three minutes," he repeated.

Tucker hurried toward the front door and knocked. "Hi, Mrs. Sherman," he said as soon as the door opened. Looking back at the drive, he saw Tubby wave and pull out, spewing gravel in all directions.

Darla Sherman smiled. "Hi, Tucker. What can I do for you?"

Tucker got to the point. "Is Ben home?"

Mrs. Sherman brightened when she saw Christy. "Christy, I didn't see you. How's your mom?"

"Thanks for asking." Christy stepped closer. "She's fine. Is Ben around?"

"No, he had a dentist appointment after school, don't ya know. I'll pick him up in ..." she looked at her watch. "In about forty-five minutes."

"Oh," Tucker sighed deeply. "I was going to ask to borrow his horse, Lightning. But ..."

"Tucker," Mrs. Sherman suddenly got excited as her eyes danced. "I tell you what ...." She pulled a woolen shawl from a peg by the door. "Come on out to the barn. You can do me a big favor."

Together, they started toward the red, bank barn to the right of the house. So wrapped up in the Lightning project, Tucker didn't notice the snow that now crunched under their feet. He wondered what Ben's mother meant by "a favor."

"The saddle and bridle are hanging on the side of Lightning's stall." She hurried ahead and slid the barn door open. "How long did you want to borrow the horse?"

Inside, the "barn smell" was like perfume to Tucker. He often wondered why someone didn't bottle the aroma. They could name it, *The Fragrance of the Barn*. The hay smelled sweet. It even drowned out the stench of the pigs and their half-grown piglets out in the barnyard. It was obvious the family kept the barn clean. Even the cats that claimed the barn as their castle seemed to tiptoe around on white, hairy slippers.

"Shouldn't take too long. A couple of us kinda sunk an eight foot by three-and-a-half-foot cement mixing tray, made of wood and galvanized tin, in the middle of Yellow Creek. We thought Lightning could pull it out."

"She could do that. Probably in a matter of minutes once you get it all hooked up, don't ya know," she agreed. "I'll call the dentist office and tell Ben to meet you at your house, so he can ride Lightning home when you're finished at the creek. Doc's office is just a couple blocks away from your house. A few minutes ago, I put a pie in the oven. If you take the horse to town, I won't have to run into Dunlap to get Ben. That would help me a lot, don't ya know."

"Sure," Tucker beamed with excitement as they went into the barn. "Christy can ride in the saddle; I'll slide on behind her, and then Ben will bring Lightning home. It'll work." He couldn't believe how it was working out … but, thought he'd better not get too excited. It amazed him how quickly an opportunity could slide downhill. Gramma often said, *Opportunities can sometimes turn into pooportunities if ya start bragging.*

"Great." Mrs. Sherman said as she turned. "I'm going to run back to the house. It's cold out here, don't ya know. Close the barn door when you leave."

"Thanks, Mrs. Sherman." Tucker nearly jumped up and down. "Hope Ben gets done in time."

Tucker saddled the horse and led her out of the barn. "Let's see … Christy, use the stirrups and get up on the saddle. I'll sit behind you and hold on to the cantle."

"The cantle?"

"The back of the saddle that sticks up."

Christy pulled her full skirt up from behind, brought it between her legs, and tucked the tail end into her waistband. With her newly fashioned riding breeches, she swung her leg up over Lightning's back, and seated herself in the saddle. "How did you know what the cantle is called?"

Tucker shook his head in disbelief of Christy's clothing creation. As for the cantle, he added, "Oh, you know, pieces here - pieces there." He reached up to the saddle horn. "Move your foot and I'll get on behind you." With that and a hearty jump, he hoisted himself onto Lightning's back behind Christy, reached around her, and took the reins.

Lightning walked at a fast pace but Tucker made sure he didn't overtax her with the two of them on the broad back. He also knew not to turn the horse around and face her north again. The previous July he had ridden Lightning and forgot the rule, "Don't point the horse toward home." Forgetting that single warning almost caused the horse to run headlong into the side of the east bound train with Tucker on her back.

Down a few houses from the Moyer house, Tucker saw Dave Mueller pacing back and forth out in front of his home. He chewed the fingernails on his left hand while twirling the end of a thick lasso-looped rope in the other.

"There you are." Dave threw his free hand in the air. "Thank goodness. This morning, I told my dad we'd have Big Blue out of the creek by the time he gets home from work."

"Okay. Get on your bike; Lightning can't carry any more weight." Tucker pulled on the reins and pointed the horse to the lower land down by the creek.

When they got near the water, flabbergasted*, Tucker stopped. Funny, how the water seemed so clear through the breaks in the ice. Yet, a cement mixer lay unseen beneath. The afternoon sun sparkled on the glassy surface of the creek.

Tucker looked at the creek. "I'm going to let you get wet in the freezing water all by yourself, Davy." Tucker was sure he didn't want to repeat the bone-chilling episode of the evening before. "You wade in and hook the rope onto the front of Big Blue where your dad had put that huge E-bolt."

"I could use some help," Dave complained. "At least I wore my bibbed hip waders."

"You have a helper, Davy … Lightning. Consider yourself lucky." Tucker and Christy jumped down and watched the operation from the bank.

Amazingly, Davy didn't stumble or drop the rope. He waded out, hooked the rope to the bolt and waded back, then handed Tucker the end of the line. "Hoop this over the horn of the saddle. Then, when I get out of the water, have the horse pull."

Tucker turned Lightning around and positioned her to pull. He looped the rope over the saddle horn and tested it for tautness. "Get out of the water, Davy."

The cement mixer turned around in the water following the tow rope, faced out, and slid up on the bank. Tucker started to unfasten the rope.

"No," Davy stopped him. "Why can't the horse pull Big Blue back to the house? Freddie isn't here, so unless Christy pushes too, there would only be two of us."

Christy's eyebrows raised in surprise. "I don't plan to push that thing anywhere."

"Then, let's do it." Tucker started toward Dave's house. "Do you want to ride?" he asked Christy.

"Thanks. That would be fun."

Dave hurried along. "I'll ride, too."

Tucker trotted along beside them and laughed. "I think walking would be good for you."

At the Mueller house, they unhooked Big Blue. "There ya are, Davy. Hope that helps things with your dad."

"It will. Thanks," he called after them.

Tucker got on Lightning behind Christy and started for home. "That went good." He couldn't believe it. There was usually a hitch in every plan.

Christy pointed toward the Moyer house. "Looks like Ben's at your house."

"Couldn't have been timed better. Perfect." Tucker smiled inside and out. It looked like some of Tucker's luck had changed.

"Hi guys," Ben called out as he waved.

"Glad you're here." Tucker nudged Christy on the arm. "You get down first."

She dismounted, bouncing on her toes as she landed on the street. "That was fun." She pulled the tail of her skirt from her waist and shook the fabric into place.

Tucker swung his leg off the horse with great theatrics and fanfare. "That was great, that's what it was." He bounced off the horse like a sheriff in hot pursuit, and landed with both feet in a horse patty. Obviously, Roman Schwartz's horse-drawn Amish delivery wagon had been there earlier or Tucker would not have his shoes embedded in the horse droppings.

Tucker looked down at his shoes, twisted them back and forth to check out all angles, and cringed. The manure was as thick as peanut butter but didn't have that rich nutty smell ... not unless the nuts rotted on the ground for several days. Sighing deeply, he sputtered, "Another poportunity."

Chapter Fourteen
Tucker at Your Assistance

After Ben road Lightning back north of the highway, not in a straight bee line but a zigzag maneuver so as not to spook the horse, Tucker sat on the side porch steps with a stick in one hand and his left shoe in the other. Gouging at the horse patty on the bottom of his shoe, the manure fell to the ground.

Christy curled up her nose in disgust. "Sure am glad I didn't step in any of that stuff."

"Christy," Gramma spoke from the door, "your momma called to see if you were here. She said your family was going to eat an early supper tonight. She wants help making bread for Thanksgiving so she can get the pie baking done tomorrow. Better head for home."

"Thanks, Mrs. Moyer." Christy turned to leave then jumped for joy. "Mom said she'd take me into Elkhart after supper. Ziesel's Department Store got in a new shipment of women's slacks. Mom said I can get some."

"Slacks?" Tucker nearly dropped some sticky, smelly patty putty on his jeans. "Christy, you never wore pants before, except your jeans."

"Right! Isn't it great?" She nearly danced around with excitement. "Mom said if they're not too expensive, I might be able to get two or three pair."

"Of pants?" Tucker stood up so fast he dropped the shoe on his almost white sock, leaving a blob of sticky brown junk. He brushed off the worst of it with the stick. Then, when he got the large pieces of gunk off the shoe, he carefully twisted the nozzle on the garden hose. A small chip of ice shot out. The water sprayed on his coat and the toes of his other sock. Luckily, most of the water landed on the soles of his shoes. When all the manure was off, he put his shoes back on, wiggling his damp socks into place. "What does your dad say about you wearing pants?"

Gramma interrupted from the door. "I think the pants would be very comfortable. Betsy said she might get some."

Christy started out the gate. "Dad said it's up to Mom and me." Waving over her shoulder, she added, "See ya later or tomorrow."

"Bye." Tucker tied his shoelaces and dried the wet soles on a tiny patch of grass near the steps.

Gramma checked the clock on the wall just as Tucker stepped into the house. "It's about 4:30. We'll eat supper at 5:30. Walter Crompton called and asked you to come down and help him."

Tucker stopped and looked up … *something to do.* "Help him do what?"

"Don't know." Gramma kept talking as she started toward the kitchen. "But, ya daresn't be late for supper."

Tucker, his coat still on, dashed out the side door, jumped on his bicycle and headed north. He heard the story at school of Walter working on his own airplane. The very brilliant, but somewhat eccentric electrician had taken his plane to his farm to work on the engine. He had to get it ready for inspection so he could legally fly it. In fact, he needed to get it back to the airport by 6 PM that evening. An aviation inspector would be there to check out the private plane for re-certification.

The problem, as Tucker heard it at school, Crompton had parked the plane in the open field behind his house. When it snowed, the sleet that fell with the fluffy white stuff during the night, thawed by the next afternoon, leaving the ground wet and muddy.

As Tucker neared Walter's house, he thought, *I'll bet that's it. Walt needs help getting the plane out of the mud.*

Tucker pedaled his bike several blocks and jumped off in front of Crompton's house. It was a nice modern, one-story home, cluttered from the garage to the barn with an electrician's stash of equipment, rolls of copper wire, and gadgets of every kind. A dispatch radio blasted and crackled from the front seat of his paneled work truck. Tucker saw Walter pacing back and forth out next to the road. "Hi, Mr. Crompton."

Crompton threw his hands in the air and gasped. "I am so glad you're here." He checked his watch again. "I have just a little time to get this thing out of the mud and back to the airport for her checkup."

Tucker looked over the situation. "What ya want me to do?"

Crompton headed for the plane's cockpit. "The strut got broken when I tried to move it a while ago. I didn't have enough speed or height due to the muddy traction. I barely got off the ground, nosed down and hit the wire fence, bending the wing strut and landing gear. I fixed all that lickety-split but don't think I have enough space to get the thing out of here."

Tucker heard every word Walter said, but still couldn't figure out where he fit in. "Okay…"

"I can't use the road for a runway 'cause the telephone poles are in the way. So … I'm going to drive the plane down the road and weave the wings back and forth. Now Tucker, I want you to take my work truck down to the next intersection, turn it sideways and block traffic so no one gets in my way or gets hurt. Then, when I finally get airborne, take the truck to the airport so I can get home. I'll leave the plane there."

"Wow," Tucker yipped. "Drive your truck? Sure." What thirteen-year-old wouldn't want to drive a fully stocked professional vehicle? Tucker ran over to the red 1940 Ford panel truck. His open jacket flapped in the cold breeze. Inside the truck, the floorboard on the passenger side smelled peculiar where Walt spilled a little from the can of crankcase oil he used in the airplane. The keys were in the ignition so starting the engine was easy. It sputtered and spit. Tucker wondered if the plane would sound the same. He suddenly had doubts about the safety of the aircraft. Still, that wasn't his problem. His responsibility was the truck. Putting it in gear, it jerked and jumped, then smoothed out as he moved it toward the single engine Cessna 172.

In the yard, Crompton hooked the plane to the truck and Tucker pulled it out onto the road. There, Walt had more space between the house and where Tucker would park the truck.

Tucker started down to the next intersection. Some of Walter's electrical materials, switches, wires, and the like, shifted and came free from their compartments. It all clanged and rattled along the way. Once at the corner, Tucker turned the truck crosswise in the street and got out so he could watch the do-si-do-dancing airplane.

Walt faced the plane at an angle to the road, so the left wing cleared the first telephone pole. Grandpop would say Walter was riding side-saddle to the road. Steering the plane back and forth, Walt tipped the airplane to the opposite angle, like John Wayne strutting down the road, and cleared the right wing.

Tucker held his breath when Walter tried to build up speed by revving the engine again. As the airplane gained greater momentum, Walt held the plane's brake and then let loose, lifting the wheels off the road a little as he moved. Higher and higher the nose struggled to gain height, attempting to clear the ground before it got to the truck.

Tucker saw the airplane grow larger as it came directly at him. His eyes stayed fixed on the approaching flying machine. *Is that thing going to clear the intersection?* The question started to repeat in his head, until he realized the possible outcome, and dove for the ditch. He landed in a heap, rolled over, and turned in time to see the plane barely clear the panel truck, at the spot where he had stood.

"Shazam!" Tucker marveled as he jumped up, whipped around, and watched Walter fly away, free above the road, on his way to the airport. Tucker scrambled to get back in the truck.

"Hold up there, Tucker," Tim shouted as he hopped out of the passenger side of Jim Straighter's sedan. Tim and Jim enlisted in the Marines together and lucky for everyone, they were home from boot camp together before shipping out. Tim opened the driver's door of Walt's truck. "Where are you goin' in Walter Crompton's truck?"

Tucker looked at Tim squarely. He had developed a stiffer backbone during the time Tim was gone. "He wants me to pick him up at the airport, so he has a way home."

"Scoot over, Tucker." Tim stood on the running board and motioned for Tucker to move. "I don't want you to drive on the highway. I'll drive ya down to the airport and Jim can follow and take us home." He got in, started the truck, and called out the window. "Throw Tucker's bike in your trunk, Jim. Then, you go ahead," Tim said. "I'll see you at the airport."

"Tim, how did you know where I was?" Tucker asked.

Tim laughed and gently bopped Tucker on the shoulder. "The whole neighborhood usually knows where you are. Of course, then there's the fact I just saw Crompton's plane flying low … and … Gramma said she sent you down here, and asked me to come get you for supper."

"Thanks Tim." Tucker appreciated Tim's coming for him. Really, Tucker wasn't afraid to drive on the highway … but knew Gramma wouldn't like it. Tucker thought about Tim in the truck and Jim behind them in the car. He puffed out with pride but didn't say anything aloud. However, he thought, *The marines to the rescue.*

Chapter Fifteen
A Hole in the Sky

Very late that afternoon, Tucker removed the Bakelite candlestick shaped receiver from the hook of the walnut wall phone and turned the crank on the right. "Carolyn," he spoke into the mouthpiece to his sister. "I didn't know you were working at the telephone office this evening."

Carolyn's voice lilted through the receiver. "I'm filling in so the operator can go home and get some baking done for Thursday."

"Good. Who answers the phone on Thanksgiving?" Tucker asked with his same need-to-know inquisitiveness.

"I don't know. That's not my problem," she said with a chuckle.

"I want to call Johnny Washington in Elkhart," Tucker said. He gave her the number and waited. When the connection was complete, he greeted, "Hi, Johnny."

"Tucker?"

"Yep. You remember my talking about going into Goshen to a movie tomorrow?"

Johnny's voice perked. "Sure do. Mom said it's okay. She can bring me out tomorrow morning and help your grandmother a little while they visit."

"Good. See you then." Tucker replaced the receiver and smiled.

After supper of Great Northern white beans flavored with pieces of sumptuous ham and served with fine textured sweetened corn bread, Tucker went out on the front porch. He left behind the lingering aroma of cooked beans hanging in the air, a pee-yew experience to some, perfume to others.

Sleet came down steadily by the time the afternoon light slipped lower in the west. Tucker couldn't tell if the sleet was more rain or snow.

The news carriers were there on Moyer's porch as they were every day. They folded their allotment of papers to distribute around the neighborhood and surrounding farm country. Grandpop arranged for them to do their work on his front porch, due to rainy, snowy, sleety days such as that one. Of course, rural Indiana had changed over the years. Even the house where Tucker lived had been a farm house at one time. Grandpop even sold acres to the township on which the school now stood. It seemed to Tucker, Great-grandpa once turned his plow on the soil that now anchored the homes of everyone around Dunlap.

"Hi Tucker," Nan Miller greeted him. Nan had been carrying the Elkhart Truth since she was thirteen. Now, a beautiful, dark-haired girl, she'd graduate from high school in the spring. She would continue with her distribution business until she went off to college in the fall. She was such a hard and faithful worker that the newspaper rewarded her with additional territory as more blocks became available. The only time she called in sick and in need of a substitute carrier was when she had mononucleosis two years before. At that time, even the back-up carrier she trained had the flu. Now, nearing the end of her news-distribution career, she was so determined to stay healthy, not even the fine, falling ice bothered her. She just said, "I don't have time for a cold today. I'll catch it next week."

"Hi Nan." Tucker liked talking to Nan because she knew a lot about college entrance stuff. Uncle David graduated from college, then seminary. But Uncle David and Aunt Karen lived in Elkhart, and while that was only a few miles away, to Tucker it felt like another state. Most of the family that remained in the neighborhood hadn't gone to college.

Oh wait, Uncle Jacob "went" to college. Accepted at Harvard University, he went to college at the end of the summer following his high school graduation in 1918. Jacob, brilliant but naïve, arrived in Cambridge, Massachusetts on Friday, played poker with some skilled upper-classmen all night, and went home with empty pockets on Saturday. Still, Tucker thought he might try college ... someday.

"Tucker," Simon Winkler called and waved from the grocery cross the street.

Tucker looked up and waved back. It appeared that Simon needed him for something special as his wave turned into a seemingly urgent, beckoning call. Tucker pulled his cap down over his ears, checked the road, and then darted across. "You need something, Mr. Winkler?"

"Sure do. Can ya come in a minute, Tucker?"

Through the door, the sweet aroma of cinnamon and ginger from the table display of Mrs. Custer's pumpkin pies greeted them. Mrs. Custer's yeasty smelling homemade bread and rolls also filled the table to nearly overflowing. Mildred Custer only sold her baked goods during the holidays.

"Gramma changed baking day from Saturday to today. She made pies and bread this morning," Tucker said as he inhaled the perfume of Thanksgiving. "I think she might have ordered some dinner rolls from Mrs. Custer though, considering all the work Gramma had to do."

"Right," Simon agreed. "Your grandmother asked me to save three dozen for her."

Tucker's eyes popped. "Three dozen? Wow! But then, I can eat a dozen of them myself." He looked around at all the specialty items Mr. Winkler had in the store for the holidays. Huge fresh turkeys crowded into the meat case waiting for pick-up. "Look at all those turkeys."

"There's more in the walk-in refrigerator/freezer." Simon crooked his finger at Tucker. "Follow me."

Tucker followed but thought of something else. "Did Gramma want me to take the rolls home?"

"No, she said they'd be in her way today. Besides, Mrs. Custer will bring in a fresh supply tomorrow. I'll save some of those for your house," Simon said as he kept walking to the Five & Dime side of the store.

Passing the sweet citric smelling oranges, Tucker reached out and touched their bumpy surfaces. They felt and smelled good enough to eat. But he just ate. Why did he feel hungry?

Simon kept on walking at a frantic pace. The boards in the old hard wood floor sang their squeaky song. "Your grandmother wants you to run over and get the rolls Thanksgiving morning. You know I'll be open until noon that day for folks to get things they forgot."

"Okay ..." Suddenly Tucker inhaled a dank, non-grocery store odor. The other side of the store smelled musty, like wet gym-socks. Overhead, a steady drip fell from the ceiling. "What in the ...?"

"That's my problem, Tucker." Mr. Winkler was nearly wringing his hands with anxiety. "I don't have the time to do anything about this. It's less than two days before Thanksgiving." He paced back and forth. "Do you have time to stop that leak? I can't get a roofer, or ceiling expert, or any other repair guy to come out until Monday."

The display tables to the right and left of the major rain puddle were dry. Those glass cubbies in the table nearer the downfall were in various stages of dampness. Above the table, hanging on the wall to the right of the wetness, was a shelf display of cookbooks. Ordinarily Tucker wouldn't have noticed them. But, one book stuck out, as if covered in neon green — The Household Searchlight Recipe Book.

"Oh, no." Tucker grabbed the book off the shelf and held it close.

Simon stepped back in surprise. "Did it get wet?"

"No," Tucker said as he cradled the book in his arms. "And, it's not going to." He handed the cookbook to Winkler. "Here, you hold this. I'll clean up all this water and go up in the attic and find the leak. Hope it holds until the roofers get here on Monday."

"Thank goodness," Simon sighed in relief as the bell on the front door announced another customer. "Gotta go. I'll put the cookbook up by the register. I know that's dry."

"Thanks." Tucker turned to go up the steps through the closed door in the corner. He'd seen the door and often wondered where it went. "Bring me some towels to clean up while I check upstairs."

"Tucker," Simon began as he looked to see who had come in. "Why is this cookbook so important to you? It's not like it's an Archie Andrews or Superman comic book."

Tucker stared at the black book with the gold lettering. "My mother had a cookbook just like that one."

Simon turned to greet Alvera Gorsuch. "Evening Alvera. Be right with you." To Tucker he continued, "Did your mom use the cookbook a lot?"

"I don't know. Gramma said she did and Gramma uses it a lot now. Mom died when I was a baby."

Simon caught his words in his throat and whispered, "I guess you're protecting the little bit of memory you have."

"The little bit of family I have," Tucker mumbled low.

"Little bit of family?" Simon chuckled as he pointed to the door to the stairs. "The whole neighborhood is full of your family, Tucker."

They both laughed. Simon flipped on the two switches for Tucker, the dim one that barely lit the stairway, and the only slightly brighter one that helped to light the attic, then went back to the check-out counter while Tucker opened the door to the stairs.

The wooden treads squeaked with every step, revealing the arthritic old age of the building. It was so dim on the stairs Tucker could barely see the next step. He imagined he was a brave knight, slipping up the turret steps to a garret high in a castle, where an evil sorcerer hid a golden treasure years before. Winding around the medieval tower Tucker peered out the open windows to the village beyond. Strange, it all looked like home.

In the attic, he shook the idea of the sorcerer's treasure and looked instead for the source of the drip. He blinked several times, but couldn't clear his vision. Even with the addition of windows on opposite sides of the open attic, the dust and dirt that covered them didn't add additional light to the second floor.

The rain is dripping down from over here, Tucker thought as he walked to the far side of the attic. "But where is it coming from?" he mumbled aloud.

The water gathered in a puddle on the floor that wasn't quite the floor. "Odd," Tucker said, talking to no one, but his need to think out loud. "Why isn't there any flooring on this side of the attic?"

Careful not to step too close, the thick wood that served as subflooring in the rest of the space was missing. Only the two-inch by ten-inch floor joists, spaced sixteen inches apart lay out before him. Below the joists, he could see the back side of the strips of old wood lath where the tradesman affixed plaster that formed the ceiling in the room below. If he stepped off the joist, he could fall through the ceiling of the Five & Dime downstairs.

For some reason, someone reinforced one of the joists by nailing a 2 X10 piece of lumber from the rafter in the corner to one of the floor joists at a 45° angle. As he studied the steady drip, drip of the leak, Tucker could easily see the problem was in the corner where the diagonal board attached to the ceiling. The water flowed down the board like a playground slide and dripped onto the unprotected plaster at the end of its journey.

"How am I going to get any place near it to fix it?" Then he remembered. Last summer, Mr. Winkler hired Tucker to help him seal the cracks in the small parking lot out front. They used tar. Tucker helped Grandpop fix a leak in the workshop once and remembered the exact process. He took off his coat and put it over a box, held his breath and began looking around the cold attic.

Over on the opposite side of the room, he pulled out some tea towels embroidered with Easter bunnies Glades Wilford stitched. He remembered Simon had sold them during the Lenten season. Tucker hated to ruin Mrs. Wilford's fine needle art but he didn't see anything else in the attic storage that would absorb the moisture. He didn't want to try to dry out the ceiling plaster with the shipment of Christmas tree skirts that would go on sale right after Thanksgiving. Besides, he wasn't sure green velvet would soak up the rain as well as linen.

Tucker carefully placed each tea towel down on the plaster lath. He hoped to use as few towels as possible while making sure he covered all the damp areas. Looking up, the real challenge hung over his head.

Suddenly, behind him came a strange *scratchy, scratch* sound as the scramble and toenail clicking of a gray squirrel sent shivers up his spine as the animal scampered up the incline to the rafters. Midway up the 2 by 10, the musty smelling squirrel splatted spread-eagle on the joist, got up and ran on. *Well, he didn't fall off the beam into next Sunday. I can do that. Of course, my toenails aren't long like his; although Gramma said they need a good trimming.*

Tucker studied the beam and the acrobatic squirrel. On the floor, someone nailed the beam to the joist running beside the area with the missing subfloor. Luckily, the joist was on the side nearest to Tucker. He wouldn't have to cross the dead-zone, as he thought of it. He figured, anyone who fell from the second floor onto display tables in the room below, would experience – the dead-zone.

The squirrel's four-point fall gave Tucker an idea. *I'll get my pants wet,* he warned himself.

Well, he talked back to himself, *I would get my pants wet if I went sledding down Duffy's Hill. And, yesterday we landed in the creek on Old Blue.* He kept talking as he walked over to the storage side of the attic. *Besides, if I get wet, I'm only a few steps from home.*

He shuffled through the boxes Mr. Winkler stored in the attic. *There, that'll work.*

Tucker found a can in a box of some other building and repair materials, with a little bit of tar left inside. He sighed in relief. Still flipping and searching through the carton, he dug through until he stopped on some shims. Winkler put them up there after he completed work on leveling the new display tables in the Dime Store a couple years back. Tucker fished out a medium size paint brush, a straight razor he found at the bottom of a box holding shaving soap and mugs, a pint size canning jar, and some heavy-weight string. He carried his treasured finds back to the angled beam.

First, with the string in his right hand, he held the end of the twine at the tip of his nose and stretched out his arm as far to the side as possible. "Gramma says that's about a yard," he mumbled. "So, I'll measure two yards for the first one." Again, he talked to the only one in the attic, himself, unless you count the squirrel. "Let's see: the jar, the shims, and the paint brush. I need one more length of string … a little longer." He hummed to himself as he measured out three more yards and cut the string with the straight razor.

Tucker threaded the shortest string through the hole in the end of the paint brush handle. He hung the brush around his neck and picked up four of the thinly cut, wooden, wedge-shaped shims. Like a bundle of Elkhart's best newspapers, Tucker bound the shims around in both directions, creating a tight wrapping. Shaping the extra string into two loops, he put his arms through the loops like a backpack. "Okay, one more to go."

Before Simon put it in the attic, he sealed the top of the can of tar by pounding it into place. Like a lever, Tucker used the end of the straight razor to pry up the lid. The extremely potent and pungent odor of the tar escaped the tin like a trapped dog pushing to get out. The fumes from the strong stench flew up his nostrils like a bird of prey, its outstretched wings tormenting and scratching Tucker's nose.

He poured the tar from the larger container into the pint jar, screwed on the lid, and tied the last string around the threads at the top of the jar. With his make-shift repair hung around his back and neck, he studied the support beam someone had put in place.

"Well, I guess I'm going to ride this pony to the top of the mountain." Careful not to slip a single step, Tucker used the first-floor joist like a stepping stone. Then, slipping his leg over the beam like he did when he mounted Lightning, he eased onto the board and sat down, straddling the imaginary saddle. With his equipment hung, mounted, and draped around him, his hands were free for pulling himself in a shuffle along the beam. After a pull, came the scoot, a pull, then a scoot up toward the ceiling rafter and the leak. The joist wood was not prepared for riding. Tucker felt slivers tear at his jeans while the wetness soaked them through to the bone. Pulling and scooting all the way to the top, he looked down occasionally and studied the back side of the plastered ceiling below. The prickly, dark horsehair the artisan stirred into the plaster to make it strong, became more distant with each two-part maneuver upward.

At the top of the beam, near the rafter, Tucker reached out and stuck his finger into a small hole next to the chimney. He smiled. It wasn't very big, just large enough for water to seep in and find the downward path to the space below. Next, he had to open the jar of tar but he didn't want to take it from around his neck. What if he dropped the glass, or what if he fell? He'd have to open the jar while it was still hanging beneath his nose. Yuck!

He slipped the paint brush from around his neck and wrapped the string around his wrist so the brush wouldn't fall if he were to lose his grip on it. He loosened the bundle of shims and pulled one free. Then, filling his lungs with one big gulp of air, he opened the jar, stuck the brush into the tar and slathered it on one of the shims. He stretched up and slapped the tared shim onto the hole in the roof and coated the reverse side with another generous amount of the smelly tar.

"Tucker," Simon called out as he came up the stairs. "Are you all right?" He looked around in the dimming light.

"I'm fine," Tucker called from his perch near the ceiling. "And ... I'm done."

"Holy cow, boy!" Winkler gasped as he grabbed his chest. "What ya doing up there? Your grandmother is going to kill me."

Tucker checked his repair work and started back down the same way he went up. "Why? I did the job that needed doing."

When Tucker placed both feet on the attic floor, Simon laughed. "Tucker, your hind-end is nearly bare. The wood sanded your pants almost to the skin." He laughed until he doubled over. "At least you didn't get any of that stinking tar on the area where your pants are supposed to be."

Tucker laughed as he danced around, trying to see the back of his denims. "Woops, these were my newest jeans."

"Let's get your coat," Winkler said as he picked it up. "I have jeans in the store. We'll find two pair in your size. And, pick up two pair of underwear or you're going to feel the cold breeze more than you did when you came over."

"Wow, thanks Mr. Winkler." Tucker was getting an extra pair of pants for his efforts.

"I'll also pay you five dollars. This fix should hold until Monday when the roofers check it over."

"I hope so," Tucker agreed. "I watched Grandpop fix the workshop roof."

Simon Winkler stopped at the top of the steps. "But Tucker, I never expected you to actually fix the leak. I just wanted the water mopped up."

"But the water would stand in puddles again in no time. So ... I fixed it."

Winkler patted him on the shoulder. "I appreciate it." He started down the steps. "And you didn't even know if you'd get paid."

"It wasn't about pay, Mr. Winkler," Tucker said, surprised at Winkler's idea. "It was about family. My mom's cookbook was going to get wet."

Chapter Sixteen
A News Bulletin

Tuesday evening

Tim wrapped his arm around Tucker's shoulder and gave him a hug as he reached past Tuck to retrieve a bowl from the cabinet. "Good to see you, little brother."

"You too," Tucker agreed. Always hungry, he waited eagerly as Tim pulled the large tin of potato chips out from under the cabinet. "That looks like a good idea." Tucker watched as Gramma came into the kitchen to put her coffee cup in the sink. "Will Uncle Jacob care if we eat some of his potato chips?"

Gramma looked in the huge one-pound tin as Tim removed the lid. "Ah, ja, it's nearly full. Ya daresn't take more than a bowl full each though."

"Sure," Tim patted Tucker on the hand as he reached into the tin, then stopped.

Tucker peeled away, filled his bowl, and took the chips into the living room where he plopped down on the floor. Grandpop sat in his Morris recliner listening to the news.

Tim reached over and teasingly tickled Tucker a little. In a flash, he grabbed Tucker's hand and flipped it over. The right thumb nail was nasty looking. The side of the nail oozed yellow puss. Tucker tried to pull his hand away when Tim asked, "What happened to you?"

"Nothing," Tucker denied. Never one to complain, he also didn't tell anyone of his dumb stunts.

Tim pulled the hand closer. "'Nothing' doesn't cause infection in the thumb nail."

Tucker didn't know what to do or say. He didn't lie to his grandparents. He also didn't tell them stuff that would cause them worry. "It happened last summer."

Tim pushed for an answer. "It? What 'it' happened last summer?"

"Well," Tucker drew out slowly as his brain worked clackety-clack. He smiled sheepishly. "There was a hammer involved." *Well, there was,* he rationalized to himself.

"Let me see." Gramma eased to the edge of her chair and leaned in his direction. Tucker stuck out his hand to her. "How long has this been infected?"

"I don't know," Tucker brushed off the injury and grabbed a few chips from his bowl. "A few days I suppose."

"How many times a day do you wash your hands?" Gramma got up and went to the kitchen. She came back with the tin of Grandma Hooley Salve and a torn piece of clean cotton from an old sheet. "Slather it on real good. Then wrap the cloth around it and tie it on."

Tucker thought. "I don't know how many times I wash my hands. I guess, when I get up, before I eat my lunch and supper, and before I go to bed."

Tim laughed. "But, Tucker, you eat a hundred times a day. I know you don't wash your hands every time you put something in your mouth. Your skin would be raw from all that soap."

Tucker opened the tin and tried to hold his head back. The smell of eucalyptus and sulfur produced a putrid odor he wanted to keep from his nose. Tucker scooped out some salve with his finger and applied it generously to his thumb. He had to admit, at least to himself, it throbbed a bit. He wrapped the cloth around the thumb to hold the salve in place and with one end of the strip between his teeth and the other end grasped in the fingers of his left hand, he tied it off. "There," he concluded just as the news announcer on the radio interrupted his usual report.

"This breaking news just came in."

Tucker dropped the potato chip he was ready to put in his mouth. There hadn't been news interruptions since the war. He remembered the Sunday morning he missed church because he was sick and stayed home with Uncle Jacob. It was December 7, 1941 when Tucker was eight years old. Uncle Jacob had nodded off in his chair and Tucker lay on the floor wrapped in a blanket, reading the comics. Radio news announcer, H. V. Kaltenborn said, "We interrupt our program to announce that Oahu is under attack by a hostile air force."

Now, nearly five years later, Tucker's entire body still shook as he remembered that day and the bombing of Pearl Harbor. This time it wasn't war. But Tucker couldn't seem to control the old fear that still haunted him.

The year was 1946, not 1941, and the newscaster's message concerned a situation far closer to home. "The local and state police departments are asking for your help. The young actress, Taffy Bean, is missing from her hotel room in Chicago and was last seen walking out the front door of the Blackstone Hotel. Officials believe she may be moving east. She may have been alone although a hotel worker observed unknown adults near her. Taffy Bean is the twelve-year-old actress who played Mimi Knight in the movie, *When Thunderheads Form*. If you see her or have any contact with her, please notify the police department."

"Holy moly," Tucker gasped.

"Tucker," Gramma scolded. "Mind your language."

"Yes, Gramma," Tucker agreed. But, for the life of him, he didn't know what he said. He knew that Gramma didn't like slang. His concern was not over the meaning of the word, "moly." His worry was whether Taffy Bean had run away or if someone kidnapped her. He hoped she would find her way home.

Chapter Seventeen
Plans Can Change

Wednesday Morning

Tucker thought for a minute. After all, he and his friends were going to a movie. Carolyn would take them. He wouldn't need the Model A. When Tim came in the kitchen, Tucker looked up. "Thanks again for helping me out with Walter Crompton's truck. I—"

"Sure." Tim filled his cereal bowl, jiggled Tucker's arm, and laughed. "You're a puzzle, kid. You help everybody in the neighborhood, and then scare them to death as you swing from a hot air balloon." He laughed again and hugged Tuck harder.

Tucker rolled his eyes up to where his imagination could take him anywhere, even for a ride in a huge bubble. "That sounds like fun."

Gramma's eyes darted in Tim's direction. "Don't give him any ideas."

"He didn't, Gramma," Tucker shrugged. "I've thought of floating above the ground before."

Tim poured milk on his corn flakes. "Gramma said you're going to a movie. What ya going to see?"

Tucker gulped down a large bite. "We're seeing *Escape from the Belfry.*"

Tim nodded, "With that cute kid-actress, Taffy Bean. She was great as the little sister in, *When Thunderheads Form.* She's the one who's missing, isn't she?"

"She sure is," Tucker drew out slowly. He hadn't put the two together, the actress in the movie they planned to see, and the girl who walked out of a hotel in Chicago. "Christy, Johnny Washington, and Freddie are still planning on going with me. Carolyn promised to take us."

"Johnny Washington from Elkhart?" Tim asked as he scooped up the last bite of cereal.

"Yep." Tucker pumped the Myers pump handle and filled his empty cereal bowl with water. He added a dab of Swan soap flakes, frothed up the water, poured boiling water from the tea kettle over it to rinse off the soap, dried it on a tea towel and replaced it in the cupboard. "Saw Johnny at the basketball game on Saturday, then Sunday at church."

Tim watched Tucker wash his dish and did the same. "Sounds like you'll have a good time."

Tucker thought some more. *Why not?* To Tim he offered, "If you want to use my Model A today, that's okay. You tuned it up."

Tim's eyebrows raised in surprise. "Thanks Tucker." Tim hurried into the entry hall where he took the steps two at a time. "I'll clean up."

Tap, tap … Tucker heard the gentle knock on the side door. "Johnny," he greeted. "Mrs. Washington, come on in." He turned toward the kitchen, "Gramma, Mrs. Washington and Johnny are here."

Gramma wiped her hands on her large baking apron as she came in from the kitchen. "Goldie," she reached out to embrace her music conductor friend. Their two church choirs shared many concerts, traveling to the other's church buildings. "Goldie, are you sure you have the time to help me? What about your Thanksgiving dinner?"

"Now, don't you worry, Rebecca. My sister, Jasmine is hosting all the family at her house this year. Each of us will bring several dishes. I'm bringing the potatoes, all pealed and cooked. I'll just have to boil them for another five minutes at her house to re-heat them, beat them, add salt and pepper, milk, and a ton of butter. My other contribution will be … the vanilla wafer cookies we talked about. After I called yesterday to ask for the recipe, I made a batch for you and a batch for me. Where did you get the recipe?" she asked as she pulled a tin from the shopping bag Johnny carried in for her.

Gramma smiled as she watched Tucker start to cut off two hunks of bread from one of the loaves in the pie safe. "Only one piece each," she cautioned. "Ya daresn't eat up all the company food. Cut from the loaf I made two days ago. The one wrapped in wax paper. Save this morning's bread for tomorrow." She ruffled Tucker's hair and smiled. "Goldie, the cookie recipe came from Tucker's mama's cookbook. The boy could eat all fifty of the cookies in one setting. So, I'll hide these. And, thank you. You're a real friend."

"The other recipe I want to borrow is the one for your bread dressing," Goldie licked her lip and rolled her eyes. "I'll break up the bread and chop the vegetables for your family this morning. Then, I'll copy the recipe and prepare mine this evening at home. I'll have time today to help you with other stuff."

Gramma finished rolling out pie dough she was working on and stopped. "Oh, Goldie, if you're sure you have time, that would be wonderful. I'm almost finished with two pumpkin pies. And, my cousin got the bread dressing recipe out of a newspaper."

Tim bounced back into the kitchen buttoning up the last two buttons of his flannel shirt. "Good morning, Mrs. Washington." Tim held out his hand and gave Goldie a side-ways hug.

"Are you going someplace?" Gramma asked.

"Tucker said he wouldn't be using his car today, so ... he said I could use his Model A." Tim gave Gramma a hug and grabbed his coat. He slipped his arm in his jacket sleeve. "Tucker's turning into one good kid."

Goldie grinned mischievously. "Yes, he is." When Tim left and closed the door, Goldie put her hand to her mouth and added, "Looks like Tim's the one turning into a good kid.

It seemed to me, he used to want to be the only dog in town that knew how to hunt."

Gramma giggled like a teenager. "Now, that's a new one. And, I agree."

• • • • •

Outside on the side porch, Tucker and Johnny almost finished the last bites of their bread. Tucker tossed a piece of the crust to Joe who jumped and caught it in midair.

Tim came out and asked, "Do you have the key with you?

Tucker pulled on a chain that hung around his neck, reached down through his jacket, and fished out the key attached to the end. "Treat it like gold."

"Around the neck? Good idea, Tucker. The ball chain holds the key, like my G.I. dog tags. Since you're not driving the A-Model very much right now, it's a good way to keep the key from getting misplaced.

"Yep," Tucker said. But inside he thought: *Who is this guy? He doesn't act like my brother.*

"See ya this afternoon," Tim added. Bouncing over to the car, he got in and went through the process Tucker was very familiar with.

"Where's he going with your car, Tucker?" Freddie asked with his hands on his hips.

Tucker waved his question off. "I offered to let Tim borrow it today." Hearing the words pop out of his mouth, he felt very grown up.

"Big Daddy is taking care of his son," Christy bowed with a flourish. "Hi guys," she added as she walked up with Rosie following on her heals. She ran her hands down her pant legs, smoothing the seam of her new slacks.

It looked to Tucker like Christy wanted him to notice the new, going-to-a-movie pants. At first, he thought he'd tease her by ignoring her attempt to draw attention to her new cloths. Then he remembered, Christy rarely got new clothes. Most of the time, what she wore, her cousin, Milly, owned first. "Are those your new slacks?"

"Yep," Christy twisted and danced around, displaying all sides of the gabardine pants. "Do you like them?"

"Yep," Tucker agreed, then changed the subject. He'd run out of anything new to say about Christy's slacks. "Joe, take Rosie home," Tucker ordered. "That's okay isn't it, Christy?"

"Sure. That's where she belongs." Christy watched Joe herd Rosie down the road. "I didn't know she was behind me. She must have tiptoed."

"Tiptoed?" Johnny asked with a snicker. "Kinda like toe-dancing?"

Christy tipped up her chin, "Yes. My Rosie is a prima ballerina."

Tucker grinned but said no more. He relaxed and watched Joe turn the corner, darting at the pig's trotters, then backing off, back and forth like a sheep dog herding wool-coats on four feet. He smiled at his super hero dog, until he saw Carolyn walking across the road from the phone office. She was not smiling.

"Hi Carolyn," Johnny greeted.

"Johnny. It's good to see you again." But Carolyn's smile was weak. Tucker knew right away something had changed.

Tucker spared no words or feelings. "What's wrong?"

Carolyn looked down and pulled her collar up around her neck. "I am so sorry, Tucker. I can't take you guys to Goshen today."

"Why?" Tucker blurted out.

"You must understand … my job is in the real, adult world, Tucker."

Tucker didn't want to sound sassy. He knew his sister had a responsible job. "I know, Carolyn."

Christy couldn't hold her tongue. "I thought we all live in the real world."

Carolyn said no more about which world they each lived in, and got to the point. "After Dalia's daughter got Scarlet Fever last summer and Dalia had to be off the switchboard, she has gotten very anxious about her daughter's health. She said Sandi is sick today and she's afraid the fever is coming back. She needs to stay home and make sure Sandi stays in bed."

Tucker felt instantly selfish and knew his cheeks had grown warm. "Okay," he mumbled. As he looked out on the beautiful morning, he saw his war dog running back, having obeyed Tucker's order. Maybe Joe was more grown-up than he. "Carolyn," he called after his sister, "tell Dalia I hope Sandi gets well real soon. You can take us to Goshen another time."

"Thanks, Tucker. You're quite a man." Carolyn turned and hurried back to the telephone office.

"Well, I'm not 'quite a man,' Christy pouted. "I don't have to be grown up and understanding," Christy admitted with her arms folded tight across her chest. "Does that mean we're not going to Goshen? I have a nice new dollar bill in my pocket."

Tucker stood and hiked up his pants. "It means Carolyn isn't taking us to Goshen today." He looked north, to where the road ran out of town and met the country beyond, where Lightening was in her stall, where Walter Crompton did the fancy footwork with his airplane, and where Grandpop used to hop on the train as it slowed a few blocks away. "I didn't say we weren't going to go to Goshen. I said Carolyn couldn't take us."

Chapter Eighteen
Riding the Rails

Johnny watched Tucker closely, tracing the trajectory of Tuck's visual target. He followed Tucker's gaze out across the tracks to where the road met the sky.

Christy, who knew Tucker better than the others and saw all his shenanigans as they transpired, burst out, "Tucker McBride, are you thinking what I think you're thinking?"

Tucker smiled. He seemed to be the only guy around who everyone called by both names, first and last. Sometimes he wasn't sure if that made him famous or infamous, in a good way of course. "I don't know what you're thinking, but I know what I'm thinking."

Freddie put both hands on his hips. "I think I know what you're thinking, too."

Johnny shook his head. "Sounds to me like a lot of double thinking. Care to let me in on it?"

Tucker pushed up his sleeve to check his watch. "The train will come through here in five minutes, slow down, and move on through." Inside, he thought of Bobby and Bobby's mom and wondered if they may be gone by now, but he had to try. He and his three friends would hop off in Goshen within walking distance of Grandma and Grandpa McBride's house. What wouldn't work about that?

Opening the door, he called inside, "Gramma, we're leaving now."

His grandmother and Goldie were around the corner in the kitchen. Gramma simply responded her usual, "Ja gut. Have fun."

"Come on, you two. Come on." Tucker coaxed the two dogs back into the house. He wanted no stragglers, hangers on, or double-crossing witnesses.

"We're leaving now?" Johnny asked as he looked in the direction the east bound interurban bus would take. "Where's the bus?"

"The bus won't come for at least an hour." Tucker checked his watch. "I don't want to wait that long."

"How come?" Freddie asked, his eyebrows raised in befuddlement. "The movie doesn't start for hours."

Tucker lifted his chin up in determination. "I have something I want to do first."

Christy put up her hands, in a "slow down" gesture. "Well, since we will all be doing *what*-ever, I would like to know what it is."

Tucker studied the ground as light snowflakes began to flutter around them. "Dad said my half-brother, Bobby, and his mom are in Goshen. I imagine they're at Grandma and Grandpa McBride's house. Bobby's mom writes to them." He shuffled from one foot to the other. "I haven't seen Bobby for … maybe six years. I just thought—"

"Well, that sounds peachy to me," Christy agreed. "Family is good. I wish I had brothers and sisters."

Tucker nodded when he remembered all the dads that were gone during the war. Families stopped growing. "Christy, your dad was drafted in early 1942. He was only away a couple of years before he got shot."

Christy's gaze dropped down, where pain mixes with memory. "Twenty-five months."

Johnny recognized the old fear and agony. "I don't have brothers either," he chimed in. "Tucker, I'd like to meet your brother. But … how are we going to get there? Your sister can't take us."

"She really wanted to," Tucker stuck up for Carolyn. "She had to work." He started walking down the sidewalk. "Let's go." He turned to the dogs, "Stay."

"Let's go where?" Christy didn't know where he was going but she followed along behind.

"We're catching the train to Goshen." Tucker marched out of the yard and turned north, toward the tracks.

Christy stopped and stomped her foot. "It doesn't stop in Dunlap, Tucker. If we're going to follow you, are we going to be swept under a racing train?"

"Of course not," he insisted. Without explaining, he led the troops forward. "The train doesn't stop, but it always slowed at this intersection. When Grandpop worked on the railroad, the train went slow enough for him to simply step on."

"I don't know, Tucker." Christy hesitated a bit as the tracks came into view. "How will we get home from Goshen?"

Johnny looked east and west. "I was wondering that myself."

Freddie smiled a Freddie-to-the-rescue smile. "After the movie, we can call my mom. She'll come and get us."

"Perfect." Walking a few more yards Tucker added, "Carolyn will be off work later, too. She might be able to pick us up."

There seemed to be a silent agreement as they neared the crossing. Each looked west, watching for the approaching train. "Don't see anything," Freddie whispered.

"It'll be a few more minutes." Christy's voice was low.

Tucker chuckled aloud. "Are you afraid the loud, rumbling train will hear us talking?"

Christy bristled. "Yes, I am."

Johnny snapped to attention as he looked west. "I hear something." He squatted down and put his hand on one of the long, never-ending train rails. "It's coming. I can feel it."

Tucker shook his head. "Are you Chief Finger-Listening?"

"That's me," Johnny stuck his chest out, boasting.

"Let's back off a little," Tucker suggested as he gestured for them to move back from the tracks. "We don't want to look like we're waiting for something."

"We are," Freddie shrugged.

Tucker motioned for the friends to join him near a fallen tree by the side of the road. Someone had stacked good size rocks in a pile near the center of the downed tree. Most of the rocks were six to nine inches in diameter. "Okay, everybody, pick up a rock and move it down there." He pointed to a spot about six feet from the original mound. "Now, we'll build a new rock heap there."

"Wait a minute," Christy stopped and stared at Tucker. "You mean we're going to move the rock pile six feet away ... for no reason at all?"

"Now, there's where you're wrong, Missy." Tucker swaggered and hiked up his jeans, like John Wayne in a western movie. "We're workers, Ma'am. We're in the business of rock moving. At least, that's what we want the workers on the train to think."

"Okay," Christy spouted. "I'll be the foreman." As the train came nearer, she pointed at the rock pile and again at the new spot. "Let's get these rocks moved."

Freddie saluted and picked up a couple of stones. "Aye, aye, Sir ... ah, Ma'am."

They each loaded their arms with rocks and carried them up to their new resting place. Tucker pretended to keep his eyes on the job while secretly watching the approaching train. Rather than going back for another load of huge stones, Tucker lingered by the new mound, which was closer to the tracks. Pretending to wipe his forehead with the sleeve of his coat and catch his breath, he watched the engine slow down as it neared the crossing and chugged on past. "Okay," he announced sharply, "jump on."

Christy ran to catch up to him; Johnny and Freddie followed. Tucker grabbed Christy by the hand as they got to the open door of one of the railroad cars. With a right-handed fling he flipped her up and through the open sliding door. He threw himself into the opening with Johnny and Freddie behind him.

The four of them rolled on the floor of the railroad car, laughing, and enjoying the triumph of their successfully "boarding" the train. Christy held her stomach as she giggled.

Tucker rolled onto his knees and looked around the space. He needed to know if he was sharing his "luxury club car" with anyone else. When he saw two extra eyes staring back at him, he leaped in the air. "Joe!" he bellowed. "I told you to stay home."

The dog hung his head, flattened his ears, and slunk down. But he didn't go over to the door again. Joe was going for a ride, and stretched out on the floor of the boxcar.

Packing crates made of wooden slates stood tight across the back end of the freight car. Some of the crates were six feet tall with red lettering on them - *Kelvinator.*

"Humph," Tucker mumbled. "Gramma's is a Frigidaire."

"Are those refrigerators?" Christy asked. "How many of them are there?"

Tucker counted. "At least a dozen. The war's been over about a year now. Guys are still coming home, getting married and trying to find homes. They need everything."

Joe perked up his ears, looked around and growled softly.

Tucker snapped his fingers in the dog's direction. "Hush."

"Seems like the war was years ago," Christy said, thinking aloud. "I guess I try not to think about it anymore." She ran her fingers over much shorter, long cardboard boxes and read from the box. "What's Harley?"

"Look at these," Freddie pointed to the boxes.

Tucker picked at the sealed seam at the top of the box then patted it lovingly. "They're motorcycles, Christy. Harley Davidson motorcycles. In fact, down here," he pointed to the lettering near the bottom of the carton. "It says they're knuckleheads. Everybody talks about knuckleheads."

Christy looked around the box car and rolled her eyes. "I think there are four living knuckleheads riding the rails right here."

"Well," Tucker stuck out his chest, boasting. "I'll be a knucklehead any day, if my first name is Harley. I'd be popular, handsome, and extremely valuable. Oh, and I'd sing great too, with a deep rumbling voice."

Chapter Nineteen
Train Going East

The four vagabonds and one wander-dog sat down on the floor of the freight car. Tucker quickly recognized the thick, well-worn wooden planks were cold, very cold. He found a few pieces of cardboard on top of one of the shorted boxes. He chose the corrugated fiberboard, placed it on the floor and used that as a seat cushion. Christy folded the thinner piece in half and sat down on it.

The scenes that passed outside were amazing. It was the same old country side they saw every time they went to Goshen, but this trip was different. The fields that rolled by and the homes and farms that nestled near the rail line all seemed like a picture show, something Tucker and his friends would see at the Bijou Theater.

The green leaves had turned to gold, just like the trees in Moyer's back yard, but they looked more elegant from the open door of the moving train than they did over on the highway. Tucker was fascinated how the small factories and businesses looked different from the alley side of the buildings. He laughed inside, remembering the fun he had last July with Uncle James. As part of his uncle's Fourth-of-July demonstration on the proper care of injuries, Tucker was able to use some acting skills. Watching other people react to his antics was always a major thrill. If he could get someone to gasp or cry out in sympathy, he had won the Oscar for The-Biggest-Fabricator*. Tucker smiled as the wind blew in through the door and spread a layer of late morning on his face.

Christy sat on the floor, pulled up her legs and wrapped her arms around her knees. "I'm still cold. Can you close the door, Tucker? It would be so much warmer."

"No!" a voice called out from behind the taller packing boxes. "It would be too dark."

Joe raced to the row of boxes at the back of the car and positioned himself for an attack if given the command. Hunkered down, he didn't take his eyes off the refrigerator crates.

Tucker jumped to his feet; his fists readied for a fight. "Who's there?" To Joe, he ordered, "Stand down, Joe."

Johnny leaped up, matching Tucker's stance, with Freddie as the third man in the trio. Christy joined the three as D'Artagnan*, the fourth adventurer with the three Musketeers.

"Wait, wait," the person in the shadows sputtered. "Hold the dog. I'm telling you, it will be pitch black in here." The voice lowered to a whisper. "I don't like the dark."

Tucker squinted into the darker area behind the crates. "Who are you?"

"T...Tallulah...ah...Tallulah B...ah Butler."

Tucker heard the stammer in her voice but didn't challenger her. Uncle Jacob stuttered a little sometimes. Pushing and mocking didn't help him to speak more smoothly. Tucker didn't know the owner of the voice but wanted to help her. "Are you scared?" He tried to be sympathetic. She already said she was afraid of the dark.

At first, only silence came from the back of railcar, accompanied by the rhythmic rattle and clickety-clack of the wheels on the iron tracks. Then, a small murmur floated on the chilling air. "Yeah, I'm scared." From out of the shadows, a round figure stepped into the streak of light streaming through the open door.

"You're a girl!" Freddie gasped.

"You're quick," the girl snapped. Looking toward the open door, she pulled the hood of her sweatshirt down farther over her forehead.

Christy walked closer and saw that the girl wasn't as big as she looked. Wrapped in blankets of many colors and designs, the stranger waddled when she walked. Christy inspected the face under the hood, shielded by blankets. "You look familiar."

Tallulah looked away and stared at the floor. "I don't know you. I don't live around here."

Christy circled around behind the girl. "There something about—" Without touching Tallulah, she peaked under the hood. "You're not as slim as her, but you look like her. Where'd you get the blankets?"

"This train is not slowing down," Johnny stated, his voice tight but his tone determined.

Freddie looked out onto Goshen as the scene clipped by. "Oh, it will."

Tucker turned away from Christy and the chubby girl. "Wait a minute." He studied the tall brown grasses that flew past like blowing wheat on a windy day. "Grandpop said there was an on-going discussion about the train stop here in Goshen. He told me it didn't stop here anymore. But I thought it slowed down, like there in Dunlap."

Christy looked at Tucker with disbelief. "You mean … you did it again?"

Johnny shook his head slowly. "Did what again?"

Christy smiled and frowned at the same time. "Tucker has a way of responding to plans like a small gremlin has leaped into his head and is playing blind-man's-bluff in the vast empty space. If he keeps his eyes closed, he can pretend he's tagging the players and winning." She put her hands on her hips. "You thought, *train*, and that was your last real logical idea."

"You're probably right," Tucker hung his head. Then his eyes started sparkling as an apparent new idea leaped in.

"We'll get off at the next stop when the train slows down. That'll work. We'll get back to the theater long before the movie starts."

"Well…" Christy drug out slowly. "No one's gonna get hurt, Tucker McBride. We're not going to jump while the train's moving fast. And, believe me, we're not going to jump into a deep river so the water can cushion our fall."

"Wouldn't work anyway," Tucker leaned one arm against the frame of the open door and grinned. "Water's not deep enough."

"It's the Elkhart River," Christy bit back.

"Right." Tucker looked out the door but saw no slowing. In fact, the train seemed to be picking up speed. "Some parts of the Elkhart are deeper than others; but, not all of it is deep enough to dive in."

"Dare I ask your plan?" She stopped as her shoulders slumped. "Oh wait. Tucker, you have no plan."

"Sure, I do. We'll get off when the train stops." He looked out again. "It has to stop sometime."

Christy started to wring her hands together. "But, Tucker, where?"

"This isn't funny," Johnny blurted out. "My mom will worry about me."

"Sorry, Johnny." Tucker meant it. He was a fun-loving kid who was always looking for the next trick or antic to play, but he never wanted anyone hurt or parents to become upset. "We'll figure something out."

Christy turned to Tallulah. "Where are you going? Will the train stop there?"

Tallulah peeled off several blankets, folded them and started a pile. "The blankets came from some of the packing crates." Walking over near the open door, she added, "And, the train will stop in Toledo."

"Toledo?" Freddie shrieked. "Isn't Toledo in Ohio?"

"Yes," but Tallulah said no more.

"Why did you hop a train going to Toledo?" Tucker asked. "Did you get on in South Bend?"

"No," she said as she added the last blanket to the stack. "I...I got on in Chicago."

"Chicago?" Tucker couldn't believe it. "Why?"

"No one would let me go home." She wiped some tears from her eyes and blew her nose. "I haven't been home in two years."

Tucker stood in stunned amazement. "Where have you been?"

Christy got close and studied Tallulah's face again. "Is it...?"

Without the blankets, Tallulah looked like any other girl Tucker's age. Slim, smart, but why did she look so familiar?

"I know why she got on this thing in Chicago," Christy smiled a sneaky smile. She reached over and grabbed Tallulah's hood attached to her sweatshirt. "See?"

Tucker's mouth flew open and his spine stiffened. He could not believe his eyes. "You're Taffy Bean."

Chapter Twenty
A Known Stranger

"Taffy Bean?" Freddie hooted. "She can't be Taffy Bean ... in the back of a freight car ... going to Toledo, Ohio?"

The girl said nothing. Defiantly, she folded her arms, stood there as her foot tapped up and down, and stared at the others.

Joe crawled closer, inching his way to the stranger. Raising his head, he sniffed at the girl and rubbed his nose on the back of her hand.

Taffy didn't pull back. "Good dog," she spoke calmly.

Tucker circled around her like he was inspecting his new A-Model Ford. "She sure does look like the actress." He stepped as close as he could get and studied her face with a squint in his eyes. "Joe approves. That's good." Finally, he asked, "If you're Taffy Bean, why are you traveling in a box car?"

She stammered a little and then pulled the hood from her hair, finally surrendering to the truth. "I...I don't want them to find me."

"Who?" Tucker and Christy asked in unison.

"Never mind." Tallulah, now Taffy, hung her head. "You can't help me."

Tucker stopped in disbelief. "Why not?"

Taffy shrugged. "You're just kids, like me."

Tucker blinked and straightened taller. "And, what does that have to do with anything?"

Taffy snapped back. "No one believes kids."

"Who doesn't?" Dumbfounded, Tucker's shoulders tightened. Gramma always believed him. It was true, sometimes he didn't tell her everything. He knew, however, he never really lied to her. "Taffy, why don't people believe you?"

"I don't know," she sighed and shrugged. "I'm twelve years old. I've worked since I was six. If I say I don't feel good and don't want to film, my guardian says, 'Grow up and quit complaining.' I've even worked with a fever."

Christy touched Taffy's arm. "I am so sorry."

Tucker wasn't stuck on Taffy's feelings. He was hung-up on one word. "Your guardian? Don't you have a mom and dad?" He felt an aching in his stomach. No mom and an absent dad sounded more like his own life than he wanted to think about right then.

"I do. I get to see them every few months." Taffy's eyes filled with tears. "But I've never been home for Thanksgiving. Not for six years at least. I'm usually doing a holiday show or a personal appearance somewhere. My little sister, Charlotte, called and asked if there was any way I could get home for some of Mama's turkey and pumpkin pie." Taffy reached out, smiled, and cuddled Joe's ears.

Tucker thought of all the exploring he enjoyed around his home and for miles in every direction. No one bared him from enjoying the crystal-clear creek in the summertime, chased him from the roar of the airport, or called him down off the roof of the school for that matter. "Who's after you, Taffy?"

"The police," she whispered.

Christy's mouth hung open. "The police? Why?"

Freddie stepped back a little. "Did you steal something on your way out?"

Taffy's back stiffened and her eyes narrowed. "If I took anything, anything at all, it was mine in the first place." She thumped her fist on her chest. "I did the work and I earned the money."

"Then why are they after you?" Tucker couldn't figure it out. He heard the words but they had no meaning.

The freckle-nosed young movie star gritted her teeth. "My guardians told the police I was kidnapped, because they didn't want to tell them I'm a run-away."

Tucker looked at Christy and shook his head. "Did you ever hear of such a thing? A girl gets a chance to act in movies, become famous, make tons of money, and then she walks away from it. Why did you run away?"

"I like acting," Taffy admitted, shaking her head as if she couldn't believe it herself. "But ..." she blinked hard. "What's your name?"

"I'm Tucker," he smiled. Pointing from friend to friend, he added, "She's Christmas Tree..."

"Hey!" Christy bellowed.

"Sorry, just givin' you the truth." Tucker nodded in Christy's direction again and made a correction. "She goes by Christy. Unless you want to pick yourself up off the ground, you'd better call her Christy." They all chuckled and Tucker finished up, "This is Johnny and that guy is Freddie." He teased again. "We all know who you are."

"Thanks," Taffy smiled faintly. To Christy she winked, "I like your spunk. Nobody tells you what to do. You get time to yourself. You're allowed to have friends, and ..."

Tucker could not believe Taffy's so-called perfect life. "You aren't allowed to have friends? What do you do in your spare time?"

"Spare time? Tucker, I don't have any spare time. I have no spending money and I can't even pick out my own clothes. What I wear must 'conform to my image' and ... I don't like my image."

"What's wrong with your image?" Freddie asked, bewildered. "You look pretty good to me."

"Thanks, Freddie." She said as her smile broadened a little. "It's not my image in the mirror, what I look like, that I'm talking about. It's who or what people think I am. I'm twelve years old and will be thirteen next month. They want me to dress and act like I'm ten. I feel like I'm in prison."

"They?" Johnny asked. "They … who?"

"Like I said, my guardians. They're following the studio's orders. Vanessa Thomas is my agent and her husband, Lloyd, is my attorney. I live with them when I'm in California, and I'm there most of the time."

It all sounded very complicated to Tucker. He thought he had a mixed-up family. Taffy's family was one confused mess of people stirred by an electric Mixmaster called *money*. "You said they follow the studio's orders? What does Moonlight Motion Pictures have to say about it?"

Taffy's voice grew tight and cracked. "They own me."

"No, they don't," Tucker insisted.

"My parents signed a contract with Vanessa and Lloyd, saying they gave up their right to have any say in my acting career. Vanessa Thomas didn't want a stage-mother or dad around. The Studio controls everything. Vanessa and Lloyd see to my daily needs, give me a place to live, and make sure they follow all studio orders to the smallest detail. Like, not going out alone without either Vanessa or Lloyd with me; only going back home to visit family after a film has finished and they decide how many movies I make each year. They set my bedtime at seven o'clock, and getting-up time at four AM so I get to the studio in time. Every day of every week is the same, every minute of every hour." Tears filled her eyes as she seemed to wilt with exhaustion. "I have no freedom … none."

"That's no fun." Tucker had to tell the truth as he saw it. But, to his thinking, working all the time and not being able to have time to explore the world, or build a rocket to Mars, was impossible to consider.

"Tucker," Johnny spoke up as he looked out to the fields past Goshen, "we didn't stop in Goshen. We didn't even slow down."

Christy jerked around to face the open door and watched the passing scene. "There's Aunt Maud and Uncle Jerome's farm house. They live east of town, well past the movie theater."

Tucker's shoulders slumped as the hot air escaped from his balloon. He couldn't believe it. Not again.

"That's okay, Tucker," Christy assured him. "We can get off the next time we stop."

"Grandpop hasn't taken the train into Goshen for a long time. He rides the interurban bus." Tucker felt empty inside. He really didn't care about missing the movie. He had the star of the show within arm's length. Maybe she could remember a few lines from the script. "Maybe the station stops have changed."

"Pow! Your mental light bulb actually popped," Freddie snickered.

Tucker's eyes narrowed as he threw both arms in the air. "At least I have enough brilliant ideas to over-heat my Edison."

Taffy closed her eyes, threw her head back and inhaled slowly. "We'll ride for a while and feel the air and sunshine."

Tucker did as she suggested; but he wasn't dreaming about the brightness of the morning. He was thinking about another opportunity lost.

Christy softened a little. "Sorry you won't get to see Bobby this time, Tucker."

Tucker shrugged and rubbed the top of Joe's silky head. The dog looked up at him and nuzzled his slightly runny nose on Tucker's wool, plaid jacket. "I know how you feel, Taffy, trying to get home. Family is important."

Chapter Twenty-One
Toledo Bound

"Listen to the rhythm of the train on the tracks." Tucker snapped his fingers to a beat he heard coming from under the boxcar. "Clickety-clack, clickety-clack, goin' to Toledo, won't come back. Got no suitcase, got no sack, goin' to Toledo, won't come back."

"Won't come back?" Christy's face strained in surprise.

"It's just a rhyme, Christy." Tucker reassured her as best he could but admitted to himself, they were still going east. "We'll get back. Maybe we'll come to a roundhouse."

"It will have to have a double loop, with all the confusion we've had so far," Freddie quipped. "I don't know whether I'm comin' or goin'."

Tucker put his hands in his jacket pockets and rocked back and forth, like the school principal monitoring the hallways after school. "Well, we were going, when what we wanted, was to go and stop, not turn around."

Freddie's eyes rolled up. "You sound more confused than I am."

Taffy looked at the refrigerator crates then found a shorter packing box and sat down. "What makes that clickety-clack sound?"

Now, that question was one Tucker could answer. With all the stories Tucker heard over the years living with his grandparents, he felt like an official railroad tour guide. "Grandpop said the joints in the rails make noise sometimes."

Taffy, a big city Hollywood girl, joined in. "Rail joints? What are rail joints?"

"Even I know that," Freddie said with a laugh. "The space where the rails lay end to end. Like your knee is a joint."

Johnny smiled a mischievous smile. "The toe bone's connected to the foot bone, the foot bone's…"

All four grinned and began to sing the spiritual together. Johnny raised his arms like a conductor. "From the top," as the choir director always said.

"The toe bone's connected to the foot bone,
the foot bone's connected to the ankle bone,
the ankle bone's connected to the leg bone,
now hear de word of da Lord." [2]

They all laughed until they stumbled into each other. Tucker fell to the dust on the floor, and like the chain reaction of a line of dominoes, each one then tumbled into the next. Joe completed the pile by flopping on top of Tucker.

Tucker lay in the heap. "Oh," he began again, picking up the thread of Taffy's question. "And, a rail squat is a crack in the rail that finally leads to a dent."

Then, there was silence except for clacking on the tracks. The morning was nearing noon when they crossed over into Ohio. The farmland looked a lot like the soil and fence rows of Elkhart County around home. Although the trees had lost all their crimson and gold leaves, the air smelled crisp and earthy. Large fields, although mostly harvested, still cradled huge orange pumpkins along the edges of the patches. The sky was blue and the mix of autumn colors everywhere reminded Tucker the next day would be Thanksgiving. He couldn't think of where the train would stop. So, there was no way to know how long it would take to get there or how long to get back. The field pumpkins made him think of Gramma's orange pies, browned on the top to perfection. Pie images slid into cranberry salad and turkey stuffing. The entire gallery of pictures made Tucker remember he hadn't eaten lunch. His stomach grumbled and rumbled adding another beat to the clickety clack of the train.

"I'm hungry, too." Christy rolled her eyes as she patted her tummy. "When do you think we'll get to wherever we're going?"

Johnny giggled and rolled his eyes. "Since he doesn't know where we're going, how will he know how long it will take to get there?"

"Oh, I know where we're going." Tucker leaned on the side of the door jamb and stared out at the passing Ohio farmland. "We must have hopped on an express train. It won't stop 'til it gets there … 'til it gets to Toledo."

"Toledo?" Johnny gasped.

"Good," Christy said as she reached in her coat pocket. "That's a big town. I'll use my movie money to buy a hamburger and a coke."

"No," Taffy motioned with her hand, "you guys won't buy anything. Order whatever you want. It will be my treat."

"I've never been in Toledo before," Johnny continued with his eyebrows knitted in worry.

"Me neither," Freddie shrugged.

"Really? But you can go anywhere," Johnny whispered.

"You can too," Tucker sputtered, then wondered what Johnny meant.

"No, Tucker. No, I can't. Most of my friends and family live in one area of Elkhart. I know which stores welcome black people and which ones are either downright mean or act like they don't want me in their store."

Christy put her arm on Johnny's shoulder. "I'm sorry, Johnny."

Tucker tried to sort it all out. Johnny, his mother, and their church choir had sung in the family's church across little Moyer Avenue from his home. He scratched his head in disbelief. "Johnny, I'm ashamed to say, I've never noticed."

Johnny smiled. "Don't worry about it, Tucker. We haven't been anywhere together. I've been in your home, your church, and your school. You've been in my home, church, and school. But we haven't gone shopping together. That's just the way it is. It's just that … I know where I'm welcome at home. I don't know where, or if, I'll be welcome in Toledo."

Tucker thought about how unfair it all sounded. Then, he came up with the only idea that popped in his head. "You'll be okay. You're one of us, Johnny. Wherever we go, you'll go, too."

"Tucker, look," Taffy tucked herself behind Tucker as they both stood at the door. "See that car?" She pointed to a powder blue Cadillac. "That looks like Vanessa and Lloyd's car."

"Here, in Ohio?" Tucker leaned in the direction of the road that ran beside the tracks for a few miles. "Why would they be here?"

"I'm from Toledo. Maybe they are going over to check with my parents." She stopped a second. "No, then they'd have to tell Daddy they lost me. Believe me … they wouldn't want to do that."

As the car passed, Tucker kept his eyes on the sleek four-door luxury car. When the back bumper was visible, he caught a glimpse of the license plate. Tucker's stomach turned a flip. The white letters on the black background clearly read *California.*

Chapter Twenty-Two
The End of the Line

Finally, miles and miles from home, across the state line, the train slowed to a stop. Tucker had been watching out the wide, sliding door. He saw the country side dissolve into neighborhoods with small factories, communities with schools, and rows of stores. Somewhere, someone was baking bread. Its yeasty, ever-so-slightly sweet aroma filled the air. Tucker didn't know how, but it made him feel warm inside, like Gramma had just taken two loaves of her golden crust bread out of the oven. Leaning out the door, the vast railroad yard stretched out up ahead, like an exploded train set that used every piece of track a kid could find in their storage box.

Tucker felt the cold wind on his face but all he could think of was home and lunch. "Grandpop said there are twelve sets of tracks here at Union Station."

"Union Station?" Freddie asked. "How do you know it's called Union Station?"

"I saw a sign, complaining about the condition of the station here in Toledo."

"Toledo?" Christy moaned. "We're in Toledo? Oh, my goodness."

Joe's ears popped up when Christy complained. "She's okay, Joe." Tucker looked at Christy and smiled. "She just feels like the rest of us."

"Not me." Taffy smiled with glee and clapped her hands together. "I'm home. My family's house is only a few miles from here."

"Maybe we could use the motorcycles," Freddie piped up as he looked longingly at the cartons. "Taffy could ride double with me."

"You mean *take* the cycles, Freddie," Tucker scolded. "That's called grand theft auto."

"No," Freddie blushed, "that's called grand theft Harley."

The train finally stopped completely. "Leave 'em be, Freddie," Tucker warned as he waited at the door to make a jump. With his body positioned for immediate flight, he paused a minute, then snapped, "Okay, everybody ... go!" Quickly, the five, plus one very smart dog, rushed at the open door and made a flying leap, landing on their feet outside that train that never stopped.

"Now...," Christy announced as she started walking, "which way to the train station and the bathrooms?"

Taffy turned around and pointed. "Union Station is right there." Putting her hands on her hips she announced, "Completed in 1886, it hasn't changed much. They call it 'Toledo's Oldest Joke,' but I kinda like it."

Multiple railway platform stations, running alongside the many tracks, blocked the view of huge, Union Station. The roof of the station house, with its several tall chimneys, and the pointed turrets of the old red brick building, peeked above the conglomeration in the train yard.

The sun was bright although the wind was cold. Taffy put her hand to her forehead. "Union Station faces Emerald Avenue on the other side of the building."

Freddie looked past the rail yard toward the station. "How do you know that?"

"Emerald Avenue meets Broadway Street about a block down." Taffy said wistfully. "Like I said, I live a little over three miles west on Broadway."

Tucker looked west and smiled. "Great. That would take us about an hour and a half to walk."

"Walk?" Christy turned her nose up. "Don't they have buses in Toledo?"

"Yes, of course," Taffy began.

Suddenly, a sharp, male voice pierced the fun of the day. "Hey ... you kids!"

"Run!" Tucker shouted as a trainman in gray work pants and work shirt waved his fist in the air and charged in their direction.

Christy was the first one over the initial three sets of tracks heading toward the station door. The long iron rails, connected by wooden ties every nineteen inches may not have been as hard to jump if they were flat. But, elevated several inches and packed around both sides with crushed stones, made it hard.

"Keep going!" Tucker shouted. Looking back, Taffy, Johnny, and Freddie were close behind.

"Ugh," Christy gasped. "There are six more tracks to go." She panted as she ran.

It was easy for Joe. He leaped and twisted and played in the train yard between the rails. He seemed happy to be out of the freight car as he stretched and moved.

The others flew up and over track after track, stumbled, slipped, ran, gasped, laughed, but most of all, they out-ran the brakeman. Christy reached for the door of the train station and jerked it open. Tucker reached over Christy's head and held the door open for the other three.

Taffy, however, balked as soon as she got to the entrance. Tucker remembered last summer riding Lightning. When the horse reared up and threw him off as they nearly got to the tracks in Lightning's mad bolt for home. "What's wrong?"

"Police, Tucker. Remember ... they're looking for me. If I wanted to parade through the busiest train station in Ohio, I would have bought a ticket and rode in comfort."

"Taffy," Tucker's shoulders sagged with impatience, "you can wait out here with Joe if you want to. Or, put your hood on and go in. The others are already looking for the restrooms."

"I can't stay out here either, Tucker. I gotta go. Wait, I know what we'll do." She wrapped her hand around Joe's collar, stiffened her arm, flipped her hood over her head, and darted into the station like a blind girl with a seeing-eye dog.

Inside, Tucker couldn't take the train station all in. "Grandpop would love to see all the carved oak, plate glass, and polished brass everywhere." The ceilings went up forever and bowed at the top for grace. "Even Mrs. Hunter, as tall as she is, would find the ceiling a mile high."

"Mrs. Hunter?" Taffy asked.

"My teacher," Tucker answered, but didn't confess aloud how happy he would have been if Mrs. Hunter suddenly walked in. He liked being in Grandpop's world of trains and station houses, although it was as far from home as he had ever been. Looking around again, he thought, *I'll bet Grandpop's been here many times*. Looking ahead, he spotted Freddie going through a door on the left about sixty feet down the hall. "Restrooms are—"

"I know where they are. I've been in this grand old lady many times," Taffy reminded him as they hurried along the hall.

"Gramma would have been here, too. She and Grandpop would use Grandpop's train pass to visit family in Toledo. I've never been here though."

Tucker spotted a uniformed policeman walking up ahead. He appeared to look at the people around him and then at a picture he carried. Tucker noticed Taffy saw the officer too. He watched as she slipped into a women's restroom and disappeared from searching eyes. Tucker thought Taffy appeared calm and relaxed, not drawing any attention to herself.

She sure is a good actress. Tucker's head was full of everything he saw. He saw Joe trotting beside Taffy and hoped Joe wasn't confused.

In a few minutes, they all gathered near the drinking fountain and planned their next move. Joe strutted along like the star of a movie, quite pleased with all the attention.

"Let's get out of here." Taffy's impatience and nervousness was becoming obvious. "I'm blind, remember. So, Tucker, we'll go out the front door, to the sidewalk, turn left, and follow Emerald Avenue up a block or so to Broadway Street and turn left again."

"Will do," Tucker announced. Then he announced the next short-term goal in one word. "Food."

Chapter Twenty-Three
A Star Shines

They only walked a few blocks when Tucker stopped and rubbed Joe's ear. "Look," he pointed to a low, white clapboard building with large windows across the front and a huge red banner. "It says, 'The Best Burgers in Toledo.' I'm starved. I'd eat the second-best burgers in Toledo if this doesn't work out."

Christy playfully jabbed Tucker in the side. "They don't say anything about French fries. Maybe we'd better look for another place."

Tucker moved toward the red cottage door trimmed in black. "Sure, there is. French fries go with hamburgers like sauerkraut goes with bratwurst."

Johnny blinked in rapid fire. "What?"

"That's good Amish food." Taffy threw back her head and laughed. "My family is one generation away from the white bonnets, black if you're not married. We have sauerkraut and bratwurst once a week in my home, or we did when I lived there."

Christy rolled her eyes. "Well, I'll let you two daydream about sausage and fermented cabbage." She pulled the door open and stepped in. "I'm ready to eat Christy-food."

"Christy-food, is it?" Freddie followed her into the little neighborhood restaurant. "And, I'll have some Freddie-food. If they have a grilled cheese sandwich with tomato soup, that's mine, that's Freddie-food."

Tucker leaned down and rumpled the well-petted hair on Joe's head. "Boy, stay here." He pointed to the sidewalk up against the building next to the door. The dog sat back on his hind legs with his paws in front of him and positioned himself to guard the door. "Good dog."

Inside, the dining room smelled like grilled beef, deep fried onions, and three kinds of pie that nested in a display case on the counter. The friends looked around briefly. Tucker was glad he had the five-dollar bill in his billfold he'd earned helping Simon Winkle with his roof. Also, the five Uncle Jacob gave him for his new shirt, lay folded and tucked in the corner of the compartment where he kept his bills. He was glad it was there; but he knew the money had to go for the shirt. That's why his uncle gave it to him. He had no idea how much the food would cost. He might even have to help Christy or the others pay for their meal.

"Harrumph*." The cook grumbled with arms crossed as he came out from behind the wall that separated the kitchen from the lunch counter and the diners at the tables and booths. He stared at the five but it was easy to see his focus was on Johnny Washington.

Taffy, ignoring the cook's distain, smiled broadly, pulled the hood from her head, and straightened her hair. "Good afternoon." She turned to Johnny with an over-acting sweep of her hand. "I see you recognize my co-star in *Kids from Montana*. Johnny Washington is anxious to taste your best-hamburger-in-Toledo so he can finish his list of the best ten sandwiches in the mid-west for *Photoplay Magazine*. And, you are?"

"Uh, Tony," the man stammered and straightened his shirt. "Tony Cassino," he spit out. "You're Taffy Bean."

"Yes, Sir," she lavished attention on the owner as if he were the most important person in the world.

"Just think, Tony," Tucker bubbled in. "You have two movie stars in your restaurant in one day. Wow. That's amazing."

"Right." Tony blushed and wrung his hands together. "Why don't you guys come back here to this big table?" He led the way to the back, left corner to an oversized table with a circular cushioned bench, large enough to comfortably hold five.

They all slid along the bench seat, Taffy, Johnny, Freddie, Christy, and then Tucker. That placed Tucker facing the door, a position he enjoyed so he could monitor the full dining room. "Thanks Tony. This is great."

"Lunch is on the house," Tony boasted. "Menus are there on the table. Look them over and I'll be back." He started to leave, then pointed toward the door. "That your dog?"

"He sure is," Tucker boasted.

Christy filled in the blanks. "During the war, he was a war-dog, a hero with real metals."

"Really?" Tony turned toward the door again. "I read about those dogs in *Life Magazine*. I'll get him some water and a couple hamburger patties."

"Thanks, Tony." Tucker sat back and relaxed. They would all eat and it wouldn't cost him anything. He thought of the roofing money in his pocket and smiled. Maybe he'd take some of that cash back home and go to Goshen to the movie on Friday or Saturday after Thanksgiving.

The group opened their copy of the menu and studied it for a second. "Grilled cheese," Freddie said as he pointed to the right side of the page.

"And tomato soup," Taffy added, running her finger over the soup-of-the-day list. "See, Wednesday, tomato soup."

Christy peeked over the top of her menu. "I have the dollar Mom gave me for the movie. The ticket would have been fifty-five cents and the popcorn 15 cents, so seventy cents. I'm glad Tony said the food was free with our two celebrities with us," she grinned mischievously. "I would have had just barely enough. The hamburger costs 55 cents, the same as the movie. The French fries are fifteen cents, and a coke is a dime. So, lunch would cost eighty cents."

"Well, if he doesn't pay for it, I will," Taffy announced. "You have no idea how much I appreciate traveling with all of you. I was so frightened."

Tucker smiled, although he thought he might pass out from hunger. He felt himself getting weaker and decided the smell of good food didn't help. "Fiddlesticks. Let's see what Tony says first." Covering his mouth with his hand, he whispered. "He's coming back."

"Have you decided what you want? Get anything. Remember, it's on the house." Tony listened carefully as each of the friends ordered their meal. He had no order pad and made no notes. When the last person was done, he turned to the kitchen and yelled, "Bertha, two heifers on a bun, one hot melted cheese, two dogs in a cradle, bowl of red soup, five taters, and five malted milks, three chocolate, one strawberry and one vanilla."

The small group was silent for a minute. Tucker spoke first, "Wow, how did you do that?"

Tony shrugged and then asked, "Would you let me take a picture ... of all of you? I'd like to hang it here in the restaurant."

Taffy's eyes grew huge as she slunk back and wrapped her arms around her middle. "Well…"

Tucker straightened up with an air of authority. "Tony, Miss Bean and Mr. Washington are movie stars; they are private people and don't want to be swamped. Please don't put up the photo until January. That's just five weeks away. Oh, and please send me a copy of the picture. I'll leave my address."

Taffy smiled. It was easy to see her relax, as her hands went limp on the table. "That would be fine, Tucker," she agreed.

"Also," Tucker added. "If anyone comes around today, don't tell them you saw Taffy or Johnny."

Tony agreed and hurried to the back room to pick up a square, Kodak Brownie camera. He came back, carrying it by the top handle, and smiled. Looking through the lens for the best position, he asked the five friends to scoot together on the bench seat. A few snaps, and that ended the photo shoot. "Okay you guys, thanks. I'll see how your food is cooking."

Tucker's eyes suddenly fixed on a man and woman who came into the diner. Well dressed and tanned, they stood out. They didn't seem like northern Ohio people or Indiana folks for that matter.

"Woe is me," Freddie sighed and slumped down on the bench.

Tucker smiled as he remembered home and his Sunday school class. "Aunt Woe?"

"Who is Aunt Woe," Taffy asked.

"Anna Frederick, from Birdie Kline's Sunday school class back home," Christy said with a grin. "She was always saying, 'Woe is me,' when she complained. So, we all called her, "Aunt Woe."

"Uncle Woe, if you don't mind," Freddie insisted.

"Good afternoon," the woman who came in the front door greeted and looked around the diner. "Have you seen Taffy Bean?" she asked. "I'm sure you know who she is."

"In my diner?" Tony mocked.

Tucker quickly reached over and put his arm around Christy's shoulder, trying to give an air of indifference to the two strangers.

Christy elbowed him in his ribs. "What ya doin' McBride?"

He nuzzled her closer and whispered in her ear. "The two at the door. Don't look."

Christy kept her eyes on the table in their corner booth, and laughed. "Oh, Tucker, you are so ... I don't know what." She was at a loss for words. Tucker wasn't Tucker.

"Annoying?" he whispered again.

"That's the word I was looking for," she said as she pulled back, laughing as if he had just told her a funny story.

Tony put his hands on his hips and threw his head back. "Sure, movie stars come in here every day. Clark Gable stopped in for coffee yesterday." He laughed. "Thanks. You really think this place is swanky enough for celebrities? I'll run an ad."

The lady looked around the now nearly empty room. "Don't kid yourself," she snapped and turned to leave.

Tony saluted with the tip of the menu he held. "Be sure to tell all your Hollywood friends about this place."

Turning back, the woman's eyes narrowed. "How did you know we're from California?"

"The tan," Tony fired back, seeming pleased to be keeping up with the snooty woman. "And, you seem to know movie stars." He shrugged. "There's no Hollywood types around here."

She nearly bumped into the man with her. "Let's get out of here."

From the back corner of the diner, a massive exhale escaped. Taffy buried her face in her trembling hands.

"Are you okay?" Christy asked as she reached over and patted Taffy's hand. "Were those two Vanessa and Lloyd?"

Taffy only nodded, with tight eyes and a worried expression.

Tucker wrinkled up his nose. "Christy, how did you know that was them?"

Christy shook her head. "Well, who else could set Taffy's teeth chattering and cause her to pull herself so far inside she covered her face?"

"Oh, right." Tucker had a hard time figuring out how Christy always knew what she knew.

"You're safe with us," Johnny spoke low. "Us movie stars stick together."

They all laughed and stretched out their tense muscles just as Bertha brought a tray full of food to the table. She spread out the feast like a king's banquet. Then, silence fell over the group as chewing and eating replaced pictures and fun.

Tucker stopped in mid-sandwich and smiled a hearty smile. "Just don't let Joe know some of you are eating a dog, with or without the cradle."

Chapter Twenty-Four
On the Way

"Tony," Taffy folded her napkin and put it on the corner of the table, "do you have a phone I can use?"

"Taffy Bean used my phone," he announced as he drew his hand across in front of him like he was displaying a sign. "I'd be happy for you to use my very own telephone." He pointed to a back hallway that led to public restrooms and where a payphone hung on the wall. "If you need change, I'll get some from the cash drawer."

"Thanks, Tony. I have a nickel." Taffy disappeared into the hall.

"Are you about finished with your hot dog, Johnny?" Tucker put the last bite of hamburger in his mouth and licked catsup from the corner of his lips.

"Sure am." Johnny polished his French fries and sucked up a deep swallow of vanilla malted milk. "These malts are huge."

"Yep," Tucker agreed in as few words as possible. "I was starved."

"Starved? Really McBride?" Christy interrupted and then she paused. "Well, maybe."

"As I was saying," Tucker blinked his eyes in exaggerated emphasis, "before I was interrupted. I was starved ... and now I'm stuffed."

"You?" Christy sipped on her chocolate malt. "Stuffed?"

"There was no answer at home," Taffy chattered as she came back into the dining room.

Tucker gulped down the last of his strawberry malted milk. "Taffy, your family isn't home?"

"No …." To Tucker, she sounded disappointed, but something else, too. Something like … excited. "This is the day before Thanksgiving. All the holiday decorations will be up in the store windows in town. Santa's workshop will be displayed outside the department store, and lights will be everywhere, even now with the sun still up … just everywhere." She caught the tears rolling down her checks with her handkerchief. "I used to love to go window shopping. My little sister and brother are the age I was when it meant so much to me. We always went to town on the Wednesday before turkey day, after Momma finished baking pies."

Tucker thought for a minute he could smell Gramma's apple pie as it came out of the oven, hot and juicy. He was full, but he was sure he could eat at least one piece of Gramma's pie.

"We could walk." Freddie put his fist to the center of his chest and burped.

"Yuck, Freddie," Christy scolded.

Taffy pulled back. "No, I can't walk home. I'd be right out in the open for everyone to see."

"They'd see you, right," Tucker agreed. "But, with your hood up, would anyone recognize you?"

Christy nodded her head. "Those clothes are far different from anything I've ever seen you in, not in the movies, magazines, or anywhere."

Johnny was quiet but nodded in agreement. "What do you wear around the house when you aren't at work but still in California? What does Vanessa usually see you in?"

"Well, not this sweatshirt, that's for sure." Taffy slipped back into the booth. "Vanessa buys all of my clothes. I have no clothes to relax in. Mom calls relaxing clothes, play clothes; and … I don't play, haven't in years."

Tucker smiled. "Well, you sure don't look like the Taffy Bean of the movies. And, you said you don't get to hang out with friends. You'll be walking with the four of us. Vanessa and Mr. Vanessa won't expect you to be with anyone. Which is safer - walking home, maybe trying to call your folks somewhere along the way, are sitting here and hoping your family will get back soon?"

"Okay, okay," she gave it. "Let's walk."

"I'll stop first at the necessary room." Christy left the table and didn't wait for a response. She wasn't asking for permission.

A few minutes later, all five of the long-distance walkers started out the red door. "Bye, Tony," Tucker called back. "Thanks for everything."

Tony waved and laughed. "Ah no, guys, thank you. Next time you're in Toledo, stop in."

Taffy stopped and turned around. Looking Tony straight in the eye, she said, "Please remember, if that last couple that was in here a few minutes ago comes back, don't tell them you saw me. Don't tell anyone."

"I promise. I'll not tell anyone," he agreed and waved again. "If it's okay, I'll hang that picture I took next week. If that's not too soon."

"Go ahead, enjoy," Taffy breathed out slowly in a whistle. "I will be home long before that."

Out on the sidewalk, Joe waited and wiggled and pranced and danced around. "Yes," Tucker soothed as he petted Joe's side and stroked the top of his head, "you're a good dog."

When everyone had their coat on, they started walking. It was a beautiful afternoon. It hadn't started snowing. For that, Tucker was thankful. "A winter day can be cold, but if the sun is shining and it's blue overhead, it's perfect."

"Emerald Street ... Logan," Tucker read off the street names, though he'd never been to Toledo. Everyone was walking along so quiet, he needed to hear someone talking, even if it was his own voice.

Turning left onto Broadway, the road sloped down and Taffy stopped. "An overpass," she gasped. "I can't see what's on the road on the other side."

Tucker looked at the train track that ran above the road. "When they planned the streets on Broadway where the road dipped, the bridge crew elevated the track avoiding a rollercoaster movement."

"How do you know that?" Freddie asked.

Tucker smiled. "Grandpop was the foreman of the bridge building crew for the New York Central railroad."

Christy looked up at the cement walls that approached the bridge along the side of the street. "Did he build this one?"

"Don't know." Tucker missed his grandfather the farther he got from Dunlap. "He could have."

"Now what?" Johnny asked.

Tucker looked at Christy, his sidekick in most of his pranks and activities. "You guys stay here. I'll climb the hill leading to the track and check out what's on the other side of the tunnel."

Christy looked past Tucker. "Wait … a police car. I'm sure they would prefer you didn't."

The black and white car with two uniformed officers inside, and a red bubble on top slowed to a stop beside the group. One of the officers in the car leaned over and rolled down the passenger window. "Good afternoon. We're looking for a missing girl. Any of you see Taffy Bean since you've been out walking?"

"The movie star?" Tucker laughed with pretty good acting skills. "In Toledo, Ohio? Doesn't she live in Hollywood"

Taffy adjusted her hood a little, and her personality at the same time. With experience from her movie, *Southern Fried Nonsense*, what poured out of her mouth next was pure Dixieland drawl. "Well my, my, my, what are y'all talkin' 'bout?"

With a tone of boredom, the officer asked, "What's your name, young lady?"

"Her?" Christy asked, looking out of the corner of her eye. "This is Tallulah Butler, my cousin from Mississippi."

"Right." The office put his finger to his forehead and motioned his partner to drive on. "If you see Taffy, call the police station."

"Okay," Taffy drew out slowly, "we certainly will. Bye bye now and happy huntin', y'hear?"

Freddie shook his head and snickered. "You've got to be kidding. Are you from Mississippi or Ohio?"

"I don't know," Taffy said wistfully and looked toward the overpass. "I don't feel like I belong anywhere."

Christy patted her on the shoulder. "For today, you belong with us."

"Thank you." When Taffy looked toward the railway bridge above the road again, she added, "That is so spooky. I have no idea what we're walking into."

"I'll go check for you." Tucker started walking toward the bridge.

"How?" Christy asked. "Or, is this going to be another case of Tucker-in-the-tree?"

"Don't be silly." Tucker took off his jacket. "There are no trees on the bridge." To Freddie he added, "Please, hold my coat."

He looked up and down Broadway Street for other police cars and the Cadillac they saw Vanessa and Lloyd in earlier. No sightings. Turning back, he saw four pairs of eyes looking at him. "Hey, don't watch me. You'll draw everyone's attention."

"Okay," Christy said as she looked around at the foot of the little grassy slope that approached the tracks on the overpass. "Over here." She led the way to a bus shelter where riders could sit while they waited for their downtown connection. She motioned to the others. "Sit."

Tucker took a deep breath when he saw the others found a way to camouflage their loitering in the area. His feet slipped on the grass where the early snow melted into a slippery slush. Sliding on the incline, he grabbed the pipe-style railing on top of the concrete abutment that held the hill from caving in and landing in the street. He pulled and tugged and managed to take more steps upward than ones he lost sliding back. His shoes were wet but his socks seemed dry. At least, his feet weren't cold. He was glad he put on his old clodhoppers that morning. Gone were the war-time steel plates, used to protect the leather on the soles from wearing out when leather was scarce. Climbing that hill, he wondered if the metal plates on the bottom of his shoes might have given him more traction.

At the top, he looked as far west and east as he could see. Usually, the day before Thanksgiving was a busy shopping day as families prepared to entertain Grandma and Grandpa. Frantic people in cars, on last-minute runs to the hardware store for screws to prop up the dining room table before the table cloth went on, all clogged the roads.

Joe sat quietly at Christy's feet. Then, like he had been planning the great prison escape, when Christy finally relaxed completely, Joe broke away and darted up the slope.

Tucker was balancing himself on the rails of the tracks, which was as high as he could climb. On the road below, he saw nothing suspicious. Others often told him, he had a talent for ferreting out danger, unless he was the center of the problem.

"Joe," Tucker snapped and nearly buckled his knees when the dog raced up, charging at him from behind. Bending over, Tucker rubbed the dog's tummy. "I'm not going to fall, unless you knock me over," he patted Joe on the head. "You've traveled all over the world, Joe. Are you afraid to get very far away from me in Toledo, Ohio?"

Joe wiggled and twisted at Tucker's feet. Prancing around, the dog's paws wedged into the spaces between the railroad ties every time he put his foot on the track. He whined when his foot touched the iron rail itself.

The crowded traffic below rumbled, screeched, and honked on their way downtown. Above the cacophony, the wind that was blowing all day, whistled in the open space above. Finally, Tucker heard something else. He didn't know how long his friends had been yelling, but their voices finally pierced the noise all around him.

"Tucker," the four screamed and pointed down track, "the train!"

"Joe, is that what your paw felt?" Tucker then realized he had no time to talk. The train was nearly on top of him. "Oh no. Here we go again. Come on boy," he yelled.

Tucker and Joe dove for the side of the track where there was about three feet of space before he hit the four-foot tall solid concrete wall. Joe stretched out like a diving champion from the high dive and landed in a heap at the edge. However, that became a problem for Tucker. His great train escape caused him to trip over the dog, fall and twist at the same time, and catapulted him over the wall. He grabbed the cold hard top plate of the bridge wall and hung on. Thankfully, the train had slowed down to a chug as it neared the railroad yard. If it were going faster, the train's draft could have caught him.

"Oh, thank you," Tucker whispered. From below the bridge he heard a cheer from the kids. In his mind, he heard Gramma, "Tucker, you get down off there." He knew he couldn't draw attention to himself by waving or someone might see he was where he shouldn't be. Even more serious, his hands were slipping. Besides, Grandpop used to say, "You can only hang so long before the limb breaks."

Tucker threw his leg over the wall and shinnied up on top. He sat for a second, just to get his breath. "Come on," he motioned to Joe to follow. Jumping up, he stood on the side-wall, ran to the end of the overpass, and slid down the little hill, like a down-hill skier on the kiddy slope.

If Carolyn were there, she would have said, "You must remember, Little Brother, Grandma is getting older. She doesn't need to hold her breath every time you decide to pull a stunt." Betsy would have raced him down the hill and would probably have come in first. She was a great athlete.

"You scared us to death," Christy scolded and swatted Tucker on the arm.

"Would you rather I let the train hit me or try to escape?" he asked as he put his jacket back on.

Taffy laughed. "Have you ever thought of becoming a movie stuntman?"

"Becoming?" Christy gasped. "Back home, his stunts are well known all over the neighborhood."

"He's never been filmed," Freddie began. "He could...."

"Just never-you-mind," Christy interrupted quickly. "He's done enough to fill several movies already."

"And, the road up ahead?" Taffy asked.

"Oh, right. That's what all this was about." He motioned toward the road and took another deep breath. "The coast is clear. Nothing seems out of the ordinary."

After a huge exhale from everyone, they started walking under the overpass. Shaded but not dark, the sun began to sneak through as they came near the opposite side. Joe had skittered on ahead and didn't sound an alarm. Tucker sighed in relief when they could see beyond the tracks. They all seemed to relax. They didn't have to tiptoe their way up Broadway Street. Besides, Joe would have looked silly on his toes. This time, they walked much faster.

Chapter Twenty-Five
So Much to See

"Not another one," Taffy moaned while pointing farther down Broadway.

Above the road stretched a second railway overpass, the iron on the handrailing was just as well-worn as the previous one. Tucker could tell by the patina on the iron surface it had been there a long time.

He bent low so he could see under the bridge. "The road dips down, the same as before, but the view is better."

"Yes, I see," Taffy agreed. "But ... it's still dark under there."

Christy bent over with her hands on the knees of her new slacks. "Taffy, it's not dark. It's just shaded, like a canopy over an Amish buggy."

"Oh, Christy, that would be fun." Taffy's frown faded as her eyes brightened. "I can write a new scene for myself. I'll be an Amish girl who drives the family buggy to the next town to visit her grandparents."

"And, she encounters the big bad wolf when she gets there?" Freddie asks.

"Freddie," Tucker stepped in. "Don't scare her."

Johnny started down the sloping sidewalk. "She couldn't find the wolf, good or bad, along the way. And, Taffy doesn't have a red coat."

Taffy laughed and gave Johnny a sideways hug. "Thanks Johnny, my faithful co-star. I needed a little laugh."

"I'll drive the surrey if you want me to," Johnny offered.

"I'm perfectly capable of driving my own buggy," Taffy said with a theatrical air.

Christy tossed her head, playing her own part in the little play. "We women are capable of driving ourselves around town." She lifted a leg like someone stepping up into a buggy and pretended to sit down. "Let's go visit Grandma."

A pedestrian pathway ran along both sides of the road under the bridge, coming and going. Separated from the busy flow of cars by a wall with empty spaces like open windows, the little tunnel provided a safe passage for those on foot.

"Come on Joe," Tucker said. He ran ahead under the overpass while the others followed in their imaginary Amish buggy. He didn't know if he ran to blaze the trail, or he ran to escape the unknown that frightened him. In the darkened gloom under the bridge, the air was colder and sent a damp chill through his bones. Tucker shook off the shudders as Grandpop's voice whispered inside him.

"Ya daresn't be afraid of the shadows, Tucker," he heard Grandpop comfort him. "The shade is just a chance to step out of the sun's glare for a while."

Tucker suddenly felt safe and warm. *Don't ever leave me, Grandpop*, he heard himself plead silently; but, vowed not to cry. A fellow just could not let others see him with tears dripping off his chin.

As they neared the sunshine again, Tucker stepped ahead and checked the other side. "Looks clear," he shouted back. "Joe isn't nervous. He doesn't sense danger."

Once the five cleared the second overpassed, they all breathed a deep sigh. They walked on for several blocks, mostly in silence enjoying the day, when they came to a cluster of stores. Taffy stopped at the door of a drugstore. "I'm going in to see if I can find a telephone."

"Joe, stay ... watch." Tucker followed Taffy into the store to make sure no one was in there who might recognize her. "I'll be right over here," he said as he sat on a stool at the soda fountain.

The counter-top was dark green marble and the emerald green continued in the leather on the stools. "Can I get you anything?" the fountain worker asked. The guy in the white hat looked like a teenager. He seemed to watch Taffy and hardly looked at Tucker.

Tucker tried to get the server's attention by placing an order. "Yes," he said as he moved his head up and down trying to catch his eye to make a connection. "I'll have a coke."

Taffy turned to look at Tucker and put her hand to her mouth like she was drinking something. Then, she mouthed the word, *Please*. She tapped her foot on the floor and said again silently, *No answer so far*.

When Tucker turned back to get his drink, the soda jerk still looked beyond him. Leaning his elbow on the counter, he nodded toward Taffy. "Who is she? She looks familiar."

"The one on the phone?" Tucker asked innocently. "Tallulah?"

"Tallulah? She sure looks familiar. What's her last name?"

"How many Tallulahs do you know?"

"Well, none. Thought I might know her sister … if she looks like her."

Taffy started to walk over to where Tucker sat. The kid behind the counter was still staring at her. When she spoke, her down-south accent came out again. "Goodness, Tucker. Who is this?"

Tucker gave an impatient eye roll in Taffy's direction and mumbled, "This always happens." He waved his hand limply from Taffy to the soda jerk. "Everybody thinks she looks like a movie star. Good grief. She's Tallulah Butler, my sister Betsy's friend."

"Are you sure?" the teen asked.

Taffy turned up her nose and stomped her foot. "Well, I declare. I guess I know my own name."

"Sorry." Tucker saw him blushed a little. "I'm Milton."

"Now, don't you worry about it, Milton. I get mistaken for someone else all the time." She took the coke Tucker handed her and made an exaggerated expression of disappointment. "Momma and Daddy weren't home yet. Let's go." She put a quarter on the counter and turned. "Two cokes at a nickel each equal ten cents. Keep the change, Milton."

Milton picked up the coin and smiled. "Thank you. But I still say—"

Tucker and Taffy didn't listen to Milton finish the sentence. Tucker was afraid he might start laughing if they continued with the hoax. He started snickering as they left the drugstore and joined the others.

Christy popped her hands on her hips and laughed along with them. "Okay, what's so funny? We're feeling left out."

Tucker pointed his thumb over his shoulder. "That crazy soda jerk in there thinks Tallulah looks familiar."

"Who'd believe such a thing?" Christy started inching her way down the sidewalk. "Let's go. It'll be suppertime in a little while."

"I'm getting hungry already," Johnny complained.

Freddie looked from Tucker to Christy as if he felt a little guilty. "Me too."

"It's a long walk to a bologna sandwich and potato chips." Taffy closed her eyes and smacked her lips.

Tucker recognized the look of hunger. "Is that a favorite of yours, Taffy?"

"Yes and no." Taffy seemed nervous, constantly searching right, and left. "Mommy always makes a quick supper on the evening before Thanksgiving, bologna sandwiches and chips. There's little time to fix a big meal after we get home from window shopping. And, there's the big meal tomorrow."

"Better quit talking about food," Tucker groaned. "Joe and I'll be hungry enough to eat an elephant."

"Well, lucky you, Tucker." Taffy skipped off the sidewalk and into the grass. "You have your dinner right here."

From over a high fence there came a terrible sound most of them had never heard before. It was a rumbling roar, like the trumpet of Gabriel.

Joe snapped to attention like a well-trained soldier and took a guard-dog position, ears up.

"It's okay, Joe," Tucker reassured him with a pat on the head. "Hot rockets," He gulped when he heard the trumpet again. "What's an elephant doing here?"

Taffy bent over laughing. "Tucker, the elephants are probably asking you the same thing. They belong here. You don't, well ... not unless you buy a ticket. It's the Toledo Zoo, silly."

"Can we go in?" Freddie jumped up, trying to see over the enclosure. "How much does a ticket cost?"

Johnny stretched to see the elephants as well. "If you're not afraid to climb over the fence, Freddie, you could see the giant beasts, eye to eye."

"And land where one of those things could step on my foot with those big flat hooves?"

"Well," Taffy began, "from my work on *Jungle Sunset*, I learned a little about elephants."

"You were in *Jungle Sunset*?" Christy asked as she struggled to see the exotic animals.

"Well sorta." Taffy threw her hand up in surrender. "It was my first movie. I had only two lines but they needed a child who could scream loud, really bellow."

Tucker turned, "It would be great to see all the animals. But we don't have time."

As they walked back to the sidewalk, Taffy continued. "Elephants are ungulates. They have toenails, not hooves.

And, they don't' have flat feet. In fact, they walk on their toes."

"They're toe dancers?" Tucker bowled over laughing. "This I've gotta see."

"No time, Tucker," Christy reminded him. "No time."

Tucker knew she was right. Still, it would have been great to see all the animals he had enjoyed reading about in Uncle Jacob's *National Geographic.*

The more he thought of Uncle Jacob, the more images of Gramma and Grandpop came to mind. All of them, getting ready for the whole family to come for Thanksgiving dinner, danced through his head like his own moving picture show. Then the goofy picture of a ballerina dancing elephant in a pink tutu crowded out the family pictures. He chuckled to himself, but had to admit, he was worried. He wondered if he would get home in time to snap the turkey wishbone with Betsy.

Chapter Twenty-Six
The Round

"How much farther?" Tucker knew they had already walked for a few hours. He was used to walking all over Dunlap, around the blocks of his neighborhood, down by the creek where they built a fort and swung across the water on the rope Grandpop braided from newspaper binding string, and miles up through the farmland to where he discovered the foundation of his family's homestead. But he didn't know if the others could walk as far as he could. He knew he was tired and they probably were, too.

"In the next block," Taffy started walking faster, "is the Walbridge Park Amusement Center. The original one burned down in 1938 but the Merry-go-round survived."

"Merry-go-round?" Freddie eyes brightened like a six-year-old who hoped to grasp the brass ring.

Tucker would have liked a ride on the round himself. Surprisingly, he felt a need to be responsible. "Let's get Taffy home, Freddie."

"Looks like there are other rides, too," Johnny added, not taking his eyes off the stone buildings or shelter houses.

Taffy ducked behind Christy as they walked. "There's another police car. They're going really slow."

"Look, Tucker," Christy added as she pointed to yet another patrol car.

Tucker saw the bubble-top cars and wondered how many more squad cars might turn up if anyone found out that Tallulah was really Taffy Bean. Joe seemed calm, so Tucker didn't think of danger. But then, uniformed police wouldn't signal danger to a guard dog.

"I have to get home before they find me," Taffy insisted. "My parents will sort this all out. The police might send me back with Vanessa and Lloyd, since they were the ones who reported me missing."

Tucker looked back at the black and white car behind them. "We'll have to get off the sidewalks, but first answer this; your parents will sort out what?"

"Daddy has read up on contract law in the last six months. He's a lawyer, but he deals more with family law: adoptions, divorce, custody … that sort of things."

"And?" Tucker didn't see what that had to do with anything.

Taffy sighed deeply. "He hoped that more information on contract law might find a loophole in my contract."

Christy looked at her with confusion. "You wanted out of your contract? You didn't want to make movies anymore?"

"I don't know," Taffy moaned. "I just wanted to come home. I wanted to see my family and be part of their lives. I wanted to go to school. I missed my friends."

As the police cars pulled to the curb, Tucker saw it wasn't the same officers as before. As casually as he could, he waved at the two and turned back to his friends. "Okay, a Merry-go-round ride it is."

"Hey, you kids," one of the policemen called, "have you seen Taffy Bean around here?"

"The movie star?" Tucker asked, sounding as dumbfounded as he could. "Here, in Toledo?"

"Sounds silly, doesn't it?" the officer said with a shrug. "Go on and enjoy your amusement ride." The car pulled away from the curb and moved on down the street.

"Then a ride it is." Tucker knew they would have to look like a normal group of friends. Like the tomato-throwing case from the church tower the other day … they had to be five normal friends, doing normal things ... not a movie star among them.

"I thought we didn't have time," Freddie snapped.

Taffy froze for a moment. "We do now."

Tucker pretended to look toward the street, past the few cars that were entering the parking lot. That didn't mean he didn't see the blue Cadillac that slowed at the entrance.

"I'll pay." Taffy reached in her pocket and took out some coins.

Tucker didn't know what to do, use the old casual tactic of slow-moving indifference or act like an excited kid ready for a carousel ride. He decided on the latter and started to run in the direction of the carrousel. *Kids are eager to get on a carnival ride.* The others walked faster to keep up, each watching the incoming cars out of the corner of their eye.

Taffy paid for five tickets and a half price for Joe to sit on one of the bench seats on the round. They all chose a high stepping, fancy carved pony, while Tucker spoke to Joe. "Up boy." The shepherd dog jumped up on the park bench type seat, curled himself around several times, and sat down.

The colorful wooden pony Tucker chose was a palomino with flowing mane and racing feet. Christy climbed on the dark horse beside him and Taffy sat astride one with red roses on the bridle in front of the two. "Try not to look out at the parking lot, Taffy. I'll keep my eye on the street."

The calliope* began as the music wound up slowly, filling the park with the familiar song of the carrousel, as the artful horses began moving up and down. *How do you look like you're enjoying yourself when your heart is pounding?* Tucker wondered. He decided to pretend his feeling wasn't anxiety. The pounding of his heart and rapid breathing, he chose to call excitement, fun-loving excitement.

He watched as the blue car slowly slithered down the park driveway. Tucker thought the headlights looked like bulging eyes, searching everywhere, seeing everything. He wanted to fix his gaze on it and know where it was at every minute. But, he couldn't, or shouldn't.

Taffy turned to get his attention, "Tucker, where are they now?"

"Turn the other way when you look over to talk, Taffy. That way your face wouldn't be seen from the drive." He thought about the image they were all making and decided to stage it a little better. "Taffy will turn away from the outside. Christy, they didn't see you in Tony's restaurant, you can turn my way. They saw me, so I'll turn toward you. Johnny and Freddie feel free to talk among yourselves since you were back in the corner of the booth."

Chattering together, laughing, riding up and down, around and around, Tucker soon saw the one car in his targeted view turn and leave. His relief was surprising to him. He'd gotten himself into many predicaments, but they were of his own creation. He had no control over what Vanessa and Lloyd were going to do next. He felt almost helpless over the situation there in Toledo ... but not quite. There were other tricks to play.

As the carrousel wound down and the music slowed to a groan, they prepared to dismount. All five stood behind their wooden horse for a minute and regrouped.

"Now what?" Christy asked as she peaked around her horse's rump.

Tucker patted the horse's mane. "They're gone. It's time to go."

Chapter Twenty-Seven
You Again?

"The Toledo Sailing Club is just ahead, on the other side of the park." Taffy pointed to the river beyond the grassy area. Picnic tables and benches stretched below snow-dusted trees and playgrounds invited a most rigorous play. "In the spring, summer, and early fall, the boats are down beyond the play area, there on the Maumee River."

"Sailing ships on a river, not a lake?" Tucker thought of the small boats on the Elkhart River at home, but there were no yachts. He also remembered the summers he spent at Lake Wawasee in Indiana. Church camp was at Oakwood Park. Cottages sat above the huge lake and classrooms waited for wiggly boys to listen to a Bible lesson before the next game of baseball. Uncle David and Aunt Karen had a cottage on one of the small channels behind the hotel.

"The sailing ships are on a river, that becomes a lake." Taffy explained as she watched ahead and behind. "Keep your eyes open. We're getting close enough to the house, Vanessa and Lloyd could turn up soon." Her relaxed expression began to change. "The water, Tucker ... in a way ... the boats are kinda on a lake. The Maumee River flows into Lake Erie."

"So, the river is like the channels at Lake Wawasee. They're the narrow, finger-like waterways that feed into the lake. People build cottages on the channels and drive their boats slowly onto the lake. Most of those boats are motor boats. Here, the boaters sail into the big lake by following the river. Hot rocket."

Tucker thought of Lake Wawasee again and a time when he was much younger. The family picnicked at the lake one summer, Sunday afternoon. The day was perfect, not too hot, and not too cold, a real Goldilocks day. While Grandpop and Gramma visited with the many aunts and uncles, Tucker swam out to a raft where the older kids were diving into the deeper water. As they all played *conquer the mountain*, one of the kids from another picnic group tried to hold Tucker under the water. The next thing Tucker knew he was waking up on the grass. He didn't believe the boy had learned drown-the-kid-next-to-you from church camp. The Apostle Paul, shipwrecked and nearly drowned, never said, "Go and do likewise."

Tucker and the four had trudged a long way. By that time, it was still several more blocks to the Bean home. His leg muscles told him it was time to sit for a few minutes. He rarely gave in to rest, but then there were many reasons to sit for a spell. Tucker knew everyone was tired of walking, because he was. The Walbridge Amusement area was behind them. The paved parking lot and long, unending sidewalk, soon turned into a grassy park that stretched from the road to the river. Of course, it wasn't green and lush. November wasn't kind to plants in the northern states. A fine coating of snow covered most of the area, like a white glaze on Gramma's yeasty doughnuts. The ground had finally gotten cold enough to keep the frost from melting. He knew they would all be getting cold too … soon.

It was a super neighborhood with beautiful houses. Kids played on front porches trying to enjoy the last days of autumn before the winter blast began. Still, it was cold. That close to the river, the wind blew heavy, thick with moisture from the water nearby.

Tucker wondered if the people who lived around there missed seeing crops coming up in the fields. When he caught glimpses of back yards, it appeared to him that family gardens took the place of wheat and field corn. During the war, everyone encouraged families to plant Victory Gardens. The folks in Dunlap did. Grandpop plowed up nearly a quarter acre for their vegetable patch. Tucker guessed many of the people in Toledo continued with their piece of green-heaven as well.

"Wait," Taffy ordered in a hoarse whisper. "Who is that?"

"Where?" Tucker thought he had been watching for anyone or anything that might look out of place.

"Down there in the block where the Yacht Club property begins."

Christy squinted her eyes. "Where does the Yacht Club begin?" She blinked a few times. "That car, way down there?" She pointed to what looked like a blue car stopped in one of the spaces of a parking lot.

"They are about two blocks past the house."

Tucker shielded his eyes with his hands. "I can't see anyone in the car from here. I'll bet it's them, though."

"I know it is them. In California, I go everywhere in that car." Taffy pulled back and searched the side streets around her. "How am I going to finally get home? I know Vanessa doesn't want me to see my parents. I certainly know my father wants to see her. I don't know if my parents even know I'm gone. My being missing, maybe kidnapped, was reported in the Chicago papers, but I haven't heard anything here."

"We heard it on the radio in Dunlap." Tucker thought for a minute. "I don't know what station it was on. It might have been out of South Bend."

"I'll bet my parents haven't heard. I can't believe Vanessa wants Mom and Dad to know. She and Lloyd promised to watch over and protect me when I was on the west coast."

Tucker felt awful. He promised Taffy they would see her home. Now, what would they do? "You know them. We don't. I know you don't trust them."

"Like I told you, I'm not welcome everywhere." Johnny began. "Now, hold on. I know you don't know where I'm going with this."

Tucker couldn't believe what he heard Johnny say. "You've been welcome at our house and church many times."

"Yes, Tucker, I always feel welcome at your place." He turned to Christy. "And, Christy I certainly felt like another friend the afternoon we all spent in Tucker's attic."

Taffy put her arm around Johnny's shoulder. "And, you're my co-star."

Johnny smiled, a little embarrassed. "I've starred in many films." His grin faded to a more serious expression. "But, guys, it's not about that." Johnny looked down the road at the car they were talking about and then at the side street across from the park. "If I felt uncomfortable in a situation, I learned to tack my way home, following a zig zag pattern."

"Sometimes we'd do that on the water at Wawasee," Tucker remembered. "When the wind wasn't with us."

"Well, the wind isn't with us now." Johnny nodded in the direction of the side road in front of them. "That's how we're going to get you home today, Taffy."

Tucker had an image of all five of them crossing the street at the same time and shuddered. "Wait. Looks like some Scouts have been cleaning up the area." He watched as three cars full of happy kids pulled to the exit of the parking lot and waited to turn. The driver in the first car put his arm out the window and pointed left*. "Follow me." Tucker turned toward the right side of the 1945 green DeSoto. The five friends were able to cross the street without notice by using the moving vehicle as a shield. Joe trotted along like a member of the adventure party. On the other side of the road, they darted up the side street and then slowed to a walk with Joe at Tucker's heals.

Johnny looked down an alley to the left. "This way."

"Oh good," Taffy nearly skipped as she hurried after him. "My house is several blocks down this alley and across the street."

Johnny put his finger to his lips. "Try to keep your voices down. Remember, we're trying not to draw attention by tacking our way to your house. We shouldn't be heard either."

Tucker searched the backyards of the houses they passed walking down the alley. "This is a good one. With few trees, the sun was able to shine through and melt the snow. No tracks."

The group walked silently onto the property beside the garage that opened into the alley, keeping their eye on the house. Continuing their shortcut through the yard, they come out in front of the house facing the next street over from Taffy's home.

Tucker turned toward Taffy's house, walking as if he was just out for an afternoon walk. A few blocks up, Tucker looked for another yard to cross. The backyards were harder to see from the front, but he chose one he hoped would be safe.

"This one should be good," Johnny checked it out.

"Oh no," Christy sighed as quietly as she could. "A swimming pool."

"It'll be okay," Johnny assured her.

Tucker motioned for them to stay back at the side of the house while he thought how they would get past the water hazard. "It has a cover on it. We could walk across it."

Christy slammed her hand to her waist and barked orders like a drill sergeant with laryngitis. "Tucker McBride, we are not going to test the strength of that pool cover and neither are you."

"Okay, okay," he surrendered. Peeking around the side of the house he asked Taffy, "Do you know who lives here?"

"Sure, my friend Yvonne, her brother, and their parents."

Tucker knew the Stuart family, next door back in Dunlap, wouldn't have cared if he cut through their yard. He didn't do it often and he certainly didn't walk in the flower beds or stomp through the garden. They had no swimming pool. To Tucker, that was a California thing, even though there it was in Toledo, Ohio.

The windows at the back of the house seemed blank, more like a photograph of a home than a warm dwelling full of people. No light glowed through the lace curtains and no sounds of laughter filtered through the door. Tucker suspected no one was home. "Maybe they're downtown, too."

Taffy brightened. "Yes, they probably are."

"We still have to take it easy," Tucker warned. "Five people running across the back yard will draw attention to Taffy. A couple of us can stroll out and move those lawn chairs there by the pool. The rest of us, find something to pick up, then continue to pretend you're picking up sticks. We'll all work our way to the back of the yard, by the garage, and slip into the alley." He turned back to Taffy, "Which house do we aim for?"

"Across the alley and one yard up." Taffy slipped from the safety of the shadows beside the two-story Dutch colonial home and casually walked over to some fallen twigs on the patio. Three of the small basswood branches from the Lindenwood tree caught under the glider, and stuck out far enough to trip someone. Christy popped out and joined her, gathering nitpicky pieces.

Tucker came around the corner, picked up a lightweight patio chair and stacked it on one of the others over near the pool. With the handkerchief from his back pocket, Johnny dusted off the chairs as Tucker stacked them. Freddie sprawled out on the glider with his feet balanced on the orange crate* someone put down as a small table. The girls gathered their small fists-full of sticks and headed toward the garage, with the boys close behind. Joe followed, dragging a larger branch of the tree in his teeth that must have fallen during the wind earlier in the day. He dropped the broken limb on the stack the girls already started.

Tucker had the habit of checking out everything around him. That was his way. With the garage window beside him, he looked in, just to see what sort of tools the man had who lived there. Grandpop had every tool one could imagine. In fact, most of the neighbors borrowed a wood plane or special wrench from him. Grandpop's only words were, "Ya daresn't loss it*."

Tucker snapped his fingers. "Yep, their car isn't in the garage, Taffy. They aren't home." With a flourish and a wave of his hand, he added, "Let us be off, Miss Bean."

Behind the garage, at the edge of the alley, Tucker reached out and pulled Christy's arm. "Wait. They're here," he pointed down the alley. "Get back." As the Cadillac inched closer, Tucker bumped the handle to the side door of the garage. *Don't be locked,* he whispered under his breath. The door scrapped on something on the floor of the garage. In the little crack in the door, Tucker grabbed Taffy and pushed her inside. "They are only looking for Taffy, not all of us."

"Huddle up," Christy ordered as she bent down as if in a football game with her arms around Tucker and Johnny. Freddie quickly joined the group as they all bent a little and stared at the floor.

Tucker checked the alley and watched as the Thomas car crept past. "Joe, on guard," Tucker ordered in a whisper.

Joe jumped in position at the end of the little sidewalk beside the garage, filling the space. With the expert training of an award-winning war-dog, he snarled as the car came near, and stood at attention.

"Let's move on," Tucker heard Lloyd say. "I don't want to tangle with a big dog." He shifted gears and moved on down the alley.

Tucker smiled. "Good. The coast is clear. Let's go."

Taffy led the way across the gravel pathway that connected everyone in the neighborhood like a loose-stitch crocheted bathrobe. They went in through the garden gate, up the sidewalk, to the concrete steps leading to the back door.

Tucker watched Taffy's excitement as she opened the door onto an enclosed back porch. He wondered what it would be like to come home every day after school to his own parents. Finally, he understood why Taffy Bean would give up fame, and travel in a dirty boxcar, just to get to her family.

Taffy's face lit up like the marque of a movie theater as she stepped inside. "Mama, I'm home."

Chapter Twenty-Eight
A Family Like Taffy's

Tucker couldn't believe what he saw stored on the walls and shelves of the Beans' back porch. His friends and family didn't live in a house such as Taffy's. Even their back porch was full of things he had only read about. Small orange beady eyes stared at him from a shelf of other yellow fishing gear. Tucker figured Taffy's dad must enjoy fishing in the Maumee River, although the spoonplug fishing lure was for deeper water. Still, the lures were new, so Mr. Bean had a few. It seemed to Tucker that every uncle in his own family fished. Uncle Jacob had the *Geographic* last Sunday and pointed out the lures to Uncle Jerry, when he and Aunt Cora where there for the family meal.

Brand new, expensive leather ice skates dangled by their laces from pegs on the wall. Tucker thought it looked like the family was getting ready for some fun afternoons on the ice. Then he remembered Big Blue and hoped his new Toledo friends would wait for the ice to get thick enough they wouldn't fall through. On the other side of the porch was a new, electric washing machine. Tucker's grandmother would have swooned over it, despite her belief that bragging wasn't proper.

Hanging on the wall was what looked to Tucker, like a chainsaw, with newly invented chipper teeth on it. According to the *Geographic*, the chain on the saw used curled teeth, that pointed left and then went over the top of the chain. He had to ask. "Taffy, why does your dad need a chainsaw?"

"Chainsaw?" she asked as she reached for the handle of the inner door to the kitchen.

Tucker explained, "It's for cutting down trees."

"Oh, in the woods, at Granddaddy's farm." She flung the door open like a grammar school girl and stepped from the enclosed porch into the kitchen. "Mama?"

"Taffy!" A woman in dark blue wide leg slacks and a turquoise, cropped cable knit sweater threw her arms open.

"Mama, it's so good to be home."

"Taffy! Oh, my goodness Taffy!" Mrs. Bean looked behind her daughter. "Where are Vanessa and Lloyd? And who—"

"I'm Tucker McBride, Mrs. Bean." He reached out his hand to her. "These are my friends, Christy, Freddie and Johnny." He pointed over his shoulder. "My dog, Joe is out there."

Mrs. Bean looked toward the back door. "Is your dog house broken?"

"Yes Ma'am. He's well-trained. He's a hero, one of the war dogs."

"Well, bring him in. The children would like to meet a hero."

Tucker went out to the back porch and came back with Joe. He pointed to the corner of the room. "Lay down, boy."

Mrs. Bean turned back to her daughter; her face bright but puzzled. "How did you get here, Honey? Taffy, where are Vanessa and Lloyd?"

"We were in Chicago, Mom, and I wanted to come home for a while." Taffy's explanation went faster and faster. "I was there for a personal appearance ... but I had no movies coming up or anything." She was nearly panting. "Vanessa just said, 'maybe' and I asked what was a maybe, and she said she couldn't remember right then. So ... I walked out the front door of the hotel, and hopped a freight train going east."

Her mother dropped the stack of napkins she had in her hand. "You hopped on a boxcar?"

"Yes, Momma," Taffy's head hung. "I thought the police would catch me if I bought a ticket for a passenger train."

Tucker wondered why Taffy's mom was more concerned about how she got there than that she was there. "That's where my friends and I met her, on the train."

"Oh, my goodness, Taffy. That was so dangerous." Her mother grabbed and held her close.

"Did I hear my Taffy candy?" A tall man in casual trousers and light blue dress shirt with a silk stripe in the fabric dashed into the kitchen. He grabbed Taffy off the floor and twirled her around. "How did you get here?"

Mrs. Bean folded her arms across her chest and stifled a laugh, "She rode in a boxcar all the way from Chicago."

"Good grief," he gasped. "That was dangerous, alone in a cattle car."

"There were no cattle." Tucker grinned and pointed to the corner of the room. "Unless you would consider my dog, Joe, cattle."

Mr. Bean turned to his daughter, "Who is this, Taffy?"

Her mother smiled and took a platter of cold cuts out of the large refrigerator, twice as big as Gramma's new electric no-ice icebox. "These are our daughter's new friends who kept her company on the way home. I remember this fellow is Tucker McBride and these are his friends."

Christy nodded a little, politely. "Happy to meet you, Mr. and Mrs. Bean. I'm Christy Tree."

"This is Freddie Cooper," Tucker pointed and then gestured toward Johnny. "This fine young man is your daughter's co-star, Johnny Washington. We're from Elkhart County, Indiana, between Elkhart and Goshen."

"I knew a Washington from Elkhart during the war." Mr. Bean patted Johnny's shoulder. "He was a good man. As I remember, he had a wife named Goldie."

Johnny's mouth dropped and tears came to his eyes. "Goldie? That's my mother's name, Sir."

"I never talk about the war, son, but I am very glad to meet you. Someday, hopefully, I'll be able to talk to you about your dad."

Mrs. Bean lowered her head and looked over her cat-eye glasses*. "And, Gregory … Taffy tells me the police are chasing her."

"What?" he bellowed and snapped back around.

Joe sat straight up. His ears pointed up and his eyes were alert.

"It's okay, Joe, sit." Tucker had never heard such a reaction, except when Freddie's dad got mad last summer when the two boys nearly blew up the Cooper's chicken coop. Mr. Bean and Freddie's dad would have quite a battle for the hog calling blue ribbon at the Elkhart County Fair.

Taffy lowered her head. "I left no note. I just walked out of the hotel."

Tucker saw Christy's eyes glance from one of the parents to the other. She finally asked, "Taffy, the Toledo police asked us twice if we had seen you, and we saw them on the road, too."

"Why didn't you tell them who you were?" her dad asked with his mouth gapping. "They would have brought you home."

"I had to get home before anyone found me, Daddy."

Gregory Bean shook his head like someone trying to shake the dust out of a mop. "But, why? You haven't answered that yet."

"Oh, Gregory, for goodness sake. Let the children sit down and have some food. We can talk about it while we eat." Mrs. Bean went into the living room and called up the staircase. "Isaac, Charlotte, look who's here."

"Char-Char," Taffy squealed as the six-year-old came into the kitchen. She grabbed up her little sister and twirled her around the room. Isaac charged in and nearly knocked Taffy off her feet. "Isaac." Taffy laughed and started tickling her younger brother. "You rascal."

"Come boys," Taffy's father motioned to Tucker, Freddie, and Johnny with a wave of his arm. "You can carry a few chairs up out of the basement for me."

"Taffy, please lay out five more places while I add some more fruit to the bowl. Christy, there's a tin of potato chips in that lower cabinet." She pointed to a large glass bowl on the corner of the table. "Please, just fill that up."

The boys and Mr. Bean came back into the kitchen, unfolded the four extra chairs, and placed them at the table. Tucker noticed, Taffy's empty chair remained in place, waiting for her to come home.

Tucker was amazed at the size of the kitchen. The maple table was large enough for all nine of them to sit around it. Gramma's kitchen wasn't big enough to hold even a small drop leaf table*. The family ate every meal in the dining room.

"Everyone," Mr. Bean began, "please take a seat. Johnny, my daughter's co-star, sit here beside me. Your father often sat beside me at mealtime in Germany before the battle that—."

"Greg, would you offer grace?" Flora Bean asked.

"Of course." He nodded at everyone and bowed his head. "Father, God," he began a comforting prayer of thankfulness for his daughter's safe return, and a blessing over the food.

Mrs. Bean picked up a plate of sliced bread, put two pieces on Charlotte's plate, then handed the bread to Taffy who sat on her other side. "Whatever is in front of you, please pick it up, serve yourself, and pass it on. Tucker, get a bowl out of the cabinet next to the stove and give Joe some water. You can tear apart some bologna and give that to him, too. I'm sure he helped get our Taffy home."

Tucker put down his sandwich and got the banquet of people-food for Joe. Joe looked up for permission to eat and then dug into his meal.

Back at the table, with a sandwich in his hand, chips on his plate, and Joe cared for, all was right in Tucker's world.

"It's possible Mr. and Mrs. Thomas might get here soon. I'm curious, if you don't mind saying, have you found out anything about Taffy's contract?"

Mrs. Bean spoke up. "Her contract? Like my husband said, he hasn't talked about the war since he got back." Her smile was warm and supportive. "But I know how it was here on the home front. Gregory's draft* was in 1942. Taffy was almost eight; Isaac was six; and Charlotte was just a two-year-old baby. My dear husband finally came home in May of 1945 with the other 90,000 members of the military."

"Mrs. Bean, I'm sorry for askin'," Tucker apologized when he saw how quiet the table became.

"No, Tucker," she assured him, "Taffy needs to hear this." Flora drank a little from her Coca-Cola. "Before he left, Gregory and I talked about the children and how I would manage. I would get a job and the Army would send home his officer's pay. But, how would we manage the children's future, the savings for their college education? Then, Taffy was in a little community play on the very weekend Vanessa and Lloyd were in Toledo. Vanessa said our sweet daughter was a natural actress and asked if we would permit her to make a movie or two. Gregory was gone and I signed the papers myself, agreeing to Vanessa becoming her agent and guardian for the short time she'd be in California. Then, there were more movies and months away from home. Now, Taffy wants to 'retire' and Vanessa won't let her."

"Is somebody knocking on the door, Mama?" Charlotte asked.

"I'll get it," Isaac announced as he jumped up from the table. His father followed close behind.

Tucker was sitting at the table in the right place to see the entry hall through the living room. He couldn't see Isaac's face but he sure saw his actions. With the door open, the afternoon sun streamed through, casting a long ray across the carpet. However, Isaac nearly slammed the door in the face of the couple who stood there. Tuck saw Isaac's dad intervene, grab the door knob, and invite the pair inside. He gestured for the two to follow him into the kitchen.

"Tucker, you know where the folding chairs are in the basement. Please go down and fetch two more. Vanessa and Lloyd Thomas are joining us."

"Oh, Taffy, thank goodness," Vanessa sighed with relief and bent down to embrace her. "What happened to you? Who took you? How did you get here?"

Taffy pulled back from Vanessa, nearly falling sideways off her chair. "I decided to walk home," she stated flatly.

"From Chicago?" Lloyd gasped with his hand slapped to his chest.

"Well," Taffy began, as she pulled up straighter in her chair than before, "you wouldn't bring me to Toledo like I asked, so I hopped on a train near the Chicago freight yards."

Tucker unfolded one of the chairs and placed it on the other side of Freddie, two seats down from Taffy. It was obvious to Tuck, and anyone else with eyes and a heart, Taffy did not want to be near Mrs. Thomas.

"Here is a plate, Vanessa," Mrs. Bean offered. "Please, take some bread and make a sandwich."

Vanessa nodded a weak smile at Flora Bean. Then, she frowned at Tucker, turned up her nose, and quickly sat down. "A freight train? You became a hobo the minute you were out of my sight?"

Christy bristled. "I think an 'adventurer' would be a better word, don't you, Mrs. Thomas?"

"And, you are...?" Vanessa asked through gritted teeth.

Tucker brightened. He tried to never let others dictate his reactions. If an adult was rude, he treated them more like an equal than he would have ordinarily. "I'm Tucker McBride from near Elkhart, Indiana, and these are my friends, Christy Tree, Freddie Cooper, and Johnny Washington."

Taffy's face lit up after Tucker spoke boldly to Vanessa. "Johnny was one of my co-stars."

Lloyd narrowed his eyes in confusion. "Which movie was that?"

When Taffy seemed to lose track of the next line in her story, Tucker jumped back in. "He was in *The Hamburger Café Mystery.*"

"I remember that one," Mrs. Bean joined in the fun.

"Right," Mr. Been added, without cracking a smile. "That one took place here in Toledo."

"I joined the Negro Actors Guild a few years ago." Johnny lifted his head high. "Fredi Washington, a founding member of the Guild with Ethel Waters, is my dad's cousin. I call her Aunt Fredi. We don't call adults by their first name. Fredi was born in Savannah, Georgia, like my father. Noble Sissle, from Indiana, is still the president of the Guild."

Everyone at the table fell silent. Tucker was the first one to break into dumbfounded amazement. "You ... Johnny Washington, joined the Negro Actors Guild?" He squinted his eyes in disbelief. "And, why is it that you joined an acting club? Other than your co-starring role in Taffy's movie."

Johnny shrugged. "Aunt Fredi thought it would be fun."

"That's great, Johnny," Mr. Bean interrupted. "I'll have to admit, I am amazed."

Tucker shook his head and stared at Johnny. "I'm ... I don't even know what I am."

"Vanessa," Mr. Bean glared at Vanessa and Lloyd. "My daughter left your and Lloyd's company and simply walked out of the hotel. Why didn't you call us? Why didn't we know?"

"Yes, well ..." Vanessa started to try to explain, "but—"

"Never mind about that now," Mr. Bean jumped in again. "Vanessa, Taffy will not be going back to California with you. She wishes to ... retire ... at twelve years old. If she wants to come out of retirement when she's older, she'll let you know."

"I don't think so, Bean," Lloyd corrected him. "We have a contract. Your wife signed it."

"I did not, however," Gregory snapped back. "My daughter has two parents."

Vanessa snarled, "Are you saying, a woman can't sign a legal contract?"

"I'm saying," Mr. Bean said confidently, "while I was out of the country she signed. I agree, nevertheless, I did not sign the contract ... too. Not instead of her, just ... too."

"Then, take us to court," Lloyd demanded as he stood up. "Vanessa, Taffy will be coming with us."

"No, she won't," Flora Bean demanded.

"The contract?" Tucker asked but didn't wait for an answer. "Gramma always says, 'Your word is better than your signature.' So, a few carefully placed words might help."

"Shut up, boy," Vanessa growled. "Mind your own business."

Joe growled through snarled teeth. He stood at attention with eyes fixed on Vanessa.

Flora jumped to her feet and snapped, "Vanessa, how dare you."

"I'm sorry, young man," Vanessa apologized, but her face did not match her words.

"That's alright," Tucker smoothed slickly. "They're just words. I would guess, they are words you wouldn't want many others to hear. They might think you're a...a ... well never mind." He took another bite of bread to finish his sandwich. "The words I was thinking of were the ones Johnny has been using in an interview. It's with a writer from *Photoplay Magazine*. The article needs a few more interviews before it's finished. Johnny will talk to the writer soon. Then, there are the words his Aunt Fredi might use to describe how the two of you won't release Taffy from her contract. Holding a child against her will isn't a good thing. And," he continued,

"I know I have relatives in several states. I guess we all do. Also, we can each talk to friends. Reputation, I am sure, is very important in your work, both as an agent and as a lawyer. Oh yes, the newspaper in Elkhart has wide circulation. The papers in Los Angeles would be really interested, too, and—"

"Stop," Lloyd barked out. "Vanessa, I cannot afford to lose my law practice." He turned to Taffy. "Consider your contract broken, Taffy."

Vanessa jumped up with her hands on her hips. "But, Lloyd—"

"That's enough, Vanessa." Lloyd demanded. "She is a child with the right to have a childhood."

Vanessa looked around at the faces that looked back hard at her. "Oh, alright."

Gregory grabbed a pen and an opened envelope from his shirt pocket, and thrust them at Vanessa. "Write, *I release Taffy Bean from her contract*. Date it and sign it."

Vanessa jotted out the words Taffy's dad dictated. She jerked the envelope over to Lloyd for his signature. Slamming her chair back to stand up, it thudded on the carpet. "If you need me in the future, Taffy," she snipped without even turning around, "you know how to reach me." She jerked her coat from Lloyd's hand and stormed out of the house.

"Tucker," Taffy cheered, "thank you, thank you, thank you."

"Tucker McBride, I am amazed," Gregory Bean came around the table and grabbed Tucker in a bear hug. "How did you come up with all of that?"

Tucker could feel his face grow warm. "Gramma says your reputation is all you really have to offer people. Keep your reputation clean."

"My dad says the same thing," Freddie chimed in. "I would be grounded if I did something to tarnish my family's name."

Mr. Bean shook Tucker's hand vigorously. "By George, I believe your grandmother is right. And, your dad as well, Freddie. Tucker, is there anything I can do for you?"

"Well," Tucker began slowly, "if I can use your telephone. But ... I am so sorry ... it's a long-distance call. Our parents don't know where we are."

"Call them immediately." Mr. Bean assured Tucker with a pat to his shoulder. "While we wait for your family to come, we'll play a game of Monopoly. It can sometimes take a long time to finish. They may be here by then."

"Oh my," Flora gasped and hurried to the phone. "You must call them right away. Here's the phone, Tucker."

The telephone sat on a side table in the living room, a squatty looking rotary dial* model. Tucker had seen that model of telephone before at the school and church, but he hadn't used one very often. He certainly hadn't ever placed a long-distance call, not on one like that or any other style. This time, Carolyn was not on the other end of the phone line to place the call for him. He'd have to have help. With instructions from Mrs. Bean, he dialed the long-distance operator. "Hi Gramma, tell Christy's and the guys' parents ... we're in Toledo."

Chapter Twenty-Nine
Family Came to the Rescue

"To jail ... again!" Christy yelped. "This is the fourth time since this game started."

"Aw." Tucker's sympathy was more teasing than sincere. "Look, Christy, I'm buying a hotel."

"I don't want to hear about it, Tucker McBride," Christy snapped.

The room smelled like ginger snaps and tapioca pudding. Tucker believed he couldn't find a better dessert or snack any place on earth. He thought of Sunday evenings at home when he would make double and triple recipes of the scrumptious pudding for the whole family.

"The pudding is delicious, Mrs. Bean."

"Thank you, Tucker," Mrs. Bean beamed. "Taffy said she heard you like it."

He looked up at the fancy clock hanging on the dining room wall. *If Uncle Jacob drives fifty miles an hour on the highway, it would take him about three hours to get here. I called Gramma around five PM. Uncle Jacob was sleeping because he worked. It's eight now ... he might not get here until nine or after... and tomorrow is Thanksgiving.* He smiled to himself. *My math isn't so bad after all.*

"Tucker," Christy jolted his thoughts, "it's your turn."

"Oh," Tucker bopped up straighter and rolled the dice. "I'm sorry we're taking up your evening, Mr. Bean. I don't know what time you go to bed."

"Sorry?" Gregory threw back his head and laughed. "Tucker, you and your friends brought Taffy home to us. And, somehow, I'm still not sure how you did it, you got her out of her contract. We'll stay up all night if we need to."

"Speaking of bedtime," Flora said as got up from her seat, "Charlotte, it's time for bed."

"But Mama, I'm playing with Joe," she protested as she snuggled up closer to the dog. Earlier in the evening, Charlotte had coaxed Joe out of the corner and into the living room, where she covered him with a blanket, plopped on top of him, and read *The Poky Little Puppy* to him.

"I know Joe has enjoyed your reading, Charlotte, but it's your bedtime." Flora took the child's hand and helped her up. "Say good-night to Tucker and his friends."

Charlotte went over, stood beside Tucker, and leaned on his arm. "Tucker," she whispered, "I don't want you to leave."

"Why not?" he asked her, scrunching down a little to her size.

"You brought Sissy home." She wrapped her arms around him and whispered, "I love you, Tucker McBride."

"Thank you, Charlotte." Tucker gave her a little kiss on her cheek. "Good night."

"Night, Tucker," she sighed. She gave Taffy a hug, and went upstairs with her mother.

Tucker looked at the clock again. Only a few minutes had passed since he checked the last time. *This is going to be a long night*, he thought.

Isaac jumped up when the doorbell rang. He shouted above the laughter and slapstick of the game, "I'll get it."

"Tucker," Christy whined again, "now, I'm out of the game."

"Ain't it awful," Tucker mocked.

Christy smacked Tucker on the sleeve and looked up as Isaac brought someone into the dining room. "Tucker..." she looked over at her friend, "your dad is here."

Tucker jumped up from the table, hit the edge of the board game flipping the game pieces, Monopoly money, dice, and everything, up in the air. The game landed in a scrambled mess on the dining table again.

Sean McBride followed Isaac into the room and stood for a minute. His voice was low and warm. "I know you're having fun, Tucker, but are ya 'bout ready? It's just as far back home as it was getting here."

"Sure." Tucker's expression was flat, drained of emotion. "Why—"

Sean smiled. "Jacob came home from work with a cold working on him," he explained. "Tim was gone, went someplace with some friends, so, your grandma called me." He looked down at the spilled game and picked up one of the dice that had bounced into the living room. "I hope it's okay that I came."

"Okay?" Gregory Bean reached out his hand to Tucker's father. "That sounds very generous. It's a long way. I imagine you worked today, too."

"Tucker?" Mrs. Bean came back down stairs after tucking Charlotte in.

Tucker was still getting over the shock of seeing his dad standing in a living room in Toledo, Ohio … to pick him up. Dad to the rescue. "Oh, I'm sorry. This is my father, Sean McBride."

Sean smiled a little and added. "I thought of bringing your Model A, Tucker. I decided it hadn't been tested for long distance travel yet."

Tucker snickered. "I'm glad. I just got it four days ago and haven't driven it for a few days."

Taffy blinked and tilted her head. "Tucker McBride, you have your own car?"

"You drive?" Mr. Bean added the next question. "How old did you say you are?"

Christy looked up from the floor where she was picking up game pieces. "He turned thirteen last Saturday."

"And … you drive?" Taffy narrowed her eyes in concentration.

"Yep," he admitted.

The room was silent for a minute. It felt awkward to Tucker but he didn't know what else to say.

Flora Bean, acting as a proper hostess, asked, "May I get you a sandwich and a coke or a cup of coffee, Mr. McBride?"

"Well ..." Sean drew out slowly.

"Sure, Dad," Tucker said as he regained his ability to put two words together. "You must be hungry. Charlotte just went to bed, take her chair."

"That would be fine," Sean agreed with a little smile.

As Flora poured Sean's coffee and placed the bread and cold cuts closer to him, it was Gregory who finally said, "We talked a lot as we played our game. I understand Tucker and his brother and sisters live with their grandparents."

Tucker opened his mouth to speak. He wanted to protect his dad, and himself, from embarrassment.

Sean raised his finger to stop him. "You heard right. My children do live with their mother's parents. Joseph and Rebecca Moyer have been great with them."

"Dad couldn't—"

"It's okay, Tucker. I'll tell it." Sean put down his half-eaten sandwich and wiped his hands on his napkin. "Tucker was only a baby when his mother died." He smiled at Tucker, put up his hand to stall and took another bite of bologna. "I'm afraid I was very weak after Margie died. I completely withdrew from everything ... my children, my work ... and stayed with my mother and dad for months. Joseph and his wife stepped in immediately and moved the children to their house. By the time I came to myself, the judge said I wasn't stable enough to take care of the children, and certainly not a baby."

"I am so sorry," Flora whispered as she looked over at Tucker.

Tucker could feel all eyes in the room turn to him and wanted out of the spotlight. For some reason, he also wanted to protect his dad's feeling. "I see Dad every once in a while," he tried to smooth things over.

"Not as often as I'd like," Sean added with his head low. "I go to your basketball games, Tucker. I sit in the darkest corner of the stands, hoping no one will see me. And, I watch you and Betsy play baseball in the lot near your house. I stay in my car at the bend of the alley." He smiled at Tucker. "I saw you get conked on the head last summer. Betsy said you had a concussion. As usual, you didn't tell your grandparents or uncle."

Tucker couldn't believe what his dad said. He had wished his own family would come and cheer him on, to say, "Good job, son," the way the other guys' parents did. "I never knew you were there," was all Tucker could say.

Flora poured Sean a little more coffee. "It sounds like you have a lot of family who love you, Tucker."

Sean smiled. "Everyone loves Tucker and he's always gathering more loved ones around him. I heard Tucker hopped the train to go to Goshen in the hope of seeing his half-brother, Bobby, while he and his mother were visiting there for the holidays. Tucker and Bobby haven't seen each other for about five years. I know Bobby would be thrilled to see him, too. Bobby's aunt, his mother's sister, said he feels isolated out there in California."

Flora handed Sean a pudding cup of tapioca and added softly, "Maybe the one Tucker really wished would come, was his mother." She turned to Tucker who was listening. "Since your mom couldn't be there, maybe you blamed the rest of the family for your feelings of loss. It's always safest to blame the ones who love us the most and won't leave us."

Christy reached out and touched Tucker's arm. "We've talked about this before, haven't we Tucker?"

"I guess." Tucker collected the rest of the game-money in silence.

"When you're finished," Sean rescued him from the deafening quiet, "we'd better go."

With everyone's help the game was back in its box in no time. Freddie put on his hat and coat and sat down by the door. His hat pulled over his eyes, his coat unbuttoned, he looked like a melting snowman waiting for the next cold snap. Johnny plopped down beside him and closed his eyes.

"Guys, I don't know how I can thank you." Taffy wiped tears from her eyes and began to wring her hands. "And you, Tucker, you … you set me free."

"It was fun," Tucker said as his chest puffed out a little.

"Thank you for the best day I've had in years." Taffy reached out and gave Christy a hug. "You are all my new friends." She grinned at Tucker and gave him a soft bop on his shoulder. "Johnny," she called out as she walked into the living room. "Are you asleep?"

"No," he said as he jumped up. "I'm wide awake."

"My new co-star," she said with a grin and a hug.

Johnny's face grew hot. "Any time."

"If your parents can bring you over, Taffy," Christy smiled with excitement. "you're welcome to come and spend a weekend at my house. It isn't as fancy as yours but we're happy. Johnny lives in Elkhart but we can call him to come over in the afternoon. Tucker and Freddie and I all live within a few blocks of each other in Dunlap."

"A weekend with friends?" Taffy's face lit up like a twelve–year-old invited to her first slumber party. "When I'm used to being home for a while, I'll call. In the meantime, we can be pen-pals*."

Christy handed her a small piece of paper. "Here is my phone number and address and Tucker's, too. He has a lot of people in his house. If you call there, you might get anyone."

"Thanks Christy." Taffy took the paper and held it close.

"Let us be gone," Sean announced as they walked out the door. Joe stayed at Tucker's heal. Sean dangled the car keys at Tucker and smiled. "Want to drive?"

Tucker nearly squealed but chose a more grown-up approach. Night had come and the darkness gathered around them making the air even colder than earlier. The sky was clear and the stars brightened the night. He would be responsible for driving them all home on that night of adventure and excitement.

Mr. Bean's mouth dropped open as he watched in amazement as Tucker got behind the wheel. "Well, I'll be."

Taffy and Isaac walked out to the car with them but had returned to the house, their hands in the air, waving them off.

Joe jumped in the front seat with Tucker beside him at the wheel. Sean walked around and sat on the passenger side of his green automobile. Christy, Freddie, and Johnny sat in the back. A full car. A full day. A full life.

Chapter Thirty
The Long Way Home

Inside the car, the Packard smelled like cigarette smoke. While no one in Tucker's house smoked, he was certainly familiar with the odor of burning tobacco after spending a great deal of time helping Butch Randolph over at the Sinclair service station across from his home.

When Sean reached in his shirt pocket and pulled out a pack of Lucky Strikes, Tucker spoke up. "Dad, if you light that in this closed car, we'll all start coughing."

"I'll roll down the window," Sean settled it.

Tucker knew his dad smoked at least three packs of cigarettes a day. He also knew it might be hard for his father to go without smoking for the three-hour ride back home. To Tucker, it didn't matter. He'd just have to be strong. "Dad, the guys in the back will be frozen out."

"Okay, okay," Sean gave in. "If I parish, just kick me out of the car. Someone will spot me and haul me away."

Tucker rolled his eyes. He had to accept the fact that his dad was being his dad again. Still, Tucker wasn't going to give in. "I'll call the Ohio street sweepers when we get to a phone. They'll remove ya before the next snow."

Sean sighed and pushed the cigarette pack back into his pocket.

The silence in the car was loud. Tucker felt uncomfortable. He tried to enjoy the night sky that stretched out above them like a giant camping tent. When that didn't help, he thought about a bright night a few summers back. It was the night he and his cousin Luke camped out under the stars down near the railroad tracks where they had hopped on the train. A radio newsman announced a meteor shower for that date. It was a beautiful clear evening, so Tucker knew they would be able to see the scatter of bright specs in the sky. When a New York Central Limited roared by, the clatter on camping pots, rattle of the ground, and thunderous power of the locomotive, sent Tucker running for home. The nighttime was always magical to him. That night on the road across northern Ohio, held the wonder of the first time he would drive a car that far.

Tucker wished he could fill the car with sound. He glanced at the dashboard and pushed the car radio's "on" button. "Wow, Dad. Car radios are expensive." Adjusting the volume, he turned to some mellow music Uncle Jacob liked listening to.

"I bought the car from a banker. The radio was in it when I got it." Sean listened to the music for a few minutes. "Better find some Ragtime, Tucker," his dad said with a laugh. "That soothing music will put us both to sleep. Here, let's see if we can find some Scott Joplin." Sean pushed a few more buttons and stumbled onto some country music.

"I know that music isn't from the *National Barn Dance*, but that will work." Tucker listened as he followed the signs from Broadway Street to where it met Route 20 heading west along northern Ohio. He knew he'd stay on Route 20 all the way into Elkhart, a straight shoot, so he relaxed. "The *Barn Dance* is on Saturday evenings."

"Right," Sean paused and listened.

The radio announcer spoke with a southern twang. "Here we are on the night before Thanksgiving. Mothers are still cooking and dads are looking for more chairs. We are entertaining you with songs from Red Foley, Lulu Belle and Scotty, and many more stars from our popular, *National Barn Dance*. Let them add rhythm to your steps and energy to your tasks."

"You were both right," Christy chimed in from the back. "You sure hold your own, Tucker. You know what you know and don't need others to say you're right."

Sean chuckled a little. "Tucker plows his own row."

Johnny and Freddie said nothing. They fell asleep only minutes after they got into the car.

Gene Autry's mellow songs filled the car. There was a country/western quality to his music Tucker loved. He turned up the volume loud enough to keep himself awake, and soft enough not to blast them all into Michigan.

Tucker had never asked his father any questions before. Life was as it was. Now that they were both held captive in the car for several hours, it might be different. "Dad, Tim never got along with you. Why?"

Sean was silent for a few seconds. "When I was younger, I didn't always discipline fairly," he admitted. "I'm sure that made Tim mad. It would have made me very angry." Sean was quiet for a moment. "I have always wanted Tim's forgiveness. If he wants to, I'll be happy to talk with him."

"You know, Dad, I was thinking about what you told Mrs. Bean, about visiting my games and Betsy's fun. I always thought you didn't come around because you weren't interested in anything the family did."

"No, Tucker. I didn't want to get in the middle between you and your grandparents. That wouldn't be fair to you. You were about eighteen months old before I was able to begin my life again. I didn't want you to have to choose between those who were raising you, and me." Sean sat silent for a minute. "One evening, I started drinking and showed up at the church after prayer meeting. I tried to take you from your grandma. All my acting-out made you cry. Some of the men, a few were my friends, had to throw me out." He was quiet again. "I'm still embarrassed about that." He turned and looked out the side window. "I was heartbroken that your grandparents kept you so busy over the years, there was little or no time for us to plan things together. What could I say?

Choose me, choose me? You had to get along with the people you were living with."

"I don't know that Gramma and Grandpop keep us busy. We always find things to do, so we kinda keep ourselves busy." Tucker felt sad inside, like he had been a part of pushing his dad out of his life. But he knew, Gramma and Grandpop meant only to love him and care for him. His father's bad behavior caused his grandparents to not trust him. "I never knew you came to any of my sports events, Dad." Tucker wasn't mad, just disappointed he had missed it all. "You could have told me. I would have been so proud."

"I'm sorry, Tucker." Sean apologized. "I did what I thought was best."

"I'm sorry, too. I guess I did sorta get mad at everybody else because I had no mother." Tucker's voice was tight as he tried to control himself and the words that might spill out. Funny, after all that talk, a peace seemed to settle over the car.

Joe finally relaxed. He scooted down between Tucker and Sean and put his head on Tucker's leg.

"Go to sleep, boy," Tucker soothed his dog. "It will be a long way until we get home."

Chapter Thirty-One
Home

It was well past midnight when Tucker drove into Elkhart, Indiana. The street lights were on in town making the wet roads and sidewalks glisten. Moisture produced halloes around the lights creating a glow that looked like pictures of lit candles he had seen in magazines and on holiday cards. When Route 20 intersected with US-33, he turned left.

Joe stirred a little, raised his head and sniffed the air. Tucker had seen that stance before. It was obvious, Joe recognized where he was.

"Yep, Joe," Tucker patted him softly, "we're almost home."

Everyone else in the car was asleep. Freddie and Johnny hadn't awakened since they got in. Christy gave up and drifted off about thirty miles back, and Sean dozed off when they got into Elkhart County. The re-play of the *Barn Dance* program was over, which left Tucker with his own thoughts.

Tucker figured Grandpop would be asleep by the time they got home. He went to bed at 8 PM so he could get up at 4 AM. On the other hand, Gramma went to bed after the 10 PM news. Still, the hour was way past her bedtime. He hoped the side door was unlocked so he wouldn't disturb anyone when he went in. If locked out, Tim used to climb in a window. Tucker knew he kept the window to his own bedroom unlatched. If necessary, he could climb up on the roof of the summer house and into his bedroom window like he did when he hung the hammock from the peak of the house and attached it to the top of the tree the previous summer. But then, maybe not.

Tucker slowed the car as they neared the corner of his world. "What on earth?" he whispered. It looked like every light in the house was on. Was Grandpop okay? His grandfather would never have permitted every light to blaze. "We're not the lighthouse by the sea here in Dunlap, Tucker," was Grandpop's usual comment.

"Guys, better wake up. We're home." Tucker turned on Moyer Avenue as those in the back seat sat up and looked around. "Joe, we're home, boy." He pulled to the sidewalk and stopped.

"Tucker, get out of the driver's seat, quick," Sean warned.

Tucker knew it would be best if the family didn't see that he was the one who had driven all the way from Toledo. He turned off the key, jumped out, and opened the back door. "Come on. It's late. We'll stop here, then Dad can take you home."

The dark night had turned cold. Snow flurries started again earlier. Tucker could feel the tiny crystals bounce off his face. He helped Christy out of the car and put his arm around her shoulder. "Pull your coat around you. It's really cold."

They trudged up the side porch steps and Tucker opened the door. "Come on in, Dad."

"Well, I'd better not." Sean slowed at the bottom of the steps.

"You know, Gramma and Grandpop always wondered why you never came in when you picked Betsy and me up to go for a ride."

"They did?" Sean slowly put one foot, then the next, on the porch steps.

Then, they all walked in to find the house full of fun and laughter. Gramma and Goldie Washington were just coming in from the kitchen with a fresh batch of warm chocolate chip cookies. Grandpop was in his chair, rocking to the sound of Uncle Jacob's violin. Betsy and Carolyn were at the table playing Scrabble. Mr. and Mrs. Cooper and Christy's parents were in the living room, Mrs. Cooper with a rag in her hand. It appeared someone had spilled some coffee on the carpet. Chatter and laughter filled the house.

When Tucker led the way through the door, Gramma nearly dropped the cookie plate. "Tucker!"

"Gramma," he said with relief as he hugged her. "It is so good to be home." Tiny leaped into his arms, wiggled and licked his face. "Hi Tiny." Tucker rubbed the little silky's tummy. "See who I brought home." Tiny jumped out of Tucker's arms as Tuck put the little dog down, and did a fancy dance around Joe.

Gramma gave Tucker a sideways hug and reached down ruffling Joe's head. "Joe was missing, too. I knew he had to be with you. I was sure he would bring you home safely. He always did."

"Tucker McBride," Betsy scolded and gave him a soft sock in the stomach. "We were worried. What's the matter with you little brother?"

"I'm just glad you're home," Carolyn reached up and gave him a hug.

Tim grinned and patted his brother on the back. "Me too."

"Tucker, they say a cat has nine lives," Betsy studied Tuck up and down. "How many have you lived up already?"

Tucker laughed and looked down, a little embarrassed. "I don't know. I don't count them. I just live them."

Mr. Cooper jumped up and gave Freddie a bear hug. "How on earth did you get to Toledo, Ohio?"

"We were going to Goshen and overshot our mark," Freddie laughed.

"Oh, Johnny," Goldie gasped. "I lost your daddy, and I thought I lost you, too." She grabbed him, hugging him until they twirled around in circles. Betsy and Carolyn joined the dance, then pulled Tucker into the fun.

Tucker watched Goldie's face. Her overjoyed smile slipped quickly into tight fear. Why was he always unaware of how his behavior would affect others? He thought he was beginning to grow up. Then he thought of the tomatoes and his Model A on the railroad tracks. "Oh, right," he whispered to himself.

"Sean," Grandpop got to his feet and extended his hand. "Thanks again. Jacob has some money for you, some gas to replace." He patted Sean on the back. "So glad you came inside this time. Tucker doesn't often get to see you."

"Sean?" Gramma walked up with the goody plate. "Chocolate chip cookie? Freddie Cooper's mother made them. She makes the best cookies in Dunlap."

Sean lifted off a cookie and took a bite. "I haven't eaten a homemade cookie in a long time."

"Ja, gut," Gramma said with a smile. "Tomorrow is Thanksgiving. If you aren't going to your parent's house for more home cooked food, you are welcome here."

Tucker could see his dad's eyes tear up. It was also hard for him to hold back tears. His own father, invited to dinner at his house, wow.

Jacob reached in his pocket and pulled out a five-dollar bill. "Sean, let me re-pay you for your gas."

Sean held up his hand, stopping the offer. "No, Jacob, thanks. I was very happy I could pick up my son. He had a real adventure, and I was able to be a little part of it."

Jacob touched his shoulder. "That's how it should be, Sean."

Tucker smiled. His dad was there to meet Taffy Bean and her family, to visit Toledo with him, and to be part of his life. He was a normal dad, doing normal things with his son, like all the other normal families he knew.

Chapter Thirty-Two
Thanksgiving All Day

When the sun was fixing to shine, and Thanksgiving morning was ready to dawn at 6:45 AM, Tucker got up. "Crackers," he snapped as he checked the clock on his dresser. "I've slept the day away. Grandpop's been up since four."

He jumped out of bed, put on his button up white dress shirt, and pulled a brown and tan V-neck sweater over his head. Woven in an argyle* pattern, it was Tucker's favorite. To complete dressing, he added the new Levi's he had earned for helping Simon Winkler, shoes and socks, and ran a comb through his dark, wavy hair. He bounded down the steps, skipped the last three, and planted his feet on the entry floor in his usual Olympic dismount.

In the kitchen, Tucker pulled the Wheaties out of the cabinet, milk from the refrigerator, and one of Gramma's mixing bowls from the shelf. "Are Aunt Cora, Uncle Jerry, and Luke coming?" he asked as he dug into the cereal. Gramma hadn't cautioned that he might spoil his dinner for a long time. As active as he was, he needed all the food he could lay claim to.

"Ja, Tucker, the whole family. We didn't know where you, Christy, Freddie, and Johnny were yesterday. We all worried so much, everyone wanted to come and see for themselves that all of you were alright."

"Uncle David's family, too?"

"Ja, Uncle David and Aunt Karen, Magda and Keith are coming."

"Oh, good. I love Aunt Karen's cranberry salad, with apples and oranges."

Gramma finished stuffing the huge turkey Uncle Jacob brought home from work, a Thanksgiving gift from the factory owner to all employees. "Aunt Franny is bringing date pudding, that wonderful cake with dates and nuts that's been in the family since before 1845. You love to pile whipping cream on top of that."

"If it's a cake, why do they call it date pudding?"

Gramma smiled and searched the ceiling for the answer. "I believe the British used to call any dessert, pudding."

Tucker nodded, but inside, he thought calling a cake, pudding, was silly. He wondered what they call pudding in England. "Where's everybody going to sit?"

"The adults will sit at the dining room table. There will be nine of us. The adult cousins, Tim, Carolyn and her fiancé, your cousin Howard and his wife Pauline, cousins Iris and Ray, James Jr – Jimmy, will sit at the two card tables pushed together, and all of you younger cousins will picnic on the floor, the steps, the coffee table … you'll all find a place. We'll pass the food then put it in the kitchen where the cousins can serve themselves like at a church pot luck supper."

"Sounds like fun," he said aloud. Inside he thought, *Yeah! I'll be able to go back for seconds, even thirds, without drawing much attention to myself.*

Tucker finished his cereal, washed, and dried the bowl and returned it to the cabinet. He started for the hall tree near the side door to collect his coat. He thought, *I feel like I've lived in this coat for twenty-four hours.* "I'm going over to the grocery to pick up your rolls, Gramma. Simon is opening Winkler's grocery early today."

Grandpop awakened from his morning nap when he heard Tucker speak. "Make sure you don't see a great looking car and wonder off, landing in Philadelphia sometime Saturday."

"Okay," Tucker called back and chuckled. Grandpop didn't often tell jokes. Tucker considered it a blessing.

He darted out the front door, down the steps and sidewalk, and crossed the street to the grocery store parking area. "Hi Simon. Hey," he said as he took the broom Simon was using and began sweeping the concrete, "that's my job,"

Simon Winkler wiped his hands on his long white bib apron, with the strings brought around and tied in front. "Okay then, when you're done, come in and I'll give you your grandmother's dinner rolls."

Tucker continued to sweep until a car pulled up beside him and the driver rolled down the window. "Wow," he said as he turned to see the sleek black four door Oldsmobile.

"Tucker," Principal Dillard yelled out his car window. "My wife, Margaret, was down helping her mother after her mom fell. I'm going down to pick her up. Do you want to ride along so I have someone to talk to?"

"Gee, I don't … where are you going?"

"Philadelphia," the Principal answered.

Tucker's mouth dropped open. "Philadelphia?"

"Yes." Principal Dillard looked at him, puzzled. "New Philadelphia is south of Indianapolis. It will be dull to drive down by myself. Margaret will be with me on the way home."

"Sorry," Tucker stammered, still shocked the principal was going to Philadelphia, just like Grandpop said. "We're having a lot of company. Have a good trip." He started to go in the store and then stopped. "Mr. Dillard," he called after him, "the car radio has some great programs on it, even into the night." He waved, then added, "Trust me, I know."

Inside the store, Simon was putting the packages of Mrs. Custer's dinner rolls into a large brown sack with a handle. "Sure is a fancy car the principal has. Not?"

"He asked me to go for a ride with him."

"In that new Oldsmobile?" Simon picked up the sack and passed it over the counter to Tucker.

"A poke to tote it in," Tucker said with a chuckle. He took the bag and smiled. "Yep. I would have liked to ride in it but it was a little too far for me. We're having a house full of company. Gramma will need my help." He started to leave, then remembered. "How's the roof holding?"

Simon puffed up with pride. "Tucker, you did a wonderful roofing job. There's nary a single drip."

"Great!" Tucker boasted. He loved to do a good job helping other people. "Gotta go. Lots to do."

With the grocery bag in hand, he hurried across the street and flitted in the door. As he took the rolls to the kitchen, there was a knock on the door. "I'll get it."

"Hi Tucker." Christy had on the other new pair of slacks she had gotten at Ziesel's Department Store, a heavy wool sweater, and the coat Tucker had gotten used to.

Tucker held the door open wider. "Come on in."

"You come out here, Tucker. I'm sure your house is a-buzz."

He leaned back into the house and lifted four chocolate chip cookies from the previous night's left-over stash. Tucker was glad Mrs. Cooper left half of them there. "Here Christy … two cookies."

The wooden planks of the porch floor felt cold as Tucker sat down on the top step. "When Aunt Cora gets cold, she says, she colder than a June bug in January. I think I understand what she means."

Christy smiled as she bit into the cookie. "My mother always says, 'I'm freezin' stiff-a-grinnin'.'"

The sky was as brilliant a blue as Tucker had ever seen. As chilly as it was, it was relaxing to just watch the people go by. Tucker smiled when he saw a few hedge apples under the Osage orange tree on the fence line and remembered they made excellent targets for his bow and arrow.

Joe came around the side of the house barking and sneezing, dog-talk for "follow me."

Tucker jumped up, brushed cookie crumbs off his jeans and motioned for Christy to join him. "We'll warm up if we walk a little."

Following the shepherd dog, the two friends walked around toward the back of the house. They sashayed past the root cellar, where vegetables, protected from the late fall ice and cold, lay buried. Why did it look so funny?

Christy stopped and stared at the leaves across the top layer of gunny sacks. "Looks like someone stumbled into the vegetable storage. Look at the deep foot prints going across the top."

"But who?" Tucker looked around. "Wait a minute. We were gone all day yesterday. Maybe someone fell. Or, Gramma would have needed an onion for the turkey dressing." He turned and started back toward the door.

"Tucker," Christy grabbed his sleeve, "your grandmother is okay. She wasn't limping today, was she? Or, last night for that matter."

He stopped in mid-stride. "No, she's fine, so is Grandpop. Whatever happened here in the yard at the root cellar, it happened this morning."

They both stood there, looking around the yard. Grandpop's workshop looked okay. The light wasn't on and no one was around.

"There she is." Tucker grinned so wide his lips nearly fell off his face. "My beautiful Model A."

"Ah yes, there it is." Christy firmly fixed her hands on her hips and stared at the monster that almost got them run over by a train.

"So … you won't be wantin' a ride in the little old lady," Tucker teased.

"Well … now, I didn't say that." Christy brushed off her pants and turned her nose to the air. "Look." She pointed at the ground behind the A-Model. "The car has been moved. As I remember, Tim drove it yesterday. Would he have taken it out many times, putting the car in a different place each time?"

"I don't know." Tucker shook his head and tried to remember. "Maybe—"

"Hey," Christy shouted and pointed at the evidence of wrong-doing.

Two boys Tucker knew to be about eleven years old, popped up from the front seat of the car, threw the doors open and started running out of the yard and down the alley. "Oscar? Vern? ... you two get back here."

They didn't stop. They kept running, slipping, and sliding on crunchy, icy gravel, to where the alley made a bend, and kept going.

Tucker and Christy bent over with laughter. "I guess Tim didn't lock the doors." They walked back to the porch, sat down, and got on to the business of enjoying the morning.

Christy sighed and smiled a wistful smile. "Do you believe the day we had yesterday? I still wonder if it really happened."

"Oh, it happened. I believe it." Tucker leaned his elbows back on the step above them. "But it does seem like a whole other world." He listened to the sound of Uncle Jacob's violin filter through the door. His uncle only played his violin on Sundays, but this was a holiday. The sweet melody of *Now Thank We All Our God* filled the air around the porch.

"So nice and calming." Christy closed her eyes as her body gave in to the music.

"I believe it happened, Christy, because I was there. But it does seem unreal." He thought a minute and added, "I always wanted to go to Toledo. Gramma has some family in Toledo."

Christy tipped her head in question. "But you didn't see any relatives in Toledo."

"No," he agreed, "but, I saw Toledo."

Tim walked up the sidewalk, carrying two folding chairs in each hand. "I have to borrow a few more from the church. You two could help." He stopped at the foot of the steps. "You never said how your great train ride went."

Christy perked up. "It was wonderful, except for the long ride in the cattle car."

"Cattle?" Tim grinned.

"Well, not cattle. But—"

"But … what?" Tim mocked. "Was it a circus train with moneys and elephants?"

Tucker shook his head with a mischievous grin. "No, the elephants were in the zoo."

"What?" Tim nearly dropped the chairs. "The zoo?"

"And the merry-go-round," Christy added. "We had to take a ride to hide from the police."

Tim's eyes bulged. "The police were after you?"

"Well, not after us," Tucker stretched out, crossing his legs at his ankles. "They were after Taffy. They thought she had been kidnapped, but she ran away."

"Taffy?" Tim gulped. "Taffy Bean?" Tim slammed the chairs down as the foot caps bounced on the sidewalk. "Thought you had grown up, Tucker. You're lying again."

"Tucker." Gramma stuck her head out the door. "You have a phone call. There's someone on the line named Taffy. Uh, Taffy Bean."

Tim gulped so hard he nearly choked as he hurried in the house and propped the chairs against the wall. Tucker followed him in, but Tim got to the phone first. "Hello, who is this?" he barked.

"Tim, get off that phone," Gramma snapped as she wiped her hands on her tea towel. "The call is for Tucker. She said she called Christy first, and tracked them down here."

"Who is this?" Tim asked again as Tucker grabbed the candlestick receiver from his hand.

"Hello, Taffy?" Tucker asked into the mouth piece of the wall-hanging phone. "Will you please say 'Hi' to my brother, Tim, so you and I can talk?" He moved slightly and let Tim hear Taffy, too,

"Hello? Tim?" Tucker could hear Taffy through the receiver.

"Uh ... yes?" Tim stammered. "Who am I talking to?"

"You asked to talk to me, Tim. I'm Taffy Bean. I called to thank Tucker and Christy for protecting me and getting me safely home yesterday."

"You sound like Taffy Bean. But Taffy doesn't call Toledo, Ohio her home. She's a movie star and lives in Hollywood."

"Tucker," she said with a laugh, "you have to listen to this guy every day?"

"Not every day anymore," Tucker leaned into the phone. "He's home on leave from the Marines. He'll be going back after the holidays."

"Well, in my opinion," Taffy smoodged, "it would be best to listen to Tucker, Tim. He was even able to talk my agent into letting me out of my contract."

"Admit it, Tim," Tucker pulled the receiver back, "you know this is Taffy Bean."

"Yes, I guess. It does sound like Taffy." Tim gathered the chairs and took them into the dining room.

"He's gone," Tucker said into the phone and then admitted, "I guess I have spread the truth a little thin in the past."

"Well, you are my hero today," Taffy admitted. "Mama even said, 'Tucker was a sweet slice of pie.'"

Tucker could feel his face grow hot. "That's because I eat so much of every kind of pie."

"You're funny, Tucker." Taffy was quiet for a minute. "Is Christy there?"

"Right here." Christy took Tim's place beside Tucker.

"Stay on the line, Tucker. This is for both of you." Taffy waited.

Tim was still muttering in the background. "I know her voice. That really is her."

"Hi Taffy," Christy spoke into the mouth piece.

"Hi Christy. I just wanted to wish you both a very happy Thanksgiving today. I am so thankful for all you did for me yesterday. But, most of all, you gave me friendship and a beautiful day."

"Taffy, I had fun." Tucker admitted. "It was a great experience."

"Me too," Christy joined in. "I talked to Mom about you coming for a visit this summer. She said 'sure'. We'll talk more about that. My mom can call your mom."

"That sounds perfect. And, Tucker, Mom and Dad told me to tell you how much they appreciate all you did for me. I can finally have a near normal life. I'll always be Taffy Bean."

"Of course, you will," Tucker said with a laugh. "Who else are ya gonna be?"

Taffy laughed. "Well, I could always find a script with a new character and some fresh lines. Oh, and Daddy said to tell you to thank your dad for coming all the way here to get you. Your dad worked all day and drove all night."

Tucker hadn't thought about it like that. Maybe Sean did need a thank-you." Okay, Taffy. Will do."

"I know you said you are having company today so I'll hang up." Taffy's voice drug out slowly. "Both of you, please write to me and I'll write to you."

"I will," Tucker agreed and then remembered how much he didn't like to write letters. With Taffy Bean as a pen pal, it might be different.

"See you next summer," Taffy reminded them.

"Sure will," Christy added.

Tucker and Christy didn't say much but grinned at each other. Tucker shook his head, "We really were in Toledo yesterday, weren't we?"

Chapter Thirty-Three
A Perfect Thanksgiving

Uncle David, Aunt Karen, Magda, and Keith were the last to get to the Moyer home. Tucker wondered if they were going to get in the house. That morning, Christy said it would just be the three of them for dinner; so, Gramma invited the Trees, too. While she was in the invitation mood, she rang Dalia, the telephone operator, who put her through to the Cooper home. Yep, Gramma added the three Coopers to the Moyer Family Thanksgiving party.

Tucker found Gramma in the kitchen where Christy was helping her take the turkey out of the oven. "Gramma, I like your idea of everyone under eighteen sitting on the floor while we eat. But, if you come in and see how the living room is filling up, there may be a problem."

Gramma and Christy followed Tucker into the over-packed living space. "Nicht gut*," Gramma said, reverting to the German of her ancestors. "What to do?"

"Well, I was thinking," Tucker said as he walked to the side window. "Grandpop has a key to the church. Why don't we carry our food over there? We could eat comfortably in the Fellowship hall."

"Ja, Ja," Gramma nearly jumped with joy. "Das ist gut*."

Tucker darted into the kitchen to make sure some of the pies made it across the street. He took a quick glance and rescued the pumpkin and sugar cream.

"Okay, everyone," Gramma tried to get their attention. She nodded at Tucker, who put down the pies and picked up a knife. When Tucker tapped on the side of a glass, Gramma began. "Everyone, pick up the food you brought and carry it over to the church. We'll have more space there. Children," she said with a grin, "carry the chairs back over there."

A cacophony of sound filled the house, from the living room down into the summer kitchen where some of the older boys searched for fermented communion grape juice. Like Moses leading the children of Israel on the great Exodus, Grandpop led the family across Moyer Avenue with the key to the church in his hand.

Tucker heard Grandpop coughing as he trudged along. Any little sound Grandpop or Gramma made created a fear for their health inside Tucker.

Howard came up from behind and patted Grandpop on the back. "Don't die Grandpa," he said with a laugh.

"Can't change God's plan, Howard," Grandpop said with well prayed-over certainty. "Just don't forget to live while you're here."

Tucker smiled as he hefted the pies above his head. He knew he was gaining Grandpop's strength. "Westward ho," he called out, like a wagon train driver, leading citizens into new territories. Laughing and chattering, he, Christy, and Freddie hurried across the street. On Tucker's heals, Joe and Tiny pranced and danced as they joined the parade. Their sense of smell seemed to set them in a whirl.

Christy darted ahead and jumped up the steps two at a time. She carried the huge bowl of bread dressing with two of Gramma's linen tea towels draped over the top to keep it warm. "See ya inside," she called back to Tucker. "I'll hurry these in so they don't get cold."

"Happy Thanksgiving, Tucker," Sean greeted as he waited for Tucker on the church steps.

"Dad? What are you doing here?" Tucker was flummoxed*.

Sean got up from the step, brushing dust from the back of his pants. "Your grandmother invited me. She said I shouldn't be alone on Thanksgiving when the family has so much."

"Dad," Tucker began as he saw Christy go inside. "Taffy called this morning." Tucker shifted the pies when he came to the steps and balanced the scrumptious crusty deliciousness on his knee where his foot rested on the step above.

"She did? They're nice people," Sean agreed.

"Her dad told her to tell you how thankful they were that you came to Ohio. He knew you were probably tired." Tucker turned to the dogs. "Go home, Joe. Sit on the porch."

Joe started for the house. When Tiny didn't leave, Joe trotted back and herded her home, moving back and forth, in and out, round-about and back to the side porch.

Sean started up the steps as Tucker stood up. "It was my privilege and joy. I enjoyed spending the time with you."

"Me too, Dad. And—," Tucker paused. He wondered if he'd be able to put into words what he wanted to say. "Dad, I'm sorry I've not been closer. Welcome to dinner."

"Thanks, Tucker. I've waited a long time to hear that." He paused like something important was on his mind. "In a few weeks, I'm getting married again. I want you to meet her and her son. You'll have a step-brother."

"A step-bother? Never had one of those," Tucker thought aloud. "I have a brother, a half-brother, and soon a step-brother. Wow." To himself, he thought, *I guess Dad wouldn't be Dad without a few more sons. Sure hope I get to know this one.*

Tucker carried the pies into the hall. He watched as Sean greeted Gramma with a thank you and Grandpop with a hand shake. But, most of all, Tucker noticed how very large his family had grown, from the small group he held in his head, to brothers he hardly knew, to everyone who filled his neighborhood. He had to admit, he wasn't alone as much as he thought he was. He had to learn to be thankful for all the people he had in his life, and remember with love, all those who were gone. His family was huge and full of love after all.

Epilogue
A Word of Explanation

I like to call *Tucker McBride's Many Lives* a family historical novel. It's based on true events, condensed in time around a theme of family and reconciliation.

Tucker McBride is my husband, Bill Rapp, as he experienced life as a kid in post-WWII Indiana. Bill grew up in Dunlap with his brother and two sisters in the home of their maternal grandparents, Albert and Perninnah Kime. Yes, Bill, like Tucker, was a very active kid and did all the antics at various times in his childhood as described in this sequel to *Tucker McBride*.

One day, Bill joined his cousin and some friends when they jumped on a freight train to go to a movie in Goshen. However, Bill knew the train wouldn't stop in Goshen. He had heard his grandfather's railroad stories many times. As they neared the small-town, Tucker jumped off, rolled in the gravel and dirt near the tracks, and walked home. The other train-riders ended up in Toledo, Ohio. This author took the Toledo segment and added the many people who depended on Bill for help, his real-life activities, and the emotional issues that surrounded his life.

Bill and his father, Edgar Rapp, reconciled later in life, when Bill was about twenty-five years old. It was included here to show how families can come closer together through forgiveness and love.

Characters in *Tucker McBride's Many Lives*:

Bill Rapp is *Tucker McBride*
> My husband, Bill, is the inspiration for Tucker McBride. Bill did most of the activities described in this book when he was young.

Brother Jack is *Tim*.

Sisters Beverly and Merry are *Carolyn and Betsy*.

Tucker's friend, *Christy* is a composite character of Merry,
> some cousins, and Bill's friends.

Taffy Bean is not a real person.
> She represents all the people who call on Bill for help, because they know he will willingly assist, and find a way to have fun in the process.

Bill's father, Edger, remarried after Helen, Bill's mother, died. Edger and his new wife, Juanita had a child, Edger Jr. Friends and family called him Joe. I call him Bobby in the book

> When Edger died, his ten-year-old son, Gary, from a third marriage, went to live with Merry and her family. He was much younger and did not live during the years covered in the Tucker McBride books.

Glossary

a-bone - A classic car bought to turn it into a hotrod

argyle - a geometric knitting pattern of several solid colored diamonds and outlined shapes on one background color

calliope - a musical instrument with organ-like keyboard, steam or compressed air whistles make the music

D'artagnan – a character in the book, *The Three Musketeers* by Alexandre Dumas (1844), a friend of three officers in the musketeers of King Louis XIV.

bitte – *you're welcome* in German or Amish

cat-eye eye glasses -

Danke schön - dutch for *thank you*

desk model rotary dial phone -

draft - military draft - The draft is when the government ordered people to serve in the armed forces, usually for a limited amount of time

drop leaf table -

dry sink -

es ist gut – *"It is good,"* in German

fabricator – fabricate - to devise or invent, someone who tells a lie

flabbergasted – greatly surprised or astonished

flummoxed - bewildered or perplexed

ja – German for "yes"

kerfuffle - a fuss; commotion

hat pin – a decorative, functional pin for holding a hat to the hair

harrumph - to clear the throat in a self-important, gruff way

hand signals – Before cars had levers to activated flashing tail-lights, indicating in which direction the driver would turn, drivers would put their hand out the window. A bent arm up pointing over the car, meant a right turn. Pointing left, straight out the window, meant a turn to the left.

jawohl – *"yes, absolutely"*

Maxwell 1925 -

mohair – fabric from yarn spun from the fleece of Angora goats

nicht gut* – *not good* in German

nein – *"No"* in German and Pennsylvania Dutch

orange crate -

packet boat –

pen-pal - a person with whom you become friendly by writing letters to each other, especially someone in another state or country whom you have never met

 pie safe - three-shelf pie safe with punched tin inserts in doors for circulation, but not large enough for bugs or mice to get in

 Radio Flyer All Terrain Wooden Wagon

rigmarole - confused or meaningless talk, or a complex procedure

rumble seat – a seat, located in the trunk of a two-door car. The trunk lid opens backwards, forming the back of the seat.

stench – a strong, unpleasant smell

trough-like (trough) – a long shallow V-shaped receptacle for drinking water or feed of domestic animals

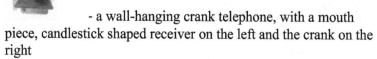

- a wall-hanging crank telephone, with a mouth piece, candlestick shaped receiver on the left and the crank on the right

- tulip chairs - outdoor or porch lounge chair

The Household Searchlight Recipe Book

The Household Searchlight Recipe Book – from The Household Magazine -Topeka, Kansas Copyright 1931. 7th 1935

Dem Bones

The toe bone's connected to the foot bone,
The foot bone's connected to the ankle bone,
The ankle bone's connected to the leg bone,
Now hear de word of da Lord.
        Johnson, James Weldon. Dem Bones. (1928)
Spiritual song. Music by his brother, J. Rosemond Johnson.
Last line has several different wordings. This is how I learned it.

Erie Canal

I've got a mule and her name is Sal
Fifteen miles on the Erie Canal
She's a good old worker and a good old pal
Fifteen miles on the Erie Canal
We hauled some barges in our day
Filled with lumber, coal and hay
And, we know every inch of the way
From Albany to Buffalo

Low bridge, everybody down
Low bridge, cause we're coming to a town
And you'll always know your neighbor
And you'll always know your pal
If you've ever navigated on the Erie Canal
(Composer unknown)

Recipes

Sugar Cream Pie
Eliza Campbell gave this to Victoria Borgman in 1984. Eliza said her great-grandmother used it.

1 c. white sugar
1 tablespoon brown sugar
1/3 c. plus 2 tablespoons flour
Pinch of salt

Mix all the above ingredients together.
Then add:
2 teaspoons butter **and add** 1 c. boiling water

Then quickly add – ½ pint UNWHIPPED whipping cream. Pour into 9" uncooked pie shell. May use a fresh, pre-made Pillsbury pie shell or your favorite. Sprinkle the whole top of the pie with nutmeg.

Bake at 400 degrees for 15 min. then turn the oven down to 350 degrees and bake for 30 – 45 minutes.

Or, Pie Crust from Better Homes and Gardens Cookbook.
Pastry for a Double Crust. Use half for this pie.
Mix together: 2 C. flour, 1 t. salt and 2/3 C. shortening
Add: 7 T cold water. Mix together to form 2 balls of dough. On floured surface, take one of the balls of dough and roll it out forming about a 12" circle. Place this crust into the pie pan. Crimp the edges. Then add filling.

Chocolate Chip Cookies (Toll House Cookies)
The best chocolate chip cookie recipe is on the back of the
Toll House chocolate chip package

Date Pudding (cake) - From Shade side of author's family.
G-G-Grandma Shade born about 1845

Mix & let cool:
1 cup chopped dates
1 t baking soda
1 cup boiling water
Cream:
¼ cup shortening
1 cup sugar
1 egg
Sift together:
1½ cup flour
1 t baking powder
¾ t salt
Mix well then add: 1 cup chopped nuts
Pour into a well-greased pan - square Pyrex baking dish
Bake 300^0 1 hr.
Use whipping cream or icing for topping

Old Fashion Bread & Celery Stuffing

Put turkey neck in a pan, cover with water, bring to a boil, turn down and cook while preparing the rest of the ingredients

Ingredients:

4 cups diced celery	1 cup chopped onion

1 cup butter or margarine
4 quarts dry bread crumbs or bread broken up small

1 T salt	1½ t poultry seasoning
½ t sage	½ t pepper

Hot broth you made with neck, or water
Cook celery and onion in butter or margarine
Combine with bread crumbs - add enough broth to moisten
Enough dressing for a 14 to 18 lb turkey
You can add chopped giblets and use that for broth for liquid
Stuff turkey loosely – don't pack tightly. If dressing sticks out of turkey, cover those areas with foil to prevent burning
Can bake in a cooking bag. Directions on box.

Vanilla Wafers

2 eggs	½ teaspoon baking-soda
½ cup shortening	½ teaspoon salt
1 teaspoon cream of tartar	1 cup sugar
1 ½ - 2 cups flour	½ teaspoon vanilla

Cream shortening and sugar. Add well-beaten egg yolks. Sift flour. Measure ½ cup and sift with cream of tartar, salt, and baking-soda. Combine with egg mixture. Mix thoroughly. Add stiffly beaten egg whites and vanilla. Add sufficient flour to make a soft dough. Turn onto lightly floured board. Roll in sheet 1/8 inch thick. Cut with floured cutter. Place on slightly oiled baking sheet (or non-stick). Bake in hot oven (400° F.) about 10 minutes. (If use non-stick cookie sheet, lower temperature.) 50 servings. – Page 128 – The Household Searchlight Recipe Book

Aunt Catherine's (Karen's) Cranberry Salad
• large box of cherry Jell-O
• 2 cups boiling water
• 1 cup sugar
• 1 package fresh cranberries – grind in food processor or blender set on chop
• 1 large or 2 small oranges – washed, peeled, and chopped
• From one of the peeled oranges, chop peeling or put in food processor
• 1 large or 2 small red apples – not peeled, but cored and diced
• 1 cup chopped pecans or English walnuts

Mix Jell-O with 2 cups boiling water and 1 cup sugar. Stir continuously to dissolve Jell-O and sugar. Do not add the cold water as stated on the Jell-O box
Add chopped cranberries, chopped apples, chopped oranges, chopped peeling, and nuts.
Stir in completely
Refrigerate until Jell-O is set.

Other Books by Doris Gaines Rapp

Novels:
*Tucker McBride (*Prequel to *Tucker McBride's Many Lives)*
Escape from the Belfry
Escape from the Shadows
Murder, She Blogged – Just in Time
News at Eleven – A Novel (Prequel to *Murder, She Blogged - Just in Time)*
Length of Days – The Age of Silence (1ˢᵗ in the trilogy)
Length of Days – Beyond the Valley of the Keepers (2ⁿᵈ in the trilogy)
Length of Days – Search for Freedom (3ʳᵈ in the trilogy)
Hiawassee – Child of the Meadow
Smoke from Distant Fires

Children's Picture Book:
Shyloe and the Mayor
Lincoln's Christmas Mouse

Collection:
Christmas Feather, one of eight short stories by eight different authors in a collection titled, *Christmases Past*

Non-Fiction:
Prayer Therapy of Jesus
Promote Yourself
Waiting for Jesus in a Can't Wait World – Advent 2014

Internet Presence
Facebook: Doris Gaines Rapp – Author Page
www.dorisgainesrapp.com   www.dorisgainesrapp.blogspot.com

Watch for ***Teacher's Guide to Tucker McBride*** by Victoria Borgman. Discussion ideas, activities, writing prompts, and investigation ideas. Available on amazon.com and barnesandnoble.com.

Activities and discussion ideas are also available on www.tuckermcbrideintheclassroom.com.

CPSIA information can be obtained
at www.ICGtesting.com
Printed in the USA
LVHW051138290820
664260LV00002B/129

9 780998 859064